Beck moan
lifted her by

Daisy wrapped he
breaking the kiss.
their connection, c ―――― ――――― along hers.
The taste of him igu――― ―er desires.

"You do that very well," she said against his mouth. "You said something about our kiss never ending?"

"I could keep this up for years." He tilted his forehead against hers. "You do things to me, Daisy-Blu."

"Good things?"

"Good. Bewitching. You make the wolf inside me want to howl."

Daisy slid out of Beck's grasp. "I almost had an interview with a hunter last night."

"Last night? You were out looking for interviews? How quickly does word get around when something like a white wolf stalking hunters happens?"

"Even faster when it's witnessed firsthand. I was in the forest. I got a few shots of the hunters running in fear from the ghost wolf, and I actually photographed the ghost wolf."

Beck's mouth hung open. Finally he blurted, "What the hell were you doing in the woods again? Alone? I thought I told you that was dangerous?"

GHOST WOLF

MICHELE HAUF

Published in Great Britain 2014
by Mills & Boon, an imprint of Harlequin (UK) Limited,
Eton House, 18-24 Paradise Road, Richmond, Surrey, TW9 1SR

© 2014 Michele Hauf

ISBN: 978-0-263-91409-2

89-1014

Harlequin (UK) Limited's policy is to use papers that are natural, renewable and recyclable products and made from wood grown in sustainable forests. The logging and manufacturing processes conform to the legal environmental regulations of the country of origin.

Printed and bound in Spain
by Blackprint CPI, Barcelona

Michele Hauf has been writing romance, action-adventure and fantasy stories for more than twenty years. Her first published novel was *Dark Rapture*. France, musketeers, vampires and faeries populate her stories. And if she followed the adage "write what you know," all her stories would have snow in them. Fortunately, she steps beyond her comfort zone and writes about countries she has never visited and of creatures she has never seen.

Michele can be found on Facebook and Twitter and at www.michelehauf.com. You can also write to Michele at PO Box 23, Anoka, MN 55303, USA.

Prologue

Two gray wolves loped across the fresh-fallen snow within a forest that edged acres of private Minnesota land. The wolves had a standing arrangement to run off their energy in the forest every weekend, a father and son get-together. A half-moon scythed the oddly clear black sky. Not a star dotted the atmosphere. Yet areas where snow had begun to tamp down the still-springy blades of grass twinkled from the cool luminescence.

The younger of the wolves always tromped ahead, challenging the elder to keep up. He was well aware he could never outrace his father, but he liked to goad him. Besides, he'd spotted a red fox and wanted to chase it until its heart gave out.

When an echoing retort shattered the calm night, the younger wolf stopped, ears shifting outward. It was a sound he had learned to fear since he could remember having fear. The sound of death. Whining, he flicked his gaze about, seeking his father. No sign of the old wolf.

Another gunshot sounded.

The wolf dashed into a race toward where he'd heard the sound. At the forest's edge the animal recognized artificial light from a mortal's vehicle. He quickened his tracks, his paws barely landing in the slushy snow until he reached the clearing where a man with a rifle approached a fallen wolf.

Snarling, the wolf leaped for the hunter, landing its front paws against his shoulders and toppling him to the wet ground. The rifle landed in slushy snow. The innate compulsion to sink his fangs into flesh and tear out anything he could manage was strong. He could break a human's bones with but a bite from his powerful jaws. Yet the wolf merely snarled and snapped at the hunter.

The hunter struggled with the wolf, slapping at its maw and crying for mercy. Fear and human urine scented the air. The wolf heard the fallen wolf's heart-wrenching whines. In pain. Dying?

In that moment of the wolf's disregard, the hunter managed to scramble out from under his aggressor.

"Damned wolves! Where's my gun?" Scrambling about in the snow, he gave up looking for the weapon when the wolf's snarls grew insistent. The hunter ran toward the lighted vehicle. "Wasn't what I needed. It didn't shift. God's blood, this trial will kill me!"

The vehicle's lights flashed across the tree trunks. Tires peeled through wet snow and soil, skidding until the rubber found traction. The car rumbled off, leaving the clearing tainted with the smell of gasoline and the echoes of the human's angry voice.

The younger wolf began to shift, its body elongating and forelegs growing into human-shaped arms. Fingers flexed out at the end of hands. Knees, bent upon the ground, sunk into the snow. Within seconds, he'd transformed from his wolf shape back to his human *were* form.

Beckett Severo scrambled over to the wolf lying in the slushy grass. Crimson stained the snow near the wolf's back.

"No. No, you can't die."

He found the entry wound over the wolf's heart. He felt the tiny beads of buckshot from the hunter's shell. One burned his fingertip. He hissed, pulling away. Liquid silver trickled within the bloody wound as if mercury.

The older wolf turned its head toward Beck and looked into his eyes.

"No, Dad, you can't..."

Beck laid his head upon his father's body and pushed his fingers through the thick winter fur. He cried out to the night until his lungs ached and the old wolf's heartbeat struggled to pulse.

The knock at the front door startled Bella Severo from her slumber in the big cozy armchair before a fading hearth fire. She'd dozed off while waiting for her husband to return home.

Heartbeat racing, she pulled the white chenille shawl around her shoulders and rushed to the door. It was well after midnight. She couldn't imagine who could be knocking now. Certainly her husband would walk right in. Her vampiric senses didn't pick up a scent, though she blamed it on the fact that she was still groggy from sleep.

Her husband, Stephan Severo, had left earlier with Beck, her son. The two always went out on weekends together. Severo generally returned early in the morning, while Beck drove to his home at the edge of town, where the woods at the back of his property framed the moon glimmering on a frozen pond. On occasion her son would stay here at the house. She loved being stirred awake in the morning to the smells of pancakes and bacon, made with love by her two favorite guys.

Tonight she'd stayed up because she had a surprise for Severo. He would be thrilled with her news.

As her hand wrapped about the front doorknob, a weird feeling tracked up Bella's spine. The blood ran from her face and her fingers shook about the glass knob. Heartbeat suddenly stalling, she gasped, clutching her chest with a hand. With the other hand, she flung open the door.

Her son stood there in but blue jeans and winter pack boots. His wide shoulders and tall stance filled the open doorway. The whites surrounding his irises were red. Tears spilled down his cheeks as he shook his head miserably. Agony clawed his fingers against his bare chest.

And Bella instinctually knew she would never be able to give her husband the news that would have filled him with pride.

Bella's knees wobbled, her head falling forward. Beck lunged and wrapped her against his shivering chest. "I'm so sorry, Mom."

She didn't hear what he said after that. Her keening wails echoed through the foyer until dawn traced through the windows and forced Bella, a vampiress, into her dark bedroom, where she stayed for the next three weeks.

Chapter 1

Two months later...

Beck stumbled to the edge of the forest, tugging up his jeans as he did so. His breaths fogged before him. The mercury had topped out at ten degrees at noon; it had only fallen since then. He'd come out of the shift and retrieved his clothes from the hollowed-out oak stump where he always kept them. Wouldn't do for a werewolf to shift to human shape without clothing to cover his shivering mortal flesh. He didn't relish the idea of walking home naked, or trying to hitch a ride.

Though, to imagine hitching naked perked up his smile. If a carload of pretty women drove by? They'd pick him up for sure.

Nah. He'd keep his clothes on. The bitter January chill did not bother him while in wolf form, but his human skin wasn't so durable against the temperature changes. Good thing he had brought along his winter coat.

He zipped and buttoned his jeans. Shoving his feet into his pack boots, he wobbled. A swirl of dizziness spilled across his vision, and he had to put out his arms to stabilize his stance. Tree stalks blurred, and for a moment the sky switched places with the snowy ground.

"Weird," he muttered, and gave his head a good shake.

Shifting took a lot out of him. More so lately. But this was the first time he'd felt so odd. Like he wasn't right with the world. Must be because he'd eaten a light lunch. Earlier in the day, his date had suggested he try a salad instead of a steak. Why he'd succumbed was beyond him.

Ah hell, he knew why. He'd wanted to impress her. Guys did stuff like that. Stupid stuff like eating leaves instead of a juicy slab of steak. Never paid off. Later, the woman had giggled while standing before her door and told him she'd see him again sometime soon.

Sometime soon? Vague, much? For not having dated in months, the step back into the pool had resulted in a cold splash to his ego. He'd added her to his mental "don't bother again" list. A guy could only listen to a woman rave about the latest fashions or which movie stars were doing each other for so long.

Turning over the thick knit sweater and sticking his arms into it to find the sleeve holes, Beck raised his arms over his head to shuffle it down over his face when something rammed into his side, knocking him off balance.

Quick footwork prevented him from taking a fall. Beck whipped around to snarl at—a pretty woman. Out here in the middle of no-place-she-should-be.

Beck's odd meter zinged far to the right.

She was petite, the crown of her head leveled at Beck's shoulder. From under a black knit cap that sported cat ears, pink hair spilled over her shoulders and onto a bulky gray sweater, beneath which perky nipples poked against the fabric, luring his interest. She clutched a pair of knee-high riding boots—she was barefoot—and blew out an annoyed huff.

As if upset because he had been the one to bump into her. Really?

Beck instinctively knew what breed she was. It wasn't a sensation he got from touching his own breed—such as vampires were capable of—he just knew when he was around another of his kind.

"Out for a run in the woods? Did you forget your glasses

at home?" He rubbed his elbow, drawing attention to where she had run right into him.

"Aren't you the funny one?" She bent to tug on a boot, followed by the other. Slender-fitted jeans wrapped her legs, and the oversize sweater fell past her hips. She looked cozy and sexy and so out of place. "I wasn't aware a big ole lug would be blocking my path."

"Trust me, the lug did not intend to get in your way. You just shift?" he asked.

"I, uh…"

Apparently she hadn't guessed the same thing about him, but quickly realization crossed her gaze as if sun flashing on metal. Pretty eyes that looked half gold and half violet and were framed by thick lashes. Her hair matched her plump lips, sort of a bleached raspberry shade. He liked it. Looked like some kind of dessert.

"Yes," she finally said. "I'm headed home. I've got a friend waiting in the car."

Beck glanced over a shoulder. He didn't recall seeing a car parked along the country road that was closest to where they stood. No vehicles out here for miles. Then he guessed she was leery, didn't want him to think she was out here alone. Yet he scented not so much caution as challenge from her. Interesting.

"I'm not going to hurt you," he felt compelled to say.

"Says the pervert before he kidnaps the girl and shoves her in his trunk." She pushed past him and walked quickly out of the forest and into the wheat field that boasted ankle-high dried stalks jutting up from the foot-deep snowpack. "Don't follow me!"

Beck couldn't *not* follow her. The road edging the field led to town. And it had started to snow in tiny skin-pinging pellets. He wasn't going to wait for her to disappear from sight before he could take off.

He paralleled her rapid footsteps.

"Seriously, dude, would you stay away from me?"

"You think I'm going to shove you in my trunk? I think you'd scratch and give a good fight if I even looked at you the wrong way."

He noticed the curling corner of her smirk, though she maintained her speedy gait. She liked him; he knew it. But it didn't matter much. It was a rare pack female who would give a lone wolf like him the time of day.

"Do I know you?" he asked. "I'm not trying to be a creep. I promise. I just— I'm familiar with most of the wolves in the area packs. I think I'd remember a pink-haired wolf. Unless this is a new color for you? I like it, by the way. The cat ears, too."

She huffed and picked up into a jog. He was tired out from his run, but Beck could keep up with her if he had to. And he wanted to. But—hell, he was winded. What was up with that? Normally shifting invigorated him.

"Who are you?" she blurted angrily.

"I'm Beckett Severo."

The pretty pink wolf stopped abruptly, dropping her hands to her sides. Flipping back her hair with a jerk of her head, she eyed him up and down more carefully than he'd taken when looking her over. "Oh."

"Oh?" Beck slapped a palm to his chest, feeling as though she'd just seen parts of him he'd never reveal upon initially meeting someone. "That *oh* sounded like you must have heard of me?"

"Uh, yeah. Something about your father?"

"Right." Beck looked away. Shoved his hands in his back pockets. He didn't need this conversation. It was still too raw in his heart. He hadn't spoken to anyone about it yet. Not even his mother.

Didn't matter who this pretty wolf was. If she knew about his father, he didn't want to listen to the pity.

The walk into the closest town was fifteen minutes. His

town was ten miles north by car. And the small bits of sleet were starting to stick to the back of his head and shoulders.

"You shouldn't run around in the forest by yourself," he said, changing the subject and keeping his back toward the brunt of the sleet. "The local hunters have developed a bloodlust for wolf pelts."

She shrugged and turned to walk, but slower now, unmindful of the icy pellets. Tugging a pair of black mittens out from a jeans pocket, she pulled them on. "I trust this neck of the woods."

"You shouldn't," he said with more authority than he wanted on the subject.

Beck was a werewolf. Like it or not, he made it a point to know what the hunters were up to. Because even though they didn't believe in his kind, and they hunted the mortal realm breed of *canis lupis*—the gray wolf—when in wolf form, his breed could easily be mistaken for the gray wolf. And thanks to the DNR delisting the wolf from the endangered species list, the hunt had become a free-for-all.

A fact he knew too painfully well.

"Didn't you hear the gunshots earlier?"

She shook her head.

"There are hunters in the vicinity."

"Maybe the ghost wolf warned them away from me?"

Beck chuckled. The ghost wolf was what the media had taken to calling the recent sightings of a tall, wolf-like creature that seemed to glow white. Scared the shit out of hunters.

"You shouldn't put your faith in a story," he said to her. "You're not safe in the woods, plain and simple."

"Well, *you* were out alone."

"Yes, but I'm a guy."

"Do not play the guy card with me. You think I can't handle myself?"

"No, I just said you could probably scratch—"

The petite wolf turned and, without warning, punched him in the gut. It was a good, solid hit that forced out Beck's breath and jarred his lower ribs. Picking up her dropped mitten, she turned and walked off while he clutched at his stomach, fighting his rising bile.

"Thanks for the chat!" she called. With that, she picked up into a run.

Beck was perfectly fine with letting her run off and leave him behind. He swallowed and winced as he fell to his knees amidst the wheat and snow.

"The guy card?" Swearing, he leaned back, stretching at his aching abdomen. "She's got a great right hook, I'll say that much."

And he was getting weaker with every shift he made to werewolf. That was not good.

Daisy Blu Saint-Pierre landed at the edge of town just as the headlights of a city snowplow barreled past her on the salt-whitened tarmac. She'd left her winter coat at home, not expecting it to snow tonight. She never took along more clothing than necessary when going out for a run. Chilled, but still riding the high from the shift that kept her muscles warm and flexible, she picked up into a run.

Her teeth were chattering by the time she reached her loft in the Tangle Lake city center. There were three other occupants in this remodeled warehouse that featured lofts on the second and third floors. She wandered up the inner iron staircase, cursing her need to not drive unless absolutely necessary. Blame it on her parents, who were uber-environmental-save-the-planet types. Her dad drove an old pickup that must have been manufactured in the Reagan era. She suspected it would be more environmentally friendly to put that rust heap out of its misery and off the road, but her father, an imposing werewolf who could silence any man with but a growl, wouldn't have it.

Once inside the loft, she stripped away her clothes, which were coated on the back with melting sleet. Leaving them in a trail of puddles behind her, she beelined toward the shower and turned it on as hot as she could stand.

The last thing she had expected while out on a run was to literally collide into another werewolf. Though, why not? should be the obvious question. The wolves in the Northern and Saint-Pierre packs used that forest all the time. Yet lately, with the hunters spreading out and some accidentally trespassing onto private land, even that forest had grown less safe.

She never ventured too near the forest's borders, and always kept an ear and nose out for mortal scent and tracks. The gunshot had been distant. She'd not smelled the hunter, and usually, when out in nature, she could sniff out a mortal scent two or three miles away.

Beckett Severo, eh? She'd heard about his father's tragic death not long ago. Killed by a hunter who must have assumed he was just another gray wolf. Must be awful for Beckett. She had also heard he had been there with his father when he'd been shot.

Daisy felt awful for punching him, but it had been impulsive. She didn't know the man, and couldn't trust him, and he'd been all in her face and trying to chum up to her. She preferred to meet her men in public places, and preferably with an advance review from a friend so she knew what she was getting into.

So maybe she wasn't an expert on meeting people. Her defenses tended to go up for no reason other than that she was uncomfortable making small talk.

Because really? That man had been one fine hunk of wolf. He'd towered over her, and looked down on her with ice-blue eyes. She'd never seen such clear, bright irises. His sun-bleached hair had been tousled this way and that. A

scruff of beard had shadowed his chiseled jaw. He'd reeked
of strength and—she could admit it—sensuality.

What a man. What a wolf. It was rare Daisy met a male
werewolf who appealed to her on more than a simple friendship basis. It was much easier to be a guy's buddy than to
flirt with him.

He hadn't known her? Probably because he wasn't in
a pack. Yet she knew about his family. Severo, his father,
had been a grizzled old wolf. Unaligned with any pack,
but respected by many pack wolves for common sense
and wisdom that had come from centuries of life. Surely
Daisy's father had mentioned Severo reverently a time or
two.

Maybe. Didn't matter. She didn't intend to bump into
Beckett again soon, so she'd have to satisfy herself with a
few fantasies about the sexy wolf.

With the way her shifting abilities had been testing her
lately, she was more self-involved than she cared to be.
Much as she preferred shifting to wolf, the faery half of her
always vied for superiority. She wasn't sure what the deal
was with that, but it was annoying. And embarrassing. She
couldn't remember when she'd last shifted around a family member. So she spent much time in her human shape,
which was all right by her, save for her lacking social skills.

She was trying to break free of her introvert's chains by
competing for a freelance internship for the local newspa-
per. Every January the *Tangle Lake Tattler* offered an internship to a journalist who offered the winning story. Story
competition was never fierce. She had two opponents. But
that didn't mean Daisy wasn't giving it her all.

Researching the story got her out into the community
and forced her to talk to others. She enjoyed it, and she was
growing more at ease with introducing herself to strang-
ers. Albeit, with a handshake. Not by charging into them
while running out of the forest.

The story she knew would be the winner was the ghost wolf. Which is why she'd been out in the woods tonight. The great white wolf had been sighted twice in the last month. Daisy suspected the creature was werewolf due to the description the local hunters circulated on the rumor mill. Save for one odd detail. Hunters had noted the wolf glowed, as if a white specter. Thus, a ghost wolf.

If it was a werewolf, she wasn't sure how to handle the story. Her breed valued their secrecy.

She'd deal with that if and when she needed to. Should have asked Beck if he knew anything about the ghost wolf. Hmm...

Good reason to see him again.

Chapter 2

Tangle Lake's annual Winter Ice Festival parade was followed with a massive community picnic in the park. Since it was the second week in January, everyone bundled up in winter wear, pack boots, mittens, caps, scarves and face masks. It was hard to be cold with the festivities to lighten the mood. Hockey was played on the nearby football field (iced over for winter), ice sculptures were judged in the town square (which was more of an oval, really), and ice bowling, s'mores over bonfires and even a quilt-off were held throughout the day.

Daisy decided next year she'd try her hand at the ice sculpting. She had no skills, but she wouldn't let that stop her from learning how to use the chain saw. She loved a good competition.

Daisy's pack always attended the festival. In town they were not known as werewolves. The humans were oblivious. And the pack principal—who was also her father—was all about community and making nice with the humans. All packs existed amongst the mortals. Garnering friendships and fitting in was key to survival.

She recognized wolves from the Northern pack pushing a sled piled with ice blocks toward the sculpting platforms. Supposedly the Northern pack had been a pretty nasty bunch of wolves in the decades before Daisy had been born. Her grandmother, Blu, had been a member then, and Blu's father, Amandus Masterson, had been the principal. He'd died—but not before first torturing Blu's vampire husband, Creed. Since the Northern pack scion, Ridge Addison, had taken over the reins as principal, everything had changed, and the pack was now peaceable toward other packs, as well as vampires.

Daisy's father, Malakai Saint-Pierre, was somewhere in the crowd, probably testing the various hot dishes offered at the bake stands and flirting with the women. Her mother, Rissa, took it in stride because Kai was fiercely faithful to her. But with a former reputation about town as a Casanova, he had no problem soaking up the female attention.

Her mother had stayed at home today in favor of an afternoon to herself. She was uncomfortable in large crowds. It wasn't because she was one-hundred-percent faery; Rissa was just quiet and didn't much understand socializing.

Daisy could relate. Her mother had bequeathed her the scarlet letter of introversion. Her four brothers had inherited their father's extroversion. They could all be somewhere in the area, though she suspected Blade had stayed away. He wasn't much for crowds simply because he was secretive.

A familiar face smiled through a bustle of winter caps. Stryke was the second-youngest of Daisy's four brothers, and was full werewolf. Trouble was also full werewolf. Kelyn was faery. And Blade was a mix of vampire and faery (the vamp was thanks to their grandfather Creed's DNA).

"Hey, sis!"

Stryke pulled her into a generous hug. The guy was a master hugger. When he hugged, he gave his all. The wise, more cerebral one of the bunch, he was the one his siblings went to when they had a problem and needed to talk.

"Why the long face?" he asked, turning to lean against the concrete bike rack where she had paused. "Not into the festivities?"

She shrugged. "I don't know. Just kinda melancholy, I guess."

"Yeah, this town isn't the most exciting. Hot dishes and lutefisk?" He shuddered comically.

"Tangle Lake." Daisy recited the town's name. "And not a tangle to it. This town is straighter than straight. The highway dashes a straight line beside it. All the streets are parallel and straight. Even the lake is square! I need a tangle, Stryke." She sighed, twisting the ends of her pink hair. "I'd even settle for a little twist."

"I hear you." Stryke's gaze traversed a nearby ice bowling match, where the participants bowled ice balls toward frozen autumn squash. "I can't wait for Aunt Kambriel's wedding this summer."

Kambriel, their aunt, who was their father's twin sister (and a vampire), had fallen in love with the vampire Johnny Santiago and planned to wed in Paris, where she currently lived.

"You might find yourself a European werewolf," Daisy said, knowing her brother's strong desire to find a woman and settle down. Yet for some reason Stryke was never compelled to put down roots with any of the women in the area. Not interesting enough, he'd often lament.

"That's the plan," he agreed. "A tangle, eh? I'm not sure you'll find the excitement you're looking for in Tangle Lake, Daisy. Most exciting thing lately— Well, hell, what about that ghost wolf? You think it's a werewolf?"

"Yes," she answered quickly. And then, "No. Maybe. I don't know. I'm doing a story on it for the local paper. Or I'm trying to."

"Whatever it is, be careful."

"I will. Do *you* think it's a werewolf?"

"Yes," Stryke said. And then, "No. Maybe. I don't know. I'd have to see the thing up close. And I'm not sure I want to. Though I can promise Trouble would like to have a go at it."

The eldest brother of the siblings, Trouble (whose real

name was Jack) had a thing for picking fights and pushing people to their breaking point. But he did it in a playful way. Unfortunately, most people did not get his confrontational humor.

"I have to go," Stryke said. He nodded toward a crowd of young women bundled up in bright ski pants and boots. Pom-poms bobbed on their heads and mittens, plus a few at their boot ties. A cavalcade of sex kittens. "Got a date."

"A tangle?"

"If I'm lucky." He winked. "You going to the fireworks?"

"Kelyn and I usually head out together. I'll see you later, Stryke."

He kissed her cheek, a cold smack that made her giggle, and strode off toward the pom-pom kittens.

Sighing, Daisy tugged out the paperback she always took along to public events and found the bookmarked page. She wore gloves with rubber tips on the fingers, designed for operating touch devices. Books were the ultimate touch device. Immersing herself in the fiction, she strolled slowly along the packed snow embankment that edged the hockey rink where makeshift teams had gathered to play. Should have brought her skates. What she wouldn't give to slap sticks for a while...

All of a sudden, someone charged into her. Daisy dropped her book and made to shove away the annoying guy, but she paused when she saw who it was. The sexy wolf she'd run into the other night at the edge of the forest.

"What is it with you and the need to ram into me every chance you get?" she asked.

"Uh, sorry. I had my eye on the puck." He tossed the hockey puck he picked up from the snow toward the guys outfitted in knee pads and skates waiting on the ice. "Besides, this is the first time I've rammed into you. If you'll remember correctly—"

"Yes, yes, I recall. So you're playing with the mortals?"

"Exclusivity to one's breed is not wise in this small town." He swept a hand toward the players who had continued the game without him. "They're a great bunch of guys. I love hockey. There you go."

"I like hockey, too, but I don't think the boys would like a woman joining them."

"Probably not. All the girls are over at the food booths making cocoa and serving us men."

Daisy's jaw tightened. "I don't serve any man."

Beck swerved his gaze toward her. "Huh? Oh. Right. Sorry, that was—"

"An asshole thing to say."

"Whoa. This is fast going down an icy slope I don't want to slip on. Let's start over." Tugging off a leather glove, he then bent to pick up her book and handed it to her. "Sorry. The pages got snow on them. Don't you have one of those fancy e-readers like I see everyone carrying nowadays?"

"I have a few of them," Daisy said proudly. "Sometimes I prefer the touch, feel and smell of a real book."

She pressed the closed book to her nose and inhaled. Snow had dampened a few of the pages, but she couldn't be upset because she also owned the digital copy of this book.

"It's so personal to hold a book in my hand. I can open it to any place I like with a few flutters of the page. I can trace my fingers down the words, rereading phrases that speak to me. The stories make my heart race and my skin flush. My toes curl when I've read a well-crafted sentence. Mmm…"

"Uh…"

She glanced at Beck, whose mouth hung open. Oh, those eyes could attract wise men on a clear winter night beneath a velvet star-filled sky.

He scratched his head. "You just made reading sound sexual."

So she had. "Books turn me on." Daisy resumed her stroll along the snowbank shoveled up around the rink.

The wolf in hockey skates followed, blades sinking into the packed snow. "Really? They turn you on?"

She nodded. She wasn't sure she'd ever find a man equal to the heroes she read about in her stories, but she held out hope. Of course, the stories *were* fiction. She knew that. But it was okay to dream. And besides, when she finally did find a hero of her own, she felt sure she'd recognize him immediately for his gleaming honor and smoldering sensuality.

"So it's one of those sex books?" he asked.

Daisy stopped and toed her boot into a chunk of snow. Oh, she pitied the poorly read. "Just what implies a sex book in your mind?" She waved her book between the two of them. "Anything with a pink cover?"

"Anything with sex in it, I guess."

He was out of his league, and he knew it. Daisy smiled triumphantly. Points to the women's team.

"Says the wolf who's probably never read more than fast-food menus and car manuals."

"Don't forget *The Iliad*. I may have been home-schooled, but I don't think there's a way for any breathing teenager to avoid that snorefest."

Daisy rolled her eyes. She wasn't much for mythology, but wouldn't admit to him that she agreed with his assessment of the classic tome. That would be too much like flirting. Of which she did not partake.

"I have read a lot of car manuals," he added. "I own a shop at the edge of Burnham."

"Hockey, cars and tromping through the forest without a shirt on. Such a guy you are."

He stabbed the hockey stick into the snow and propped both wrists on the end of it. "I can't tell if you're admonishing me or trying to flirt awkwardly."

"I—" Stymied, Daisy turned her gaze away. She did not flirt. Because if she did, it would be exactly as he'd implied—awkward.

One of the men guiding the puck across the ice with the mortal crowd called to Beck to return. He waved and said he'd be right there.

Shoving up the sleeve of his jersey to reveal the long thermal sleeve beneath, he winked at her. "If you're in the mood to test your flirtation skills later, come find me."

"I, er—"

Without waiting for what would surely be the awkward reply of the century, Beck tromped off, blades cutting hashed tracks toward the ice.

Daisy couldn't help but notice the flex of his quadriceps with each stride. Clad in jeans and a fitted long shirt, over which he wore a big loose hockey jersey, the attire highlighted his awesome physique.

"Nothing new," she said to herself. All the wolves in the local packs were ripped. It was the very nature of a werewolf to be so muscular.

Unless of course he was Kelyn, her youngest brother. Who wasn't actually a werewolf at all, but rather, had inherited their mother's faery DNA. He was lean and lithe, yet her father deemed him the most deadly of all his boys. Faeries were swift and malicious, Malakai would often say.

Daisy hated to think of Kelyn as malicious. And he was not. She hoped he wouldn't develop a complex because of her father's words.

No longer interested in the book, she stuffed it in her coat pocket and wandered under a massive willow tree where a half dozen tween girls were sipping hot chocolate and cider from thermoses and texting on their cell phones, fingertips bared by half gloves.

"Why is your hair pink?" one of them asked as Daisy walked by.

"Because my mom dropped a can of paint on it when I was born," she offered, smirking. "Why is yours red?"

The befreckled girl shrugged. "Yours is pretty. I wish mine wasn't so ugly."

"Yours is gorgeous," Daisy offered. "Don't ever let anyone tell you differently. It's good to be unique, not like everyone else."

The girl sat up a little straighter. The friend beside her, sporting a hot-chocolate mustache, nodded in agreement.

"What's the best food to get today?" Daisy asked the group. "I'm in the mood for something sweet."

"Try my grandma's chocolate peanut butter brownies. Over there." One of them pointed toward a table draped in red, around which dozens loomed. "She's selling them cheap."

"Thanks." Daisy waved them off and wandered toward the food tables, her boots crunching across the snowpack.

Unique, eh? She smirked at her encouraging words. But not so unique that a woman's body couldn't make up its mind whether or not to be werewolf or faery. That wasn't unique; that was just pitiful. She had to get it figured out. But she had no clue how to do so.

When she reached the table, she had to wait in line, and when only halfway to the front, a tall, blond man approached her and offered her a treat. "These are awesome. I figured you'd like to try one."

"Are you following me?" she asked as she accepted a brownie as heavy as a small kitten. She got out of line. "You were just on the ice."

"And then I was not. I always answer the call of my stomach. Even if it sets me back a cool ten bucks for two brownies."

"What? These cost five dollars apiece?" The girl had said they were cheap. Shady sales tactics at that.

Daisy bit into the thick, moist chunk of chocolate and

peanut butter and sighed one of those after-orgasm kind of sighs.

"Right?" Beck agreed. "Well worth the expense. I may never eat my mother's brownies again. Ah, that's not true. I'll chow a brownie any day. Even the five-dollar kind. Now I need something hot to wash this down with."

"Over there." She pointed to a refreshment stand. He grabbed her by the free hand and led her toward where she had pointed. "Did I say I wanted something to drink? Dude, we are not on a date."

"I know, but I figured the brownie should earn me some chat time with you. I'll get us some cider, and there's a tree over there that's calling our names."

"Do you even know my name?"

He paused from digging out his wallet from a back pocket. "Uh...I guess not."

"Bring cider," Daisy said.

With a wink that surprised her probably more than it did him, she wandered over to the tree.

With the brownie gently clutched between his jaws, Beck headed toward the tree where the gorgeous pink-haired wolf sat. Reading while others partook of the festivities? She was a curiosity to him, and he liked that he couldn't figure her out.

He bit off a bite as he sat, catching the brownie in his palm. She snagged the foam cup of cider before he'd even settled against the trunk.

"I should have gotten two," he said.

"That's okay, I only want a sip." She handed him the cup.

Beck peered into the cup. It was half-empty. "A sip?"

She shrugged and finished off her brownie. He wanted to tweak those cat ears on top of her hat, but instead he wolfed another bite.

"So who do I have the pleasure of sitting with under the maple tree this chilled and frosty January afternoon?"

"Daisy Blu," she said, and offered a hand to shake.

Beck gripped the cup lip with his teeth, and with brownie in one hand, shook with his free hand.

"Saint-Pierre," she then said.

He dropped the cup and it almost spilled in his lap, but he made a fast-reflex save. "Uh, Malakai Saint-Pierre's daughter? The pack principal who makes swords for a living?"

She nodded, licking her fingers clean of chocolate crumbs.

"I thought he only had the boys."

Beck scanned the picnic area, filled with mortals and paranormal breeds of all sorts and sizes. Living in the next town ten miles north, he didn't know a lot of people in Tangle Lake. He kept to himself far too much. But everyone knew about Malakai Saint-Pierre.

"Four boys," Daisy said. "But I was here first. Who you looking for? Don't worry, my dad's not around. At least, I don't think he is."

Beck stood and nodded that she follow him around the trunk. "Let's sit on the other side of the tree, okay?"

She settled next to him with a laugh. "Are you afraid of my father?"

"I wouldn't say afraid, more like leery with an edge of self-preservation. Dude's not the sweetest wolf in the pack."

"Yeah, he's not too keen on unaligned wolves. Which is what you are, am I right? You being Severo's son?"

"Not for lack of your father trying to get me to join your pack."

"Really? My dad has invited you to join us? Why haven't you done so?"

"I have nothing against the Saint-Pierres. Or any of the local packs, for that matter. Joining a pack doesn't feel right to me. My father was always adamant that a man didn't need a pack to stand up for what was right within the werewolf community."

"I've heard about your father. Severo was a good man. But I have to point out the serious flaw in your sneaky attempt to hide out."

"What's that?"

"Now we won't be able to see my father coming."

"Shit. Maybe we should—"

Daisy placed a hand on his knee just as Beck attempted to stand. The woman's hand was warm, even in this weather, and her heat crept quickly through the jeans and to his skin. Nice. He settled against the snow-encrusted tree trunk.

"I'd scent him before he got too close," she said. "I'll give you advance warning if you need to run." Then she smiled and tucked a swath of hair over her ear. "I shouldn't be talking to you, either. But I like a little risk in my life now and then."

"Don't get enough from your books?"

"Not exactly."

"Is that why you think it's a good idea to run in the forest all alone? You really should take someone with you."

"I'm a big girl. I'll be fine. You going to eat that last piece of brownie?"

Beck held up the piece, and Daisy made a remarkable snatch with her teeth. She giggled, pressed her fingers over her mouth, then snagged the cup of cider from him, as well.

Licking his fingers clean, he could but shake his head. This one, as much as he should stay the hell away from her, he wanted to learn more about. Because getting close to Malakai Saint-Pierre's daughter could prove a lesson in Stupid Things Guys Do. But at the same time: kitty ears, pink hair and an irrepressible giggle. How to resist that?

She looked at him now with such curiosity that he

matched her gaze with an intense stare. "What?" he implored.

"I was just thinking there are probably icebergs in the Arctic the same color as your eyes."

"Wow. Look who just got their flirt on."

"I wasn't—uh..."

He waited for her to realize that she had indeed been flirting. Didn't take her long. She busied herself with the ends of her hair. Ha! She liked him.

"So what do you do, Daisy Blu with the kitty ears who wanders about with her nose in a book?"

"You mean like work? I am a budding journalist."

"Is that so?"

"I'm competing for a freelance position with the *Tangle Lake Tattler*. I've always wanted to be a writer, but I'm not so good at making up stories. I like digging for facts, learning the truth."

"A noble pursuit. So what truths have you dug up lately?"

"Well, Mrs. Olafson, who lives at the corner across from the courthouse? She's growing marijuana in her backyard shed."

Beck faked a shocked openmouthed gape. Could he touch that pink hair? Just a careful slide of his fingers over it without her noticing? Because if she wanted to flirt...

"Thing is, she has no clue what it is. I couldn't bring myself to actually write about it. Besides, I've got a bigger, better story I'm working on that I know will win me the job."

"Much luck to you. Isn't often you hear of pack princesses working."

"No one calls me princess unless they want a black eye."

"Duly noted. So you're the modern working-class prin— er, wolf chick, eh?"

"I'm half faery."

"Is that why your hair is pink?"

"No one will ever pull one over your eyes."

"A faery wolf. I like it."

"So what do you do? You said you're not from Tangle Lake?"

"No, I'm up in Burnham. I have a garage just off the highway. It's not open to the public yet. I'm working on some friends' cars right now. Want everything to be perfect and have a career plan in place before I put up signs. I get a lot of business just by word of mouth anyway."

"If I drove more than once every few weeks, I'd bring my car to you just because you were so nice to share your last sip of cider." She handed him the cup, empty, and served him a wide grin that teased him for a kiss.

But that would be too risky. Her father was a pack leader. And princess or not, Beck knew she wore a flashing *no touch* sign as a tiara.

"I should have bought two cups." He snickered and leaned his head back against the trunk. "So journalism is a full-time job?"

"Hardly. Only a few hours here and there. When I'm not pursuing a career, I'm also a sculptor."

"That's cool. You enter the ice sculpture contest?"

"Next year. That'll give me the winter to learn how to use a chain saw."

It wasn't difficult to imagine her wielding a chain saw. Not after that powerful right hook she'd served him in the field. She was petite but packed a punch. "What do you sculpt?"

"Anything with recycled metal. My dad's a blacksmith. I used to watch him forge swords when I was a little girl. Always wanted to be able to manipulate metal the way he did. One day when he was welding on his old truck, I asked to help, and I've been welding my designs ever since."

"Welding? That sounds macho."

"Yeah?" Daisy bent up her arm, making a fist. An impressive bicep bulged beneath the sleek white winter coat.

"I grew up with four brothers. I don't think I could do feminine if I tried."

"You're doing it right now." Beck traced a strand of her hair back over her ear. Score! It felt as soft as it looked. She flinched and gave him the curious eye. "Sorry, just wanted to touch it."

"It's hair, dude."

"And you're kind of defensive, you know that? Is it because of the 'you shouldn't talk to an unaligned wolf' thing? Or is it that I just don't appeal to you?"

"You appeal to me," she said quickly. She sat up, tilting her head down and closing her eyes. Shaking her head, she said, "I didn't mean to say that. It just came out."

"You like me," Beck teased. He dipped his head to catch her straying gaze. "It's because I seduced you with brownies, right?"

She punched him playfully on the biceps. Beck winced. It hadn't been quite as gentle as she may have intended it to be. So he fell over to his side and moaned.

"Yeah, and don't you forget it," Daisy said.

The sass that ran through her veins just needed a little prodding to rise above what he suspected was a bit of a shy streak. He hadn't seen her talking to anyone here at the festival. And if she had a boyfriend, she wouldn't be talking to him right now.

"So what do you sculpt?" he asked, moving closer so their shoulders touched.

"Anything that I'm feeling at the moment. I'm working on a project for the wolf sanctuary up north. I use lots of abandoned scrap metal. Right now I'm into recycling bicycle chains."

"Really? I have a whole box of bicycle chains at the shop. They're yours if you can use them."

"Of course I can."

"Stop by anytime and pick them up. I'm at the shop most of the day, and if not, I'll let Sunday know they're yours."

"Sunday? You mean Dean Maverick's wife?"

"Yep. Sunday used to have a shop when she lived in North Dakota. She's a gearhead like me. My shop is the only place she's got to get her grease on."

"And her husband doesn't mind?"

"Dean's a cool guy. We chat when he stops by to pick up Sunday. Not all in the packs are against the lone wolves like me, you know."

"I'm not against you. I just don't understand why you don't feel the need for family that a pack offers."

"I have family with my mom and my—" He hung his head. Now was no time to step into that bleak memory. "You want another brownie?"

"No, thank you. I should get going. I promised my mom I'd stop by with some treats from the picnic."

"You going to the fireworks later?" he asked.

"Possibly. Will you be at your shop this afternoon? Maybe I could stop by for the bike chains?"

"I'll be there in a few hours. But this is the deal—I'll give you the chains if you'll watch the fireworks with me tonight."

She crossed her arms and made a show of considering it. Her lips were the same shade as her hair. Beck bet if they kissed, she'd taste cool like ice but would warm him up faster than s'mores melting over a bonfire. Would she really turn down his offer? She seemed independent, yet certainly she was shy.

"I might have a brother along with me. Kelyn and I always watch the fireworks together. We usually find a quiet spot at the top of a hill."

"Oh. Well, I wouldn't want to intrude." Nor did he want to bring the wrath of the Saint-Pierre family upon him for talking to their precious daughter.

"We'll play it by ear. I'll stop by your shop later, and then we can decide, yes?"

"Sure. I'm north on 35."

"I've seen the shop. I know where it is."

She took off, tugging the book out of her back pocket as she skipped across the snowy field that hugged the rink where the men slapped the hockey puck back and forth.

Beck stood and brushed the snow from his jeans. "First date with one of the brothers as chaperone? I don't know about that."

Chapter 3

Beck's shop was about ten miles out of city limits. The next town, Burnham, was four miles beyond his shop. Daisy knew the Darkwood was in the vicinity. Her brother Blade lived at the edge of the haunted forest that locals told tales about. Even the paranormal breeds avoided it for its fearsome reputation.

Though the road was hugged by tall birch trees interspersed with thick pines, Daisy found Beck's shop easily and pulled in her Smart car before the shop's opened garage doors. While most fix-it garages in the area featured random junkers parked here and there, tires stacked against walls and general disorder, this area was well-tended. The snow had been plowed and banked, and there was an orderly parking area with cars tagged on the license plates, likely for pickup.

Stepping out into the brisk air, Daisy's breath fogged before her. She'd bundled up in cap, mittens and winter coat. Striding toward the opened doors, she scanned for signs of life inside and called out Beck's name. Instead of a handsome werewolf popping his head up from behind the raised hood of a truck, the blond dreads of a very familiar familiar swung around the front quarter panel of a red F-150.

Sunday winked at Daisy. "Hey there, sweetie!"

"Sunday! Beck told me you worked here, but I didn't expect to run into you." Daisy looked about the neat shop that featured four car bays. Tools hung neatly along the walls, and tires were stacked in a corner. There were even red-

and-white-checked curtains on the door window that must lead to the office. "Does Dean mind that you work here?"

The self-confessed grease monkey laid a wrench on the engine and wandered around the side of the vehicle. Grease smeared Sunday's pale check. Daisy had known her since she'd been born because of the cat-shifting familiar's friendship with her grandmother. She considered her an aunt, even. Of all the women in the family, she got along with Sunday best. Probably because they were a couple of tomboys.

"Why should Dean mind?" Sunday asked. "I don't let my man tell me what to do. Unless it's in bed." She winked.

Daisy fought against rolling her eyes.

"So why are *you* here?" Sunday asked. "Shouldn't you be more respectful of your father and his very obvious dislike for an unaligned wolf?"

"My dad doesn't know I'm here. And you won't say anything to him."

Sunday quirked a brow, but her easy smile held the kind of knowing that all women shared when a man was the topic. "There's nothing to tell. Beck's a good guy. Just because he doesn't feel comfortable joining a whole group of wolves after living in a small family his entire life shouldn't make him a pariah."

"Exactly," Daisy said, relieved that Sunday had put into words what she should have said.

Behind the car bays, a big-screen TV flashed a news report that featured area gray wolves scampering across the screen.

Sunday noticed Daisy's interest and turned up the volume with a remote she tugged out of her pocket. The report was on the local wolf hunt. It had only been a few years since the DNR had passed legislation to allow hunters free rein on the gray wolves that had been removed from the endangered species list.

Thing was, the mortals didn't care what happened to the environment when they reduced the wolf population. Not to mention the devastation to the wolf packs. They were killing wolves that belonged to families. Fathers, mothers and pups. And the loss to the pack was no less heartfelt than a loss to a mortal family. Of course, the hunters never looked at it that way.

It made Daisy think of Beck's loss again. Poor guy.

"So, having car trouble?" Sunday prompted. "I wouldn't be caught dead in one of those clown cars. I can't imagine it has traction on an icy road."

"I try not to drive too much in the winter. But no trouble, as far as I know. I wish I was mechanically inclined like you. None of my brothers are, either."

"Not like they need it," Sunday said. "Those Saint-Pierre boys are too fine to get all greasy fixing engines."

"Whatever. I'm just here to pick something up," Daisy said, trying to ignore the news. Though she shouldn't. This was her story. But she was distracted by the obvious. "I'm not here for, you know, a date or anything."

"What's that about this not being a date?" Beck rounded a yellow sports car (sans windshield) at the end of the shop. A large cardboard box was hoisted on top of his shoulder. "I thought we were going to the iceworks tonight?"

Sunday tilted another eyebrow quirk at Daisy, and it was accompanied by a knowing smile. So much said. Daisy's neck flushed warmly.

"We hadn't confirmed that. Are those the bicycle chains?" she asked, to change the subject.

Beck set the box on the floor before the pickup, and both Daisy and Sunday bent to inspect the contents. Dozens of chains slicked with grease snaked within the box.

"This is awesome," Daisy said. "I can use these."

"Best way to get the grease off is with Simple Green," Sunday said.

"I know. I've done it before."

"How's your art stuff coming anyway?" the familiar asked.

"My work in progress is turning out a lot cooler than I'd hoped. I plan to donate the finished piece to the wolf sanctuary up in Ely."

"Cool."

"And now with these, I'll be able to finish it sooner than expected. Thanks, Beck."

Daisy swung around toward Beck, arms out as if to hug him—her family hugged a lot—then she paused, and dropped her arms. Right. Not ready for that kind of contact. At least, not in front of the familiar.

"Uh, how much do you want for them?"

"I've already stated my price." Beck crossed his arms and peered down at her with his arctic-ice eyes.

He meant accompanying him to the fireworks tonight.

Daisy blew out a breath that fogged before her, even standing within the garage. Attending the midnight iceworks near the ice castle on the lake was a family tradition. And the only way to really enjoy it was to bundle up, snuggle next to another warm body and sip hot chocolate from a thermos. She could completely imagine doing that with Beck.

She glanced to Sunday, who put up her palms and strode around the front of the hood, disappearing from view. "Not listening," the familiar called out. "But check out the news."

Both swung their heads toward the TV, where the female newscaster was talking about the ghost wolf that had been scaring hunters witless. A pair of hunters had sworn off hunting for wolves and anything else, including deer.

"The thing was big and nasty," one of the hunters said to the camera. He gestured widely with his red flannel-coated arms. "And white and filmy like a freakin' ghost."

Beck chuckled. "Ghost wolf. That's a good one."

Daisy wished she could have been the one to interview the hunters.

"But it was solid!" the other hunter chimed in on a shaky voice. "It slapped the shotgun right out of my hand. I ain't never hunting again."

Beck's smile captured Daisy's attention. He was proud of what the ghost wolf was doing. Either that or he was amused by the redneck hunters getting their justice and repenting. Both were good reasons to smile, in Daisy's opinion.

"Whoever or whatever the ghost wolf is," she said, "it's doing all the wolves in the area a big favor by chasing away the hunters. I hope he keeps it up."

"He?" Beck asked as he picked up the box and started toward her car. "You called it an it first. How do you know it's a he?"

Daisy ran up to unlock the trunk. Surprisingly, the tiny car held a lot in the back end. "I don't know if it's a he, or an it, or a ghost. But this whole story has superhero under-tones, don't you think?"

"Superhero?" Beck winced. "I don't know about that."

"The underdogs, which are the wolves *and us* in this case," Daisy explained, "need a defender to protect them. And suddenly from out of nowhere comes a hero on a quest to set things right. I love it!"

"Yeah, but I'm guessing the ghost wolf doesn't have a cape."

"You don't need a cape to be a superhero. Just a focus and a desire to do good. That is my new angle."

"Your angle?"

"I did tell you I'm trying to win an internship for the local paper."

"You're doing a story on the ghost wolf?" His expression changed so suddenly Daisy wondered what she'd said to offend him. "I renew my warning for you to be careful and stay out of the woods unless you bring someone along with you."

"And I renew my assertion to being able to take care of myself. You are *such* a guy."

Beck sighed and shook his head. He did appear genuinely concerned, but Daisy was trying to prove herself here, so she disregarded his anguish. She could do anything the boys could do. Oftentimes better.

"So can I pick you up later?" he asked.

"Um, I guess I could call my brother and cancel with him."

"Really? So it's a choice between your brother, whom you've gone to this event with before, or the lone wolf?" Beck winced. "You should probably go with the safer bet."

"Yeah, but that'll never get me the tangle I want."

"The tangle?"

Oops. Where had that confession come from? Deep inside, where the yearning part of her ignored her armor of introversion and just wanted to get tangled, that was where. If she didn't stop blurting her secrets out to Beck, she'd tell him about her shifting troubles, too. No way. That was mortifying.

Daisy nodded toward the trunk, indicating he set the box inside. "I gotta go. I have some research to do online before tonight."

He settled the box into the trunk and stood back to look over the box. "I cannot believe that fit."

"Thanks, Beck. I appreciate it."

"Where do you live? I'll pick you up around ten."

The man would not take maybe as an answer. So she'd let it happen. Beck would make a much better date than Kelyn. She gave him her address, which he entered into his phone.

Walking around to the door, Daisy paused and turned to find Beck standing right before her. His breath fogged out. Ice eyes took her in. The moment felt as if he should kiss her. And then it did not. It wasn't right. Sunday wasn't far away, and even if she said she couldn't hear anything, Daisy knew that cats had as excellent hearing as wolves did.

She held out her hand, and Beck stared at it awhile before

conceding and shaking. "Later. Uh, will there be brothers at this event tonight?"

"Probably. You scared?"

"Should I be? What's the one's name? Trouble? I should probably keep a good distance from anyone with a name like that."

"Trouble is all bark and no bite. Blade is the one you won't see coming until it's too late."

Daisy slid inside the car and turned the key to fire up the engine. As she backed out, she smiled and waved. Sometimes brothers came in handy. Couldn't let him think it was going to be easy courting her, could she?

But really? The guy was courting her. How cool was that?

Beck went over the brothers' names in his head as he pulled up before Daisy's building. Kelyn. Had she mentioned he was faery? Faeries were no problem. And Trouble was not the one he was supposed to worry about? But Blade was? There was another brother, as well. He didn't know his name.

But he did know the father's name. Malakai Saint-Pierre. The man's name was as much a mouthful as he was a menace. The wolf was big, and he made swords for a living. Freakin' swords. He'd asked Beck on two occasions to join the pack, once a few years ago, and then only a month ago when he'd seen him in town at the local hardware store. Both times Beck had felt disdain in the man's growl.

He couldn't do it. Severo had lived free and alone, but he had been the best wolf Beck had ever known. His father hadn't needed the approval of a pack. He'd lived life on his own terms and had thrived, earned respect from his fellow breed and married the woman he loved and had a son—

With another child on the way.

Beck squeezed his fingers about the steering wheel. His

father should have been here for the birth of his second child. The hunter needed to pay.

The stir of his werewolf twisted inside. It straightened his spine, prodding his skin to form goose bumps. Beck growled. Now was no time to shift, so he redirected his thoughts.

He shut off the engine and stretched out his legs. Focusing on the pull at his hamstrings diverted the werewolf's urge to run free. He normally experienced a twinge of the werewolf when upset or angry. But lately? It was growing stronger. More insistent.

Concentrate on Daisy. Glancing over the brick building's facade and arrowing his gaze up toward the third floor, Beck muttered, "What am I getting myself into?"

Did he need to mess around with Malakai Saint-Pierre's daughter? He'd never let a pretty face distract him so easily. And then again, he'd always let a pretty face distract him. Anytime he went out into the world, whether walking through the grocery store or standing in line (even with a date) at the movie theater, he appreciated a pretty woman. If a guy didn't notice the beauty walking around him, then there was something wrong with him.

But he hadn't dated seriously in months. Not since his father's death. The salad chick last week had been a fruitless attempt at jumping back into the social game.

He'd gone through the grief process rather quickly. Or so he felt. Lately, he was more concerned about his mother. Didn't have time to worry about himself. He was fine. He missed Dad dearly. But he had to move on. For his mother's sake.

So getting back into the groove with this date tonight felt right. Like he was moving forward.

As long as Daisy didn't learn about the other thing he'd been involved with lately, then everything would be golden. Hell, he'd have a tough enough time acting accordingly if any of the brothers were wandering around the fireworks, so he didn't have to worry about the other thing coming up.

Jumping out of the truck, he landed on the compacted snow. He wore his Arctic Cat overalls and a warm matching coat, plus gloves, pack boots and a knit ski cap. It was already bitter cold tonight. And he intended to test the whole *touch not the princess* theory. He looked forward to holding Daisy close to keep her warm.

Grabbing the flowers he'd worried over for a full five minutes at the grocery store, he headed inside and up the stairs to the top floor, just as she'd directed him to do. It was an old warehouse that was slowly being retrofitted for apartments, and so far Daisy and a few other residents were the only ones in the building.

"Nice," he muttered as he topped the stairs and took in the open framework that exposed the original ironwork and ducts. Not what he'd expect a woman to choose.

Daisy was the opposite of the usual sexy, soft, slinky woman he preferred. She punched, too. Entirely unexpected, but she had warned him he'd get a black eye for calling her princess. And the pink hair? He liked it. It looked like cotton candy.

Unzipping his jacket because it was hot up here, Beck knocked on the door, then whipped the flowers around behind his back. He waited a few seconds, listening. All wolves could hear well, and if she had been in the shower, he'd hear the running water and start to imagine that water slicking over her skin—

"Those for me?"

He spun around to find a pink-haired pixy wolf standing behind him, a smudge of black across her cheek. She wiped her hands down an old gray T-shirt, imbuing it with more grease.

"Uh, yes?"

He held out the fluorescent blue daisies. The color was

god-awful, but they had made him think of her. "For Daisy Blu, blue daisies."

"That's so…" She wrinkled her lips into a moue as she accepted the horrible bouquet. Sporting wilted leaves, with one of the flower heads chopped off, it had been the best of the bunch. A guy couldn't find any better in the middle of January in a Midwestern Minnesota town.

"Thank you," she breathed, in a more impressed tone than he had expected or deserved. "It's sweet that you got them because of my name."

"You don't have to act all happy about it. They're an ugly bunch, but—"

"No, I love them. Come inside." She opened her door and he followed her in, but stayed on the rubber mat inside the doorway. "I'll put them in water, then get ready," she called as she disappeared around a corner.

The vast loft ceiling was two, maybe even three, stories high. He loved the wide-open space. Immediately before him lay the living area with couch, TV and armchairs. To his right must be the kitchen that he couldn't see from his position. Off to the left and behind the living area, he saw something big covered with a sheet. Tools and a workbench stood nearby.

"I'm sorry." Daisy appeared before him, twisting her hair about a finger. "I completely lost track of time. I was over at my neighbor's. Her old stove is trying to kick the bucket, and she won't invest in a new one. I had to pull out the heating coil and give it a good talking-to."

"That works with appliances? A good talking-to?"

She shrugged. Such a pretty pink little pixy wolf. He could kiss her right now. Run his fingers through her hair, pull her close and taste her mouth until he forgot his name. But she probably read about that kind of stuff in her books all the time.

How to win over this particular woman, who was like

no woman he had ever dated before? The flowers had been stupid. Should have gone for one of those paperback romances he'd noticed in the checkout line.

"Give me ten minutes," she said. "I'll go wash my face and change quick. You can sit on the couch."

He lifted a foot. "Uh, I should stay here. My boots are wet."

"Suit yourself. In that case, I'll make it five."

She scampered off to the back of the loft. A king-size bed sat against the wall, and near that an iron bar suspended from the high ceiling served as a clothes rack. She pulled a few items from it then disappeared into the bathroom, which appeared to be the only room that was actually walled and private.

Beck squatted down and took in the place. The window at the end of the bedroom was curved to a peak at the top, sort of cathedral-like. Cool. And probably romantic as hell to lay snuggled in bed together watching the moonlight.

He smiled and rubbed a hand over his grin, but realized he didn't need to hide his reaction to the sexy thought.

Beyond the window, the rest of the place was clean and industrial. It was the ultimate bachelor's pad. Big, spacious, minimal decoration. Nothing froufrou. And there was a welder's torch on the bench over by what he assumed was the covered artwork.

He'd like to see how she was using the bicycle chains. Hell, he'd like to see anything she wanted to show him, so long as that meant they got to spend some time together.

"What about the brother?" he called when she stepped out of the bathroom five minutes later, pulling her hair back and twisting it into a ponytail.

"Brother? Oh, right. Kelyn is going to look for me there. He's got a date tonight, too. So we're on our own." She scampered up before him, dressed in snug gray jeans and an oversize black sweater that looked softer than a kitten. "You okay with that?"

"With having you all to myself? I think I can deal."

"Great." She pulled on some snow pants, a coat and a black knit hat with the cat ears on the top and long strings that hung down over her coat and ended in big black pompoms. "What's wrong? You're staring."

"You're just so cute," Beck said.

Daisy punched him in the arm. Apparently this woman's way of dealing with compliments was with violence.

Good, he thought. She'd keep him on his toes. If not leave a permanent bruise on his biceps.

Grabbing a tote bag from the kitchen chair, Daisy led him through the doorway. Toggling a cat ear on her hat, he closed the door. "This way, kitten."

"Oh, do not kitten me," she said as she locked the door behind them.

"You prefer pixy wolf?"

"Pixy wolf?"

"Yeah, you look like a pixy."

"Apparently you have never seen an actual pixy. They're no bigger than six or seven inches and have pointy ears and a nasty manner."

"Then nix the pixy reference. How about faery wolf?"

"Why don't you try Daisy?" she suggested, and shuffled down the stairs.

Beck nodded. Hell, he was nervous. He felt like he'd never been on a date and he was doing everything wrong.

Chill, man. Relax and get to know the girl.

What was it Beck had heard about faeries and their wings? Something about touching them being a sexual turn-on.

"Nice," he muttered.

Chapter 4

They'd found the perfect perch on a hilltop and up against a rock, just behind the masses of people who had gathered at the park. The ice castle sat before the lake, its neon lights reflecting on the shoveled lake surface. The fireworks would begin when they turned off the multicolored spotlights on the castle, usually around eleven.

Daisy poured Beck a cup of hot chocolate that she had made before going to help her neighbor with her stove. The brew smelled so good, she took a sip before handing Beck his cup.

"Had to check," she said. "Make sure it's not too hot for you."

"Thank you, mother."

"Hey, I'm a chocolate freak, so you know. And I don't share my chocolate with just anyone."

"Then I'm honored. To sharing." He tilted his cup against hers, and they drank the toast.

"What?" Beck stared at the cup, mouth open in awe. "This is..." He took another sip, eyes closed and a satisfied murmur rising. "This is the most amazing stuff I've ever tasted."

Daisy bristled with pride. "Why thank you. It's a recipe from my aunt Kambriel."

"Did she steal it from the gods?"

Daisy chuckled. "Actually, one of her friends works at Angelina in Paris. It's a ritzy place known for its decadent hot chocolate. The recipe is a lot of work, but in the winter

I make it at least once a month and freeze it for emergencies. It's necessary to me, like breathing."

"I love it. I love you. I love your aunt. Do you think she'd marry me?"

"She's getting married to a handsome vampire this summer."

"That's too bad for me. What about you?"

"A marriage proposal on our first date?"

Beck sipped again, his eyes closing in bliss. "Yes, please?"

"You stick with love for the hot chocolate for now. I'll reconsider your offer at a later date. Besides, love is so easy."

"You think so? I suppose I did confess love kind of quickly. But seriously, are there witches in your family? I think you've put some magic in this hot chocolate."

"No witchcraft. No even a smidge of faery magic. Just tender loving care. Love it all you like. You can even love me if you want to. Because the real challenge is in liking a person."

"How so?"

Daisy pulled up her knees to her chest and held the hot cup beneath her face. The scent was heady. "When you like someone," she explained, "you enjoy spending time with them. You can hold conversations and never get bored of what the other is saying. Or you can just be next to one another in silence and not feel the need to talk. You tolerate their bad habits, and admire their good. Trust me, like is hard work."

"I agree. To like!" Beck tilted his cup against Daisy's. "So your aunt is marrying a vampire in Paris, eh? Fancy. And a werewolf pairing up with a vamp? Cool."

"Kam's a vampire. My grandpa Creed is vampire, so, well, you can figure things out."

"I can. My mom is a vampire. Though she was mortal

until a nasty bitch of a vampire transformed her after she
met my father."

"She's Belladonna, right? How is your mother doing?"

Beck took another sip, pausing for a while. She studied him from the side. The barely there stubble on his chin
wanted a shave because his good clean looks demanded it.
But she guessed he kept the stubble for that hint of danger,
and it was probably warmer in the winter. He had the all-
American tousled blond-and-brown hair, and that killer
smile. And if she looked into his blue eyes long enough,
she'd surely fall in *like* faster than a falling star.

She'd forgotten what she'd asked him, so when he finally
answered she had to think back.

"Fine," he said.

"Fine?" His mother. "Oh, right. That's good. And you?"

"Me? Don't I look fine?"

"You look more than fine." The words came out in a
dreamier tone than she'd intended.

"Is that so?" Beck wrapped an arm around her shoulders and pulled her against his side. "You look a little cold.
Drink up."

She did, and the hot chocolate filled her gut with a warm
explosion that loosened her nerves and coaxed her to settle
against him a little snugger. They both wore cold-protective
snow wear, so she'd never feel his body heat. But she could
smell him now. A little bit of chocolate and a lot of sensual wildness. His aftershave wasn't too strong. She liked
it. Woodsy and warm. Like an old leather book found in
the hollowed-out trunk of a tree on a hot summer evening.

Mmm, she'd like to crack open his cover and delve deep
into his pages. She bet his story was filled with adventure,
action and some steamy sex scenes. She could hope.

"So where's this brother I need to worry about?" he
asked.

With any luck, Kelyn would not find them tonight. Not

that Daisy expected her brother to actually look for her if he was on a date. If they happened to see one another, then he'd probably wave across the crowd.

"Oh, I'm sure he's got an eye on us even as we speak," she said, then regretted that tease. "Kelyn's cool. If he sees us, just wave."

"Right. Why do I feel as if I have a target on my head, and there are four—five, including your dad—wolves who want to shoot holes through it?"

"I have no idea. You're the one getting all worked up over nothing. Haven't you dated a wolf from a pack before?"

"Nope. You did get the whole lone wolf part about me, right?"

"If you think it's such a bad decision, why are we here right now?"

"Because always making the right decision is boring. Sometimes the wrong one is a hell of a lot more fun. And not getting to learn more about you would be worse than losing my head to one of the Saint-Pierre boys," he said. "Besides, you've already forgotten. I love you."

"Right. A victim of my witch's brew. I can dig it. Love me all you want. Just don't expect me to fall head over heels in like with you too quickly. We don't even know one another."

"That is going to change. Let's talk."

"So what do you want to know about me?"

He toggled the kitty ears on her cap, then tugged the string hanging over her jacket. "What's a cute wolf like you doing without a boyfriend? I can't believe I didn't have to fight off a ton of wolves at the picnic to get near you."

Daisy shrugged. "I'm…" She sighed. The truth was she probably pushed men away simply by being who she was. And yet there were more days than most that she had no idea who she was. Wolf or faery? "I'm not so much shy as kind of content with my aloneness. If that makes any sense."

"Not really."

"I'm not like most women."

"You mean most women don't get excited over greasy bike parts and know how to fix the heating element in an old stove? Who would have guessed?"

"You tease, but next time your stove goes on the fritz…"

"I'll know who to call. So you like doing things with your hands. Nothing wrong with that."

It pleased her that he hadn't said boy things. She'd grown up with the tomboy label. Competing against her brothers for her father's attention had been as natural as breathing. And that had required a hard skin and masculine interests. The tomboy persona hadn't bothered her until her twenties when she'd noticed the women in their pretty dresses walking with their handsome lovers. Femininity was so easy for them. Walking in high heels? Daisy would rather jump in mud. (Which was always a blast.)

And really, dealing with the werewolf in her was always an issue when dating mortal men. But she loved being a wolf, so she wasn't about to complain. Though, her wolf was "one of the boys."

"My father taught me a lot about blacksmithing and working with metals," Daisy felt the need to explain. "And if you grow up with brothers, well then."

Beck leaned into her a little more, just enough so she could relax against him without worrying about toppling over. "I think it would be awesome to have so many siblings."

"I can't imagine what it would be like to be an only child. I suppose your parents spoiled you?"

"I'm not sure doing chores every day, chopping wood and helping my dad tend our land could actually be labeled spoiled. Though I confess I am a momma's boy. She taught me how to cook. I can make a mean wild rice Tater Tot hot dish."

"Ohmygoddess, seriously?" Daisy twisted to fall against Beck's arm and curled her mitten-clad hand about his forearm. "I love hot dishes."

"Like I love your hot chocolate?"

She nodded. "I could marry it. So long as it doesn't have cream of mushroom soup in it."

"I'm not much for mushrooms."

"I knew there was a reason you appealed to me."

"I promise to protect you from any and all mushrooms we should ever encounter. And so you know? I would do anything for this hot chocolate." He held up the empty cup. "Tell me what you want and it's yours, oh pink-haired faery wolf."

Oh, she could think of a few things she'd like him to do for her—all of them involving privacy and snuggling before a warm fireplace. Daisy couldn't resist the lone wolf's allure any longer. "How about a kiss?"

Beck opened his mouth to reply, but at that moment the crowd erupted in an excited whoop. The lights on the ice castle blinked out. Immediately following, a multicolored firework dazzled in the sky, twinkling, lingering and spilling over the iced lake. More sparklers followed at a rapid pace, accompanied by the crowd's oohs and aahs.

Daisy snuggled against Beck's chest to watch. "I've come here every winter with my parents, and then with friends." She pointed to a particular small firework that spun like a Chinese whirligig. "But this time it feels more... magical."

"I like the sound of that." He slid down parallel to her so their faces were inches apart. "Now about that kiss."

Daisy tilted up her chin. Their breaths fogged in a mingled cloud. She closed her eyes, anticipation scurrying heat through her system. Beck's mouth touched hers. The cold night made the first touch icy but fun. She giggled, but didn't stop the kiss. He slid his hand behind her head as he

deepened their connection. Warmth radiated through her
system, and she forgot that it was colder than a deep freeze.

His stubble brushed her chin. When she breathed
through her nose, the woodsy aura that surrounded him
filled her senses and transferred her to that hot summer
night she'd been thinking about.

Nothing had ever felt as good as Beck's mouth against
hers. Not even winning a race against Kelyn, who was
amazingly swift. This kiss was all hers. She hadn't needed
to compete for it. It was a prize she'd not known she needed
until now.

Above them the fireworks glittered up the sky. Beneath
them the compacted snow crunched as their pack boots slid
over the surface. Beside them, the thermos of hot chocolate
rolled across the snowy ground and hit the booted toe of a
man who had just arrived hilltop.

"Daisy Blu?"

She broke away from the delicious heat of Beck's mouth,
wishing she hadn't heard her name and that she could kiss
him again and again, but the voice was too familiar. And
it wasn't a brother.

"Ah, shit," Beck said under his breath.

Daisy twisted to sit and looked up at the dark-haired
man towering over them. "Hey, Dad."

Chapter 5

Daisy got a hand up from Beck. She noticed Beck did not stand tall before her father, but instead bowed his head, showing submission, as was expected when a lesser wolf stood before a pack alpha.

Most men might stand up to Malakai, to grandstand in an attempt to show him he couldn't be pushed around. Those men generally walked away limping or bleeding.

Much as her anger for her father tightened her muscles, Daisy appreciated that Beck showed her father respect.

"Hello, Mister Saint-Pierre," Beck said.

"What the hell are you doing here with my daughter?" Kai asked.

"Daddy, please."

"Quiet, Daisy. I'm talking to Beckett." The taller wolf was dressed in a leather jacket, his long curly dark hair pulled back behind his head to reveal his square jaw held in a tense frown. "Are you two on a date?"

"Uh…" Beck looked to her.

"Of course we are," she broke in. "And will you stop treating me like I'm a teenager? I'm a grown woman. I can see whomever—"

Kai's hand landed on Daisy's shoulder, a staying move that he'd employed as she'd grown up. A means to show her he was not to be trifled with, and must always be respected. It was his gentle way of showing authority.

And she quieted.

"You won't be seeing this lone wolf," Kai said, his gaze

fixed to Beck's, who had trouble holding the alpha's stare. "Isn't that right, Beckett?"

"Uh, sir." Beck's shoulders rolled back. He tucked his thumbs in his pants pockets and looked Kai straight in the eye. "I don't want to cause any problems, but I think Daisy can choose whomever she wishes to date."

Daisy smiled inwardly. *Go, Beck!*

"Are you trying to tell me how to run my family, boy? My pack? Because it sure sounds like it."

"No, sir. I— It's our first time out together."

"And you thought it was okay to kiss my daughter?"

"Daddy," Daisy said under her breath. "Do not do this."

The fireworks had ceased. The night sky grew dark with few stars. The waxing moon hid beyond the tree line. While the humans tromped back to their cars, the trio of were-wolves held position at the top of the hill. Daisy scented her father's anger, and yet, there was a tangible softness to it. Similar to how he reacted when she'd made a mistake when she was little. Like maybe he was puffing up to show aggression in display but didn't mean it as much as he showed it.

But she hadn't made a mistake this time. At least, she didn't want it to be a mistake. She could understand that her father wouldn't want her hanging around an unaligned wolf, but to approach her when they'd been kissing had been too much. She wanted to tuck tail and crawl off into the woods.

"I'll take Daisy home," Beck said.

"No, you won't. I'll drive her home," Kai asserted.

"I brought her here. I won't abandon her," Beck said, his shoulders tilting back a little farther.

"I said I'd take her home, boy."

"I want Beck to drive me, Daddy."

Malakai Saint-Pierre twisted his neck to look down at Daisy. The menace in his gaze could never be softened, and it did not fail to strike at her heart. She swallowed back her bravery and bowed her head. When would she be able to break free of her father's influence? Was it even possible?

"Get in the car, Daisy," her father said.

Beck bent to pick up the thermos and handed it to her. "I'm sorry about this."

"No, I am," she offered. "This isn't how things should have gone tonight." Inhaling a deep breath, she swept her gaze over her father's stare then wandered down the hill.

She hated leaving Beck at the hands of her father. And what had he done? He'd only wanted to get to know her better. Rare was it a guy actually asked her on a date to do something, as opposed to wanting to go straight to her house to make out on the couch. She craved the wooing process. And that kiss. It could have been amazing had her father not shown up.

Glancing up the hill, Daisy saw that her father was already on his way down. Whew. He hadn't given Beck a chewing-out. Her father was not a cruel man, but he was feared for the very reason that his physicality was remarkable. It was the rare wolf in this area who could stand against him, alpha or otherwise.

Daisy got into the old pickup truck and pulled the door shut with the duct-taped handle. As her father got in, she tucked her legs up to her chest and twisted to face the window. The engine rattled, and the truck took off.

"He's arrogant," Kai said after they'd driven a few miles.

"He's kind."

"I've invited him to join our pack too many times."

Daisy swung her head around and met her father's brief glance. "How many is too many? Two? And the one time he was grieving his lost father."

"Two too many. He's refused both times. Says he doesn't need a pack. That's arrogance, if you ask me. Stay the hell away from him, Daisy Blu."

Beck had every right to refuse her father. Daisy could

imagine that if he had grown up with a father who had been
a lone wolf, then the idea of a pack must be odd to him.
Overwhelming. Perhaps even threatening.

"You're not going to stay away from him, are you?" Kai
asked softly.

Daisy bit her lower lip to fight the tears that threatened
to spill down her cheek. She wanted to do the right thing
in her father's eyes. But her right and his right weren't in
alignment now. And she was a grown woman. Too old to
still have her father tailing after her, approving or denying
her choice in men.

"Daisy?"

"I don't know," she finally said.

Kai's sigh rippled through her skin and twanged at her
heart.

The afternoon had been designated for research. Scanning the internet, Daisy tried various search words, starting
with "ghost wolf," which brought up nothing. The data on
werewolves provided for interesting reading, some laughs
and a lot of head shaking. Eventually she typed in Fenrir,
the name of a Norse god who was the son of Loki.

"The ghost wolf obviously isn't Fenrir," she said as she
scanned the information. But there were some similarities.
A monstrous wolf often depicted in paintings as white or
ghostlike, he could not be restrained, save by a delicate rib-
bon named Gleipnir.

Though it was fascinating, it wasn't getting Daisy any
closer to results. The article needed facts, or in this case,
some kind of legend to compare to the ghost wolf, at the
very least. The creature was larger than life. She needed
to communicate that on the page.

"I need a picture," she said. "That would be the ultimate scoop."

When her breed shifted to their werewolf shape, they

could not be photographed. Well, they could be, but none had been that she knew of. They were fiercely protective of their secret. And should a hunter manage to snap a photograph? A quick slap of claws destroyed the camera.

What would ultimately show up on film, she wasn't sure. Nothing, much like a vampire? Or a ghost image of the werewolf? If the ghost wolf was already transparent or some kind of filmy state, the results on film were unimaginable.

She eyed her winter clothes hanging by the door. "I'll go out early in the evening."

The majority of hunters would be packing up and returning home for supper at that time, yet the ghost wolf sightings had been just after dusk.

Wishing she could give Beck a call and invite him along, Daisy waffled on the idea. Her father had been adamant about her staying away from him. Yet she'd been impressed by Beck standing up to her father. He'd cowered initially, to show respect, but hadn't been about to yield to Kai's demands without stating his own position.

"I could like him," she said to herself, remembering their conversation about love and like last night. Like was the goal. Love would simply be a happy bonus.

Beck had felt humiliated standing before Daisy's father last night. He should have stood up to the elder wolf, but it had been the right choice to show respect for the man, despite his intrusion on their date. He'd learned from his father that a man must never jump to hasty violence or make judgments of a man he did not know. If Saint-Pierre didn't want him to date his daughter...

"Hell." Beck wandered the edge of the forest a mile from where he'd parked. "He'll kill me if I see her again." Or at the very least, tear him a new one with a slash of claw.

But he kind of thought Daisy liked him. Make that love.

Like was something even better than love, according to her. He agreed with her definition of it, too.

Man, did he like her hot chocolate.

Did she want to see him again? She hadn't called. But then, she didn't have his number, nor did he have hers. He'd thought about stopping by her place today, but didn't want to push it. Certainly, Malakai would scent him if he showed up anywhere near his daughter's home.

Was he going to let some big boisterous wolf scare him away from the girl? Was she worth the risk?

Beck nodded. The kiss hadn't left him. He could still feel her at his mouth, sighing into him. Clinging to his clothing and leaning in closer. Sweetly hungry. And her kisses had tasted like chocolate.

"I'm going for it," he muttered. Because he knew a good thing when it kissed him.

Now, with the sun tracing a vibrant orange line on the horizon, he shed his winter coat and boots and pulled off his sweater. Steam lifted off his hot skin as the cold assaulted his torso and arms. He stored a waterproof backpack in a hollowed-out oak trunk. The worst thing after shifting back from werewolf form was to find his clothes sitting in a puddle of snow that had melted from the lingering body heat.

Shoving down his jeans, he shuffled barefoot in the cold snow, and when he was naked he stretched back his arms and head, breathing in the crisp night air. The world was gorgeous, and he loved breathing it in. But the very reason he stood here was enough to make him want to punch something.

And then he knew he didn't have to. His shifted form would take care of matters nicely.

A gunshot in the distance alerted him. He judged it a few miles off. This time of day, most hunters were packing it in and heading home.

No time to waste.

Bending forward and narrowing his focus inward, Beck began to shift. His human skin stretched and prickled as fur grew in the pores and his bones lengthened. Claws grew out from his paws, and his hind legs formed into the powerful werewolf's legs. His maw grew long, and ears twisted into long, furred beacons that picked up every movement and sound from mouse to fox, to…hunter.

Beck's werewolf rose to an imposing height, sniffed the air and homed onto the scent of human.

Daisy kept the hunters in view, while hoping to stay out of their line of sight. She wore a vivid orange hunter's vest over her winter coat. She'd no plans to shift tonight—not with armed hunters in the forest. But she certainly didn't want to be so incognito that she invited a bullet.

Her camera wasn't the best at taking night shots. And now as she leaned against the base of an oak tree, fumbling with the settings, she wished she did have something more high-powered. She'd never win the internship by handing in grainy night shots.

Thinking it would have been awesome to have someone along to keep her company on this cold dark evening, her mind drifted to Beck's sweet smile and those entrancing blue eyes.

So maybe she was getting her flirt on with him. Felt kind of awesome.

He hadn't called her today. She didn't know what his number was. She thought he might have stopped by. Her father must have put fear in the handsome wolf.

Daisy decided if Beck never showed again, then that meant he wasn't deserving of her interest. Only a wolf who dared defy her father would be worthy of her time. At least, that was the romantic version she played in her head. In reality, she knew Beck was better off staying away from her and avoiding Kai's wrath.

Too bad. Beck's hasty confession to loving her because she had a talent with hot chocolate had won her over. The way to a man's heart was through food. And she wasn't beyond utilizing such tactics. But as well, his kiss was not to be overlooked. If she never felt his kiss again, the world might never again be as bright. Heck, she'd seen fireworks during that kiss. It didn't get any better than that.

She knew where his shop was. Nothing was stopping her from driving over to see him. "No," she muttered. "He needs to come to me."

A gunshot alerted her, and she whipped her head around, along with the camera. Set at its highest zoom, she peered through the lens and spotted movement. She'd turned the flash off.

There were two of them. Hunters. She saw the shotguns they held. Not aimed at anything because the wooden stocks were slung against their shoulders. And they were running for their lives.

Tilting the camera to the right, she caught a blur of white tracking through the birch trunks in the hunters' wake.

"The ghost wolf." Daisy tracked the blur, snapping shots repeatedly.

The frightened mortals ran within a hundred feet of her. She recognized the hunter in the lead. He had bright red hair and was known in town simply as Red, a Scottish farmer transplanted from his country to Minnesota through love and marriage. She didn't recognize the man behind him, but he yelled for Red to hurry and get to the truck.

Then she scented the wolf. It was angry and feral, and so close she could hear its breathing. Steady, not taxed, and punctuated with vicious growls. Shaped like a were-wolf, she estimated it grew two feet taller than even her father when he was shifted. It was indeed white, but a sort of filmy white, perhaps even transparent.

Remembering her mission, Daisy clicked a rapid succession of shots. When the hunters exited the forest and slammed the truck doors, the wolf paused at the tree line. It smashed out its fists to the sides, cracking the tall birch trunks, and howled. It was like no wolf howl Daisy had ever heard. The haunting noise climbed up her spine and prickled under her skin. She shivered, and sank down against the tree trunk in fear.

Her camera hand dropping to the snowy forest floor, she cast her gaze upward as the white werewolf stalked toward her.

The truck peeled away on the icy country road, its back end fishtailing until the chainless tires achieved traction.

And Daisy wished she had hitched a ride with the idiot hunters as she looked up into the ghost wolf's red eyes.

Chapter 6

Werewolf eyes always glowed golden when shifted. Daisy had never seen the likes of these before. This wolf's eyes were redder than a vampire's feast.

She swore under her breath. The camera slipped out of her hand and slid across the slippery snowpack. The werewolf must recognize her scent as wolf—she hoped. But was it even the same breed as she? It was like her, and yet not. Bigger and bulkier, its shoulders and biceps curved forward in impossible musculature and ended with talons coiled into fists.

And its coloring was surreal, not of this realm. Glowy and pale, but not see-through, as she had guessed. Iridescent. From Faery? Only Faery things glowed as this wolf did. Or maybe a god such as Fenrir? Couldn't be. According to the legend she had researched, that god had been chained until the end of time.

Its white leathery nostrils flaring, the wolf scented her, then whipped its head back and reared from her. Growling low in warning, the wolf stepped back and stretched out its arms. Emitting a long and rangy howl, it sent shivers throughout Daisy's body. She clutched her arms across her chest and tucked her head.

With a stomp of its massive foot, the ghost wolf took off into the forest, leaving its tracks imprinted deep in the snow near her feet.

Daisy breathed out. "Holy shit, that was close."

Holding a shaking hand before her, she assessed her

heartbeat. Ready to bust out from her ribs. She shook her head. She'd take her father's wrath over another meeting with the ghost wolf any day.

And then she checked her fear. The wolf hadn't hurt her, hadn't even moved to touch her. For all she knew, it could be of her breed.

"I can't be afraid," she said. "Only girls cry."

By the time she arrived back in town, Daisy's heartbeat had settled. The fear had segued to an adventurous exhilaration during her walk. She'd stood face-to-face with the ghost wolf! Her brothers would be stunned.

With adrenaline tracing her veins, she wasn't content to go home and crawl into bed. Instead, she headed toward the west end of town where she knew Red lived. She marched up to the front door, passing the truck that hissed out steam from beneath the hood. Seeing a light on inside, she knocked.

Red answered immediately, frowned, then looked over her shoulder. As if she should have brought along an entourage?

"You it?" he asked.

"Uh, I'm Daisy Saint-Pierre, Mister Red. I heard about you seeing the ghost wolf," she tried.

"You bet I did."

"Would you mind answering a few questions for the *Tangle Lake Tattler?*" She whipped out her notepad to make it look official.

"Hell no. I ain't talking to no one but Kare11 News. I called 'em. I thought you were it, but apparently not." He pushed the door closed, but Daisy wedged a shoulder against it and shoved inward. "Nobody but the big news," he reiterated, and this time managed to shut the door completely.

Daisy stepped back and stared at the door. Kare11 was the most-watched news channel in Minneapolis.

"Shoot. I should have gotten here sooner. He must have

called the station as they were driving back. Couldn't have been that scared if he was thinking about his fifteen minutes of fame."

Daisy wandered down the path back to her car just as the Kare11 News van pulled up. She recognized the blonde reporter who got out and directed her cameraman toward the house.

The woman rushed over to Daisy and shoved a microphone in her face. "Are you related to Red MacPherson?"

Daisy shook her head. "I'm with the *Tangle Lake Tattler*."

The reporter lowered the microphone. "Red didn't give you the scoop, did he? I told him this was my story."

"He didn't. But I had to try."

The woman sucked in a perfectly highlighted and blushed cheek and sneered. "Tough luck." She spun about and marched across the shoveled sidewalk in her high heels.

Who wore high heels and a business skirt at eleven o'clock at night in the middle of January? Daisy sighed. A reporter who was always prepared to get her story, she decided. There was a lot she had to learn about the business of journalism.

But she did have one thing that might scoop them all.

Rushing back to her car, Daisy pulled away with one hand on the wheel and the other clutching her camera.

The following afternoon, Daisy opened her front door to find Beckett Severo standing there, smiling sheepishly. The frustration that had been building all day as she'd tried to understand the Photoshop program to enhance her photos slipped away. A more intriguing distraction had arrived.

And a sexy distraction, as well.

"Beck." She shoved a hand over her hair. Hadn't looked at it since stepping out of the shower this morning. Yeesh. "I wasn't sure I'd see you again after, well, you know."

"Do you want to see me?" He remained behind the

threshold, hands shoved in his front pockets. "I mean, should I be here?"

"Yes." She took his hand and tugged him inside. "I didn't want to influence you one way or the other so I didn't make the first move. Also, I don't have your phone number."

He tugged out his cell phone and pressed a few buttons, then handed it to her. "Let's remedy that right now. Type in your number. If you give me yours, I'll do the same."

She grabbed her phone from the counter and handed it to him. Typing in her digits, she entered simply Daisy Blu, and not her last name. She didn't want anything in there to remind him of her father.

"I don't want to disrespect your father," he said, handing her back her phone and reclaiming his. "But I couldn't stay away."

"Why is that?"

"That I don't mean any disrespect to a pack principal?"

"No, I understand that completely. And I have to say I'm glad that humiliating episode did not keep you away. It must have been my hot chocolate that lured you back, right?"

"While I admit that wicked brew could certainly provide a strong lure toward you, that's not the reason. How can a guy walk away from pink hair and fluttery lashes like yours? And you're not like most women. You're smart, and you have interests in things beyond shoes and celebrities."

"I don't know what torture king expects us to walk in those wobbly high-heeled shoes."

"I like you in pack boots and your kitty hat. Can I, uh…" His eyes danced over her face nervously. Then he splayed out his hands. "We never got to finish that kiss before your father showed up."

Indeed not. The man had an excellent memory, and thank the goddess for that.

Daisy stepped up to him and tilted back her head because he was tall, and she wanted to stare into his eyes all day. Until such a view didn't matter, and she closed her eyes and tipped forward onto her tiptoes.

He met her mouth with his. A warm, sure kiss that belonged nowhere but now. She gripped the front of his sweater, beneath the open coat, and when he spread a hand up her back she leaned into him. He was so warm, and strong. The muscles beneath her hands were hard as rock, and she curled her fingers against the curve of his pecs. Yet at her mouth, everything was not hard but eager and searching. Inviting and exploratory.

He smelled like caramel and coffee. Whatever he'd had to drink before coming here, it was delicious. Beck moaned into her mouth and lifted her by the hips. Daisy wrapped her legs about his waist without breaking the kiss. He dipped his head to deepen their connection, dashing his tongue along hers. The taste of him ignited her desires. Her skin prickled, and her nipples tightened. She almost grinded her mons against his stomach but stopped herself. This was only their second kiss. And actually, it was just finishing the first kiss.

"You do that very well," she said against his mouth. "You said something about our kiss never ending?"

"I could keep this up for years." He kissed her eyelid, then tilted his forehead against hers. "You do things to me, Daisy Blu."

"Good things?"

"Good. Bewitching. You make the wolf inside me want to howl."

At that moment a wolf howled on the television turned to low volume before the couch.

Daisy laughed. "Appropriate timing."

"You watching a nature show?"

"No, I've had the news on while I've been trying to figure out how to make a computer program pair up with my camera."

Behind them the news anchor reported on last night's encounter between two hunters and the ghost wolf.

"Karell can suck it," Daisy said. She slid out of Beck's grasp and picked up the TV remote and clicked it off. "I almost had an interview with one of those hunters last night. I should have told him I was with Karell. He'd only speak to them. How's that for sucky?"

"Last night? You were out looking for interviews? How quickly does word get around when something like a white wolf stalking hunters happens?"

"Pretty fast. But even faster when it's witnessed first-hand. I was there." She spun, and her enthusiasm over what she'd witnessed last night made her bounce on her toes. "In the forest. I got a few shots of the hunters running in fear from the ghost wolf, and—you'll never believe this—I actually photographed the ghost wolf. They're too blurry, though. Nothing I can use unless I figure out the computer program. I'm so not tech savvy."

Beck's mouth hung open for so long, Daisy wondered if he'd slipped into a sort of catatonic state. When finally he swept a hand before him and clenched it into a fist, he blurted, "What the hell were you doing in the woods again? Alone? I thought I told you that was dangerous?"

"I'm fine. See?" She spun before him, not about to let the big tough male treat her like a helpless female. Been there, done that. Learned to punch the lug in the gut. "And you know what? The ghost wolf walked right up to me. Sniffed me, even."

"Daisy! It could have killed you."

"Oh, I don't think so. I'm ninety-five-percent sure it's a werewolf. Except bigger. And stronger. Its muscles were just so much…" she caressed the air in the shape of the wolf "…more. And you know, it really does kind of glow. It's white and transparent. Maybe iridescent—"

"I can't listen to this. Daisy, what would your father

say? Does he know you go wandering in the woods alone
at night where hunters are waiting to shoot their prey? You
being just such prey."

"I'm no man's prey. I wore an orange vest. It's not the
hunters I worry about. Besides, I went in human form because I needed to get the shots. Why are you getting so bent
out of shape about this? I'm a reporter. Or I hope to be. I'm
doing what is necessary to win the internship."

"Daisy, reporters don't risk their lives by standing before a wild animal."

"I think they do. At least, this reporter does. But I didn't
fear the ghost wolf. Not for long, anyway. In fact, I know it
wouldn't have harmed me. I felt that from it."

"Must have recognized your scent."

"What? How could it? Recognize it from when?"

Beck shook his head and wandered over to the long table
before the windows. Her notes, books and various sketches
were scattered beside the laptop and a digital camera.

He gripped his hair and paced. "I don't think it's wise.
We don't know anything about this ghost wolf. And even
if you think it's werewolf, it's not like us, Daisy."

"Yeah, I'm trying to figure that out. Let me show you."

She slipped around behind the table where half a dozen
books on myth and even some volumes written by paranormal breeds listed a variety of the known and fantastical
creatures that existed within this mortal realm.

"I haven't found anything exactly like what I saw. At
first I thought it could be an incarnation of Fenrir, but I
doubt that. This one comes close." She tapped a page in an
open book that featured Chibiabos. "It's a Native American
legend, and this area of the state is steeped in Indian tradi-
tions. There's a reservation not far from here. Or this one."

She pulled another book before her and Beck leaned
over, though it didn't seem as if he were interested, but

rather distracted. And not in a good way. She could sense his tension and smell not so much anger as concern.

"Here." She picked up the picture she'd printed out earlier. "This is the best shot I could get of it."

He took the photo and looked it over. It was a blurred image of something white. Could be the abominable snowman for the clarity. If she hadn't seen it with her own eyes, she'd never be able to look at the picture and say, *Yes, that's a werewolf.*

"What do you intend to prove by getting a picture?" he asked. "I know you want the internship, and that requires a winning article, but why this story?"

"It's what I know."

Beck frowned.

"Okay, I know I'm treading dangerous territory with our breed. We're all about secrecy."

"And for good reason."

"Right, and I get that. But the ghost wolf is already out there. The humans are making it out to be some evil creature. But I think of the ghost wolf as more of a superhero."

"Right, your hero in a cape theory. It's nonsense, Daisy."

"I didn't say he wore a cape." But that he'd dismissed it as nonsense hurt. Daisy lifted her chin. "And I want to make sure it's not hunted as a monster, but rather honored as something that made the hunters take a pause to rethink their motives toward mindless killing. The ghost wolf is helping the wolves."

"A noble goal, but..." Beck sighed and turned to sit against the table, facing her. He clutched the table edge and leaned forward, entreating, "What if one of these nights a hunter's bullet goes astray and you get hit? Daisy, this story is not worth the risk."

"So long as it's not a silver bullet, I'm good."

"Silver—Daisy. Wait." Beck stood, his hands pressed together, going to his face. "Silver."

"Right. That's the only thing that can kill us."

"Yes, but…fuck."

"Beck? What's wrong?"

She could sense his increased heartbeats. As well, her heartbeat sped up. What had she said? His mood had shifted from concern to something like angst. He must be thinking about his father. She had heard he had been with him when he'd been murdered.

"I don't know why I haven't been pursuing this all along."

"Pursuing what?" she asked.

"The shotgun shell that killed my father had silver in it."

"That's odd. Aren't most shells filled with lead shot?"

"Exactly. So the hunter had to have made it special. And to use silver…he had to have known what he was hunting. Who would do something like that?"

"You think it wasn't a human?" Daisy asked. "Vampire?"

"Huh?" He found her gaze, as if coming up from the depths, his eyes focusing on hers. "No, it wasn't a vampire. I jumped on him that night, held him down. He was human, and though I was in wolf shape at the time, I felt his fright."

"That's to be expected if a wolf attacks you."

"I didn't attack him. I just…kept him away from my father's body."

Daisy sucked in her lip. They were moving into intimate territory, and she felt the need for caution. It hurt Beck to retell this information, but that he trusted her to reveal a few details was immense.

"I have to go check on something," he said. "This is big." He started toward the door. "I'm sorry. I had come here to spend some time with you. But this is important."

"I understand. I have your digits now." She rushed to beat him to the door and pressed her shoulders to it as he arrived before the threshold. "I want to help you, Beck."

"I don't need any help. And I don't want you getting

shot in your quest for a picture of a creature that could very likely kill you. Will you promise me to stay out of the forests? Please, Daisy?"

That wasn't something she could promise. And she was smart; she knew when she was in danger, and she hadn't felt it yet. Not even when the ghost wolf had walked right up to her.

She touched Beck's cheek and traced his stubble-darkened jaw. His thoughts were miles away, back at his father's side as he'd died in the forest. She didn't know how to deal with grief. It hadn't touched her life. And it had only been a few months since he'd lost his father. He seemed normal and stoic on the outside, but could he be a bundle of agony on the inside?

"Have you spoken to anyone about this? Losing your father?"

"Why? I'm not a weepy girl, Daisy. Something bad happened. I'm dealing. If anyone needs help, it's my mother. She's— Hell. I've got to go. I'm sorry about this."

"Don't apologize. I just… Can we make another date? Tomorrow night? I'll cook if you come over."

"I'd like that. You like wine?"

"Sounds good. Bring red. I'll make meat and potatoes."

He bracketed her head with his palms and bent his forehead to hers again. "You could win my heart, you know that, Daisy Blu?"

"I'll give it a try."

"You don't need to try, just…be you."

He kissed her again, this time holding still at her mouth. She thought she felt his heartbeat in that touch. And in the seconds that her heart stood still, Daisy knew she would try for that win, whether or not he wanted her to.

Chapter 7

Beck found his mother in the kitchen cleaning the copper-tiled backsplash behind the stove. Why she cooked was beyond him, but he was glad to see her not sulking in the big easy chair where she and Dad had always snuggled. She looked good, actually had color in her cheeks, and greeted him with a genuine hug and a kiss.

"How you feeling?" he asked.

"I'm well." She patted her growing belly. "I have a doctor's appointment tomorrow."

"Do you want me to come along with you?"

"No, you don't have to. But you're a sweetie to offer. Did you go to the iceworks the other night?"

"I did."

"By yourself?" she asked in a tone that implied she had already deduced the answer.

"Why do you ask?"

"I haven't been a complete hermit since your father's death. I talk to Blu on the phone once in a while. She said her son Malakai was all in a huff because he saw his daughter with my son. I only have one son—at the moment—so…"

"I've told you Malakai asked me to join his pack, and that I refused."

"You can join, Beck. You don't have to be like Severo."

"I don't feel a strong need to do so. Can we just drop it, Mom? What matters is that I think I like Daisy."

"Daisy?"

"Malakai's daughter. I was with her at the iceworks. But I don't want to piss off her father, so the whole thing is kind of sticky."

"Well, you already have pissed off Malakai. So what's to lose, eh?"

Beck caught the sparkle in his mother's green eyes. "Are you suggesting I see her without her father's approval?"

"I'm suggesting you do what makes you happy." Bella rubbed her belly. She was about four or five months along. "Life is so precious. You should enjoy it while you can." Sucking in a breath, his mother looked away so quickly, Beck knew it was to hide tears. "I was just on my way back to do laundry," she said softly. "I'm going to fold the load before the clothes get wrinkled."

"That's cool, Mom. I stopped by to get a few things from Dad's shop, if you don't mind?"

"Take anything you like." Her voice wobbled as she headed down the hallway.

Beck wished it could be easier for his mother. He considered giving Ivan Drake a call. The vampire had been the one to finish his mom's transformation after she'd been attacked and bitten by Evie, his father's nemesis. Drake had taught Bella the ways of his kind, and they'd been friends ever since. Severo had admired the vampire for his kindness to his wife.

Bowing his head at the lingering scent of sadness in his mother's wake, Beck sighed. Yeah, he'd give Ivan a call today. Maybe Ivan could lift his mother's spirits. At the very least, the vampire could make sure she was getting enough blood so the baby could develop. A doctor's appointment? He hoped she was going to the doctor who had delivered him. A werewolf M.D. who treated all breeds except humans.

Wandering down the marble-floored hallway that hugged the foyer, he arrived at the steel door that opened to Severo's shop. Inside was an arsenal that the old were-wolf had kept for sentimental reasons. Severo hadn't used a weapon in ages, but was ever ready for those werewolves or vampires who thought they could tussle with him.

Beck's father had suffered in his lifetime. Severo had watched hunters murder his parents when he was a child, and had been caught in a hunter's trap himself. He'd limped because of that injury. Those hunters had been vampires. Vampires who had hunted werewolves for the sadistic thrill of it, not for their pelts or the bounty offered by the state.

Similar to the idiot human hunters who currently tracked the Minnesota wolves. The DNR claimed they were harvesting the breed, keeping their numbers down.

Harvesting. Beck hated that word.

Thing is, nature had a way of doing that just fine on her own. The harvesting was murder, plain and simple. And if any hunter dared to be honest, he was going after the wolves for sport, a new hunting experience and a unique trophy for his case.

And Beck would do what he could to stop it.

As he entered the shop and flicked on the light, a chill swept over his shoulders. Last time he'd been in here, he'd held his dead father in his arms. Beck had laid Severo's human body on the steel worktable and had plucked out the bits of shot that had pierced his heart. The silver had run through his veins. Impossible to clean away. All while listening to his mother's wails not far off down the hallway.

Beck's heart was racing with every step he took toward the steel table. The images of that night grew clearer and bold in his thoughts. His father had gasped once or twice as he'd driven him home. Still alive, struggling for breath. He'd been dead when Beck had gently lifted him into his arms to carry into his mother's house.

Falling to his knees before the table, Beck gripped the edge and pressed his forehead to it. He squeezed his eyelids shut and gritted his jaws. Why had it happened? He and his father had always played it safe, keeping to the private land Severo owned, and where they knew hunters were not allowed.

Someone had stepped out of bounds and onto private property. And that someone had used silver to make the kill shot. He hadn't given it a second thought that night. But then, Beck had only been trying to hold it together while he'd made his father's body presentable for his mother to look over.

When one of his breed was killed in wolf or werewolf form, it shifted back to its *were,* or human form, just before the heart pulsed one last time. To watch that shift had torn Beck's heart out as surely as the hunter's shell had pierced his father's heart.

A hunter who must know more than Beck had initially imagined.

Finding clarity through determination, Beck scanned the tabletop. It was clean. He'd wiped it down after wrapping his father's body in sheets in preparation for the funeral the following night. Dozens of wolves had arrived to witness the burning of Severo's body at the pond's edge at the back of their property, including many from various local packs. Beck hadn't known all of them. But he appreciated that his father had so many friends. Or rather, had earned the respect of so many, despite his lone wolf status.

He couldn't recall seeing Malakai Saint-Pierre there. But then, he hadn't looked for him, either.

Now he brushed his arm across the cold steel worktable. Then he bent and searched the floor and spied three tiny beads—shotgun pellets—that must have rolled to the floor. He picked up the pellets. They looked rusted—no, that was dried blood.

A teardrop splashed his hand, but he sniffed back more. He had to be analytical about this and keep emotion stuffed

deep. Laying the pieces on the table, he reached up to click
on the overhead lamp. Inspecting both, he saw that they
were silver, but most shotgun pellets were that color. The
third bead was larger and looked clear, almost like glass.
Yet there was something inside it, as if encased in a delicate womb.

Beck grabbed a bowie knife from the shelf above the
counter and gently crushed the hilt of it onto the bead.
Glass cracked, and beneath the hilt a tiny droplet of silver oozed out.

He was careful not to touch it. Once silver entered a
werewolf's bloodstream, it was only a matter of minutes
before it infected his entire system. Death could result in a
nasty inner explosion, or a slow, painful smothering from
within.

Hell, to think about it wrenched his heart so painfully,
Beck clutched his chest. His father had suffered in those
long minutes as he'd driven him home. If only he could
have done something for him.

He would do something now. He had to find a hunter in
the area who used silver in his shotgun shells. These odd
glass-encased pellets had been specially made. They didn't
look like something that even an expert could manufacture.
If he let his mind wander they looked…futuristic. Where
to find such a thing?

If he asked around at the local shops, he might get lucky
and find the person who had ordered in glass-encased pellets.

It was a start. To a revenge his father deserved.

Hours after her son had left, Bella answered the front
door. At the sight of the tall, dark-haired man who stood
there, she broke down in tears.

"Bella, I should have come sooner." Ivan Drake stepped

across the threshold because he'd been welcomed into her home a long time ago, and wrapped her in his arms.

Pressed against his comforting body heat and enclosed within his strong arms, Bella let her body go weak. She trusted this man, this vampire who was also a phoenix and witch. He had been the one Severo had trusted to complete her transformation after she had been viciously attacked by vampires. He had taught her how to be what she was. She loved him as a mentor and friend.

He lifted her in his arms and carried her into the living room, avoiding the easy chair where she and Severo had often snuggled and watched movies together. Setting her on the couch and kneeling before her on the floor, he grasped her hands and pressed her fingers to his mouth. He held her in his eyes, their silence so easy.

Beck must have called him. She was glad her son had done so.

"I'm here to talk. Or not talk," he offered. "Whatever you need from me. Dez sends her love."

Ivan's wife was a beautiful, centuries-old witch whom Bella also called friend.

"Ivan," Bella gasped. Though it had been months, the smothering clench on her heart never ceased to choke her up. "I miss him so much."

"I know. I've never lost someone close, so I won't lie and say I can understand. That's why I want to be here for you. Whenever you're ready to talk, to let it all spill out, I'll hold you and catch your tears."

"It's not me I worry about," she said through sniffles. "Beckett hasn't had anyone to talk to."

"I'll find someone for him to talk to. But I know you, Bella. You worry about everyone but yourself. You look too pale. When's the last time you drank blood?"

She dipped her head.

"That's what I thought." He slid up to sit next to her, and

clasping her hand in his, he turned up his wrist and bit into the soft underside. "Drink, Bella."

And she did until her heart began to feel the tiniest flutter of life. It would never beat so bold and bright as it once had when Severo was alive. But she knew she needed to take care of herself, and the baby.

Wine bottle in hand, Beck paused before knocking on Daisy's door. He'd vacillated about coming here, and then his heart had pushed him out the door faster than his good sense could argue the worse points of that decision. Because...

Because he was an idiot. Because he wanted some pretty werewolf to kiss him again? No. And yes. And no. It was more than a visceral attraction to a sexy woman that stirred his desires. It was what he'd told her. She was different. And something about Daisy Blu pulled him toward her when all he wanted to do was put up his fists and fend off the softer emotions that vied against the tangle of red and violent emotions that stirred in him lately.

And if all those reasons did not exist, he wanted to keep her safe from her pursuits regarding the ghost wolf.

Shaking out his arms as if after a round of punching the boxing bag out back of his house, he nodded and then knocked. "This is good," he pep-talked. "I can do this."

When the door opened, Beck was hit by a cavalcade of sensual notes. The savory rosemary and sage of roasted chicken. The soft melody of some pop song dialed to low volume. The warmth of the air beckoning him forward. And the visual that so didn't mesh with what he had expected.

Daisy's hair was unbound and spilled over her shoulders in soft pink waves. A sparkle of rhinestones glinted at the crown of her head. A thin strand befitting the werewolf princess she claimed not to be. The usual bulky sweater hung past her hips, and black leggings led to toenails that flashed bright purple polish.

"Daisy?"

She punched him gently on the bicep. "Don't say anything. I found this in a drawer. Do not use the *P* word."

"Uh, okay." *Pretty? Pixy? Princess?* All of the above. "I love it."

"Love is easy, wolf."

"Well, I can't commit to like just yet. So what's with the sparkles?"

"You don't love it."

"I do, I just—" Had expected his usual pink faery wolf, sans any glint of feminine sparkle.

"It's not a tiara, it's just—"

And he leaned down to kiss her, because if he let her continue she might come up with another ridiculous excuse for him not to like her. *Love* her, that is.

He spread a hand through her hair and crushed it in his fingers. It smelled sweet as candy. Combine that with the roasting chicken, and he was hungry.

She ended the kiss and blinked at him. "Why are you so cool?"

"I'm not cool. I just don't live my life based on other people's opinions of what that life should be."

"Like joining a pack?"

"Exactly. And even though I know this is going to hurt, I have to say it. You look like a princess."

He caught her punch in his palm with a smack, and quickly kissed her again. "I win that one."

"I hate losing."

"I suspect that about you. Okay." He spread his arms, exposing his torso to danger. "Take your best shot."

Daisy wound up, and he winced in expectation, but she dropped her fist. "No." She took the wine bottle from him. "I'm not feeling it anymore."

He stroked his thumb across her cheek, as if he could feel the warmth brightening there. "I'm sure the feeling will strike again."

She smirked.

"The whole place smells amazing." He wandered into the kitchen, where two places had been set at the counter and the blue daisies had wilted. "Okay, that's just pitiful." He grabbed the vase and turned around. "Where's the garbage?"

She pointed over her shoulder. Beck plucked out the dead flowers and tossed them in a closet that hid a garbage can. "I'll bring you new ones next time I see you. A natural color, even. Promise."

"I'll look forward to it. Now, sit. Let me test out my culinary skills on you. I don't cook as often as I'd like to. My dad taught me, so I do have some talent."

"Your dad? Doesn't your mother cook?"

"Only bakes. She's into sweets big-time. Dad does all the hunting, so he insists on cooking, as well. Sweet potatoes with a pomegranate glaze," she said, spooning the side dish onto his plate. "I hope you're hungry. I think I made enough for four."

"I'll eat the whole chicken if you need me to."

"We are going to get along just fine," she announced, swinging around the end of the counter to sit beside him.

The meal was amazing. Beck wasn't sure if it was Daisy's culinary skill or just that a home-cooked meal always won over his heart and stomach. He ate everything she put on his plate. And she kept filling his empty plate with more.

As Daisy chattered about how she liked living in town because everything was but a walk away, but really wanted a place out in the country like her father owned, Beck's mind drifted. Standing in his father's shop this morning had worked a number on him. He couldn't erase the image of having to carry Severo home and show his mother.

And then he thought about the ghost wolf. Would the creature ever be able to completely stop human hunters from pursuing the natural wolves and his breed?

He wondered if Ivan had gotten around to his mother's house. She was thin, and needed care. Should he move in with her? Make sure she ate and took care of the baby? He wondered which of her friends might be willing to move in for a month or so, just until she got back on her feet.

There was so much to consider. And now, this beautiful woman sat beside him, oblivious to the torment in his head. She was sweet, and kind, and pretty, and he wanted to kiss her and then push her up against the wall and tug down her leggings and thrust into her, losing himself within her. Finding a solace that could comfort him, if only for a moment in time. Without a care in the world…

"Beck?"

"Huh?"

"You seem distracted. I'm sorry. I shouldn't talk about my work so much."

"It's not that, Daisy." He set down his fork and pressed the heels of his hands against his eyes. "I don't think this can work."

"This? You mean…?"

"Us." Hell, he shouldn't have said it. But better to say it now than to string her along. What an asshole. Taking advantage of her kindness and her cooking.

"There's so much going on right now." His thoughts blabbered out quickly. "You're so good, Daisy. And I'm a fucked-up mess. And my mom…" He stood abruptly. "I don't want to drag you through my drama."

"Beck, I don't want you to leave."

"I think I should."

"It's my dad, isn't it?"

"Your dad? No. Yes. I don't know. I wanted this to work out. You're such a pretty faery wolf. And your chicken is the best I've ever eaten. You sparkle. Your conversation is interesting. But right now things are so crazy in my life."

Could he just grab her and kiss her until all the crazy thoughts slipped away?

"You've been through a lot," she said, fumbling with the ends of her hair. "But I'd like to be here for you. Beck, I really want to spend time with you."

"And that's dangerous for you. At least, right now it is. I have to go. I'm sorry. The meal was so good. I don't want to be the kind of guy who walks out on a girl, but…"

He tugged on his coat and marched out the door. "So sorry," he muttered. "I'm the wrong wolf for you," he added, knowing she could hear him, but not sure how to face her.

Chapter 8

Denton Marx looked over the various ingredients he'd gathered over the past few months for the allbeast spell. Each was contained in a small glass jar capped with a screwable tin lid. Marvelous technology, that lid. He needed something like that in his own time.

Alas, to think of his own time—and the woman whom he had lived with in that time—never ceased to raise his ire. Too much time had passed. Sencha must believe he had stopped trying to rescue her from that horrible nonplace where she had become trapped.

She had once told him about the Edge. Witches feared it only if they traveled through dimensions and time. And as a wandersoul, Sencha traveled through time quite often. She was possessed of a soul that wandered the worlds and times, ever searching, until it found that one other soul it felt comfortable enough to remain with, and cease the wandering.

His soul.

Yet even after finding him, she had continued to travel through time because it pleased her. And she had taught him how to do it. He had drank her blood in a ritual that allowed him to actually travel through time on his own, but only once or twice before the magic was depleted. He'd used it to obtain the weapon he must now use to get the final ingredient to the spell.

He would kill a werewolf, and then he and Sencha could be together again.

* * *

Daisy pulled on her snow pants and zipped up her coat. She slipped the orange hunter's vest over that. It was dark out, but if a hunter's flashlight beamed over her while walking amidst the thick foliage, she wanted to be seen.

Sighing as she locked the front door behind her, she wished tonight's supper hadn't gone over so horribly. Beck had practically pushed her out of the way to leave. Something must have set him off, because he'd sat and eaten and talked with her for almost an hour before deciding it wasn't going to work.

Had she talked too much? That wasn't like her. She rarely gabbed anyone's head off. It was easy to let loose and be comfortable with Beck. She'd probably let her hair down too far. She'd freaked him out by wearing the crystal headpiece. It had once been her mother's. Finding it in a drawer had made her smile, and she'd felt the urge to pretty up for the guy. She should try to tap into her feminine side more often. It may be necessary to win the guy.

And she wanted to win him.

"So I don't have feminine wiles," she muttered. "Screw it."

Stepping outside, she gasped at the below zero weather and sucked the permafreeze into her lungs. Rushing to her car, she set her camera on the passenger seat and fired up the engine. Thank the goddess for heated seats that warmed quickly. In no time she was snug as a bug. Pulling away, she wondered if she should drive by Beck's shop on the way out of town.

She shook her head.

As much as she had wanted to grab him, pull him close and offer him the comfort she sensed he needed, she'd also felt the distance he'd asked for was the better bet. He was struggling with loss.

Maybe this distance was best for the both of them?

Daisy sighed. Seriously? She was hot for Beck, and

she'd thought he was for her. She'd been hoping their kisses would advance to something more tonight. What did a girl have to do to get a little between-the-sheets action from a handsome man? Was a skirt a requirement?

"Can't be. Just give him space," she said, turning onto the country road where she usually parked.

Fifteen minutes later, she stalked through the forest, camera in hand. The scent of humans was strong. They were nearing her, but perhaps still a quarter of a mile away. And then the other scent rose, and Daisy flicked her head around to home in on it. The feral scent was familiar and strong.

"The ghost wolf. It has to be."

Finding a wide oak tree trunk, Daisy positioned herself against the rough bark and waited. If another pair of hunters dashed past her tonight, she'd be ready.

The hunters did run by, fifty yards off. The luminous ghost wolf pursued them. Daisy's camera snapped repeatedly, and the zoom was set high. As well, she'd adjusted the f-stop and ISO according to an article she'd read online for better night photography. She really should use a tripod, but she'd be thrilled if these shots showed more than a white blur.

As long as she tried, she may come up with at least one or two good pictures out of the dozens she was taking.

Headlights popped on, beaming through the woods, but not lighting where Daisy stood. She scampered from tree trunk to tree trunk, positioning herself for a better shot. The hunters pulled away in a cloud of snow spit up by tire chains. Rock music blared through the closed truck windows.

The ghost wolf had struck again. Its howls echoed in the air, pricking up the hairs on Daisy's skin.

Where was it?

Daisy noticed the feral scent had risen. It was moving closer to her. She maintained her position against the tree trunk, unwilling to risk spooking the wolf. When she heard its huffing breaths, she sensed it was less than thirty feet away. Over near the massive copse of white birch whose trunks had been marked at her head level by moose antlers.

She dared a peek around the tree where she stood. The big white werewolf had slowed to a walk but wasn't coming toward her. Was it possible it wasn't aware of her presence? Bending its muscular body forward, it dropped onto all fours. It looked as if it would begin to shift.

The ghost wolf was a shapeshifter?

Well, of course, if it was a werewolf. Daisy just hadn't put two and two together. So the wolf could be a man. Who was it?

Clinging to the bark with one hand, she readied the camera with her other.

The ghost wolf howled, thrusting back its massive head as its body contorted into the shift. It was never painful, unless the wolf resisted the shift—but it did appear to others an agonizing experience. Within seconds the body had changed, losing fur and claw and taking on skin and the features of its *were,* or man shape.

"Holy crap," Daisy whispered.

She couldn't force herself to take a picture of the naked man lying there on the snowy ground before the tree trunk. He heaved in a breath as if exhausted, then crawled to the tree and pulled out a backpack from the hollowed-out trunk. When he turned around to sit and dress, he suddenly lifted his head, sniffing. He'd scented her.

What to do? Reveal her presence and risk his anger? Or attempt to run, only to be surely caught if he pursued?

Either way, he wouldn't be pleased.

Daisy stepped around the tree trunk, putting herself into his view.

The wolf swore.

"Beck," Daisy said.

Chapter 9

She'd watched him change.

The remarkable, luminescent creature who instilled fear in the hearts of many hunters was really a man. Daisy dropped the camera in the snow. Slowly, she approached the naked man sitting before the birch trunk.

Beck put up a hand. "Daisy, wait. Let me get my pants on."

She nodded and stayed her position.

"Turn around?" he asked.

"Oh. Right." She turned and listened as he pulled up his jeans.

He was still breathing heavily. Huffing, as if exerted. Normally coming out of a shift from werewolf was exhilarating. At least, it was for her. It stretched her muscles nicely and worked out any kinks that may have developed over the days since the last shift. Much more fulfilling than if she brought out her faery wings.

"Okay."

She turned at his voice and saw Beck stumble backward, catching his palms against the papery birch trunk and collapsing into a sitting position again. He tilted his head back against the tree and closed his eyes.

"Beck? Are you okay?"

"I'm fine. Just…it takes a lot out of me. Give me a few minutes to catch my breath. Come back to this form completely."

She crept closer and knelt beside him. His eyes still

closed, he breathed in deeply, his chest expanding and stretching the gorgeous muscles. His biceps were tight, the veins cording them in graceful curves and ropes. He perspired, even sitting in zero-degree weather. His face was beaded with sweat, and his hair stood up at all angles.

When he opened his eyes and met her curious gaze, he shook his head. "I didn't want you to see this."

Daisy's held breath released in an exhilarated sigh. "But I did."

He nodded, closing his eyes again. "That you did."

"You're the ghost wolf," she added enthusiastically.

How cool was that? She'd discovered the secret behind the ghost wolf. He really was a werewolf, as she'd suspected, and—he was the man she wanted more than anything right now.

"How is this possible?" she asked. "Are you like me? A werewolf?"

He nodded. "It's a long story."

"I want to hear it."

"So you can write an article and print it for the humans to read? I don't think so. Daisy, I didn't want to drag you into my mess."

"You didn't do any dragging. I stepped into it. And grant me the right to make my own choices and speak to whom I wish, and date whom I want."

"I'm not your dad, Daisy. I'm just a guy who wants to protect you from the dangers of…" he spread his arms and let them drop at his sides "…this."

"How are you a danger to me? I saw the ghost wolf— you—the other night. You scented me. I think you recognized me."

Because in werewolf state they hadn't complete control over the human mind. Smell was the key sense. They were more animal in that shape, and they sometimes recognized friends, but sometimes did not. It was a good thing, because once back in human form, to remember having pursued and killed a rabbit, or even a deer, would not be cool.

"You would never hurt me," she said. "But why haven't you done something to the hunters yet? You've only been scaring them."

"I don't want to hurt anyone, Daisy. I want to scare the living crap out of them and hopefully, in the process, change their minds about ever killing wolves again. If I were to harm one, that would bring me down to their level."

"Beck, you're so right. I'm sorry. I shouldn't have insinuated that you could be so cruel. I can't believe it's you. I'm so glad it's you."

She lunged into his arms and hugged him, nuzzling her face against his bare shoulder. He was hot and smelled of musk and salt and the fresh tinge of snow and ice. Delicious. And sensual. "I won't tell anyone. I promise. But you have to tell me how you are able to do this."

"I will. Soon."

"Right. I won't push. And I won't take notes. Promise."

"Daisy, what are you doing to me? I walked away from your place today, thinking that was it. Much as I wanted you in my life, I knew it was better to keep you out. Safer for you. But now…"

"It's hard to get rid of me."

"You think?"

"Beck, now more than ever, I understand you're in a tough spot with everything going on in your life. I'd love for us to have a relationship. But if you're more comfortable with us just being friends, I can do that. I just don't want you out of my life."

"Your father will have an argument for that."

"Yeah, well, he's not here right now."

"Are you sure? Because he seems to turn up when we least expect him."

"Very sure." She leaned up and kissed him.

Moving to straddle him, she deepened the kiss and he moaned against her mouth. The ridiculous heat of him compelled her closer, and she wished she weren't all bundled in winter clothes so she could share his body heat. Then she corrected her lusty thoughts because she shouldn't push. If this was what he was willing to give her right now, she had to accept that.

"So we can be friends?" she asked.

His eyes traveled back and forth between hers. He smirked and tugged the end of one of her cap strings. "From you I need more than friends. If that's okay."

She nodded eagerly.

"Good, because I don't kiss my friends. And don't forget, I love you." And he kissed her again, pulling her into the exhilaration of the unknown.

Beck pushed his hands through her hair, and her cap fell off and tumbled down her back. There beneath the tree-filtered moonlight, they kissed like tomorrow was to bring the end of days. And it felt exciting. Daring. Dangerous. She was kissing the ghost wolf! And he wanted to be more than just friends.

Daisy could deal with that. But she knew she had only brushed the surface of Beckett Severo. The man was complicated. And that didn't begin to define the ghostly werewolf that he was able to shift into. She would learn him. But she'd be careful, and respectful of his need to guard his privacy and protect himself.

Honestly? She'd try hard to respect his barriers. But this touching, kissing and tasting one another was fast plundering all barriers.

"I want you to touch me," she gasped as he licked her lower lip. "I'm wearing too many things."

"I want to touch you, too. I want to put my hands all over your skin and read you with my touch."

"Mmm, I like the sound of that."

"See? I like to read, too," he offered with a wink. "But not here in the woods with me sitting in a pile of wet slush. Want to come home with me? You can open your cover for me and let me do a little reading."

"Keep talking."

"Yeah, talk. We need to do that, too. I think talking should be at the top of the list."

"Then let's go."

They stood, and Beck shoved his feet into his boots. Daisy handed him his sweater and coat, regretting his need to cover those awesome abs.

"Did you see which way the hunters went?" he asked.

"They ran out toward the east access road. I didn't recognize them." And she knew, as werewolf, he wouldn't be able to recognize their faces while in human shape, but their scents he should know if he encountered them again. "Was it the one…?"

He shook his head. "I don't think so."

How weird was it that Beck had the ability to become the ghost wolf to stalk the very hunter responsible for his father's death? Had he always been this way? Or had his father's death changed him so drastically that he had literally become a monster?

"Did you check on the silver? You said you were going to do that."

"Yes, the shell that killed my dad was handmade, laced with tiny glass pellets filled with liquid silver. I've never seen anything like it. It looked technologically advanced. Which means whoever killed my dad was purposely hunting werewolves."

"That's insane. You think a human knows about us?"

"Lots of humans know about the things they shouldn't know, Daisy." He grasped her hand. "Where did you park?"

"That way." She pointed over her shoulder. "Should I follow you to your house?"

"Or I could bring you back to pick up your car later."

"Good plan."

And she didn't want to let go of his big, wide hand. Not now that she'd gained some of his trust. And now that he was leading her to his home, where she would learn the truth about the ghost wolf.

Beck's first thought as he drove toward home with the pink-haired faery wolf sitting beside him was a feeling of relief. Now she knew. Someone knew. He didn't have to carry that burden alone anymore.

But he should. It was his burden. He'd asked for it. It could endanger anyone he got close to.

Yet his brain battled to keep the relief, along with the gratefulness that swept through him when Daisy clasped his hand and smiled quietly at him as they cruised down his street. He lived ten miles from where he'd been stalking the hunters. The land out here was selling too rapidly. He'd have to move soon if his neighbors got closer than the three-mile distance they were at now. He valued his peace and privacy. All wolves did.

Behind the house he'd built a few years ago, a four-acre pond had frozen over for the winter. The beavers were hibernating as well as the bears. He did not shift and hunt on his meager twelve acres. Because again, the neighbors were too close. And in this neck of the woods, seven out of ten humans owned guns and felt it was their right to shoot at anything they feared or didn't understand.

Which was pretty much anything on four legs. Two legs, if it glowed.

Someday he'd move up north into the Boundary Waters, where a wolf had more freedom because the vast acreage offered privacy. But to move so far from his mother, especially now when she was so fragile, felt wrong.

"I like this area," Daisy said. The truck's headlights

beamed across the thick woods that surrounded his house. "Quiet?"

"Very. You ice skate?"

"I, uh, yes?"

He chuckled at her reluctance. Parking, he swung around and raced to Daisy's door. She'd opened it by the time he got there, but she did take his hand to get out of the truck. Baby steps, he decided, would endear him into her trust.

"You can skate on the pond behind my house," he said. "It freezes thick. And I'm guessing you might be into hockey."

"I am a pond hockey champion. There's not a Saint-Pierre in the county who can beat me."

"An accolade I'm sure your brothers keep to themselves, eh?"

"You know it."

As they approached the house, a rabbit scurried across the snow cover, stitching tracks in the snow. Beck opened the door, and Daisy stopped inside on the rug and stomped the snow from her boots. He kicked his boots off beside hers.

"I'll get a fire going." He strolled into the living room and opened the hearth. A stack of wood he'd refilled this morning offered dry pine. He started a log on fire and closed the screen.

Daisy had shed her outerwear and stood in socks, tight gray leggings and a cozy purple sweater that looked two sizes too big for her, yet compelled Beck to pull her in for a snuggle.

"You always look like you need a cuddle," he said. "You and your pink hair and soft clothes. And these lips."

She turned up that raspberry sherbet mouth to him. "What was it you said about my lips?"

"They fit mine nicely." He kissed her quickly, because his brain was beginning to spin again. Sure, he'd invited her here to make out. But he'd also invited her to talk. And the talk, while necessary, would take a lot out of him. "Hot chocolate?"

"You know the way to my heart." She followed him into the kitchen and slid onto a bar stool.

Beck sorted through the cupboard, pulled out two small plastic cups and displayed them to her. "It'll never rival your magical elixir. Just Keurig."

"My brother Blade likes that coffee," she said. "I didn't know you could make hot chocolate with the machine."

"I can make cider, too, if that floats your boat."

"Chocolate, please."

It took but minutes to warm up the coffeemaker and brew the first cup, then the second.

Daisy cast her gaze over the kitchen's inner timber walls. "This house is cozy."

The furnishings were all clear-stained timbers with bright, patchwork cushions. The coffee table had been hewn from a single oak trunk. The hardwood floors had been made from reclaimed redwood. All natural or recycled.

It truly felt like home to Beck. His father had loved to sprawl on the couch and listen to Lynyrd Skynyrd while Beck had worked on taking apart a carburetor in order to learn how it worked.

"It's a home," he offered. He slid a cup toward Daisy. "Give me your rating."

She took a couple sips. "Not bad for powder. I'll give it a six."

"I'll take the six. But that makes yours a twelve, hands down. Let's go sit on the couch."

He put another log on the fire and joined Daisy, who had curled her legs up and settled onto the couch. She touched his cheek as he sat and turned her finger to show him the ash she'd wiped off his skin.

He rubbed a thumb over his cheek.

"Let me," she said. Licking her thumb, she then rubbed his cheek until she pronounced, "Gone." She leaned in, eyes closed, and scented him. "You smell so good."

Beck's skin tingled. It was difficult not to go straight to horny around her. Hell, why not?

Because they needed to talk. And talk would lead to trust. Trust was important before they could take this relationship further.

Setting her mug on the coffee table, Daisy then took his and set it aside. She climbed onto his lap and kissed him. Chocolate and winter, that was her flavor. She was sinuous and warm and so soft under his roaming hands. Beck glided his hands up her back and around to cup under her breasts. She didn't balk at that touch, so he spread his fingers over the small curves. He wanted to lick them.

Too fast.

But he sensed if she moved a little bit closer, she'd feel his need because he now had an erection that wouldn't stop.

Pressing his palms to her cheeks, he stopped her deep kiss. "We have to go slower," he said. "Just until…"

"I get it. You're the ghost wolf. I have a lot of questions."

He nodded. "Hand me my mug."

Chapter 10

An hour later they sat beside one another on the floor before the fire, their backs to the couch, their feet tangled together. Beck hadn't let go of Daisy's hand the whole time. She didn't ever want him to let her go.

He'd explained it all. It was fantastical. And that was saying a lot, considering Daisy's heritage. She thought she'd seen and heard it all.

In the immediate days following his father's murder, a streak of revenge had coursed through Beck. And yet, he was not the sort to commit retaliatory violence. Sure, he sought the hunter who had killed his father. But to kill him? Never. There had to be a way to prevent him from killing other wolves. He'd wanted to instill fear into the hunter—all hunters—and perhaps even save a few gray wolves in the process.

But he hadn't known how to do that. So he'd gone to a faery.

Faeries were not the first choice a person should go to for help. Daisy knew that too well. She'd grown up listening to her parents tell the tale of how they had met. How Malakai had been cursed by a malicious faery, and how her mother had been cursed as a leenan sidhe—a faery who fed on the vita of others until they literally died—because she'd broken off an affair with the Unseelie king, Malrick.

One should never dabble with faery magic without certain knowledge that it could never end well.

Daisy believed that Beck had not known what he was

getting into when the faery had offered to give him super-natural ability to shift into something that would frighten mortal men.

"What did she ask in return?" she asked now that Beck had laid it all out.

"I'm not sure."

Clasping his hand against her chest, she nuzzled her head against his shoulder. "Beck, faeries never give away their boons. There is always a return favor in exchange."

"I know that. She wants a favor, but she didn't specify. She doesn't want repayment until I've accomplished my task."

"Which is?"

He quieted and looked down at their clasped hands. "You know. I...wanted revenge for my father. A life for a life."

"You said you couldn't imagine killing another."

"I can say that to you now. But in the days after my fa-ther's death?"

She nodded. That he'd confessed such a thing was im-mense. Awful, but trusting. She wouldn't question him for having murderous thoughts at a time when grief had surely overwhelmed.

"I did it when I was grieving," he explained. "I could never harm another person. Even the man who killed my father. It would make me as evil as him."

She kissed his knuckles and smoothed her thumb over his warm skin. That he was able to think like that now, with his father only dead a few months, was remarkable. She wagered whether any of her brothers would hold a death wish infinitely if someone took Malakai Saint-Pierre's life.

"Will you ever forgive the hunter?"

"Forgive him?"

"Seems the thing to do to close the grieving process. Maybe. I don't know."

"You don't know. And I have grieved. So let's drop it, okay?"

"Sorry." Who was she to suggest proper ways to grieve? Though she suspected Beck had not gone through the grieving process because his claim to have done so had been defensive.

"You didn't seem right after you'd shifted to *were* form in the forest," she said. "You stumbled."

"Lately I'm totally racked after a shift. It's weird. Usually I feel more alive and vital after a shift."

"As you should."

"Shifting to the ghost wolf drains me."

"There's always a price to pay for magic. Beck, what if continuing to shift to the ghost wolf kills you?"

"I'm fine, Daisy." He pounded his chest with a fist. "Feel better than ever now that I've rested."

"Exactly. You shouldn't have to rest after shifting from werewolf. That's not normal."

Brushing off her concern, he stood, picked up the empty mugs and padded into the kitchen. "You don't need to worry about me. I'm not exactly a normal werewolf, if you hadn't already noticed."

He'd tossed up an emotional barricade. But Daisy allowed it. She wanted to tender his trust with care. And really, she was no expert on compassion. She was most comfortable hanging with the men and practicing duels with Kelyn. Emotional support? That was out of her skill set. But even so, she wanted to be there for Beck because it didn't seem like he had anyone else to confide in.

"So you're going to keep scaring the hunters?" she called toward the kitchen.

He paused from placing the mugs in the dishwasher, glancing toward the window over the sink, darkened by the night. He didn't answer her.

Daisy wasn't sure she wanted to hear his answer. Did he

believe his own words that he could never kill? She prayed that he did. But that wasn't the problem, was it? Maybe the ghost wolf had plans of its own?

"It's almost midnight," he offered, returning to stand over her. He gave a hand, and she stood. "Probably should be getting you back to your car."

She nodded. He'd hit a limit on sharing. She was cool with that.

"If I invite you over for supper again," she asked, "will you stay for dessert?"

"I promise I will. I'm sorry for the quick escape the other day."

"It's cool. It's gotta be kind of freaky dating me."

"Because of the big bad wolf who is your dad?"

"I know you respect him. But you have to also understand if I don't push back at my dad now, he may never let me go. I'm his only daughter. I'm sure it's tough to see me in the arms of an unfamiliar wolf."

"Who is not in a pack."

"You don't think you'll ever join a pack?"

"Maybe I'll start my own someday?"

She kissed him. "It doesn't bother me that you're a lone wolf. So don't let my dad's voice have any room in your head, okay?"

"Too many other voices in there right now as it is." He handed her her coat, and she hung her snow pants over an arm. Didn't need them for the ride home. As they strode outside to the truck, Beck said, "You promise you won't tell anyone I'm the ghost wolf?"

She nodded. "But I still need to do the story for the competition. This is a chance for me to get a job, Beck."

"Daisy."

"You can't understand what it would mean to me. My father believes I should never work. And I don't have to, thanks to the investments he's made in my name. But I'll always feel tied to him, like I owe him. Do you see now what making my own money would mean to me?"

"Sure, but isn't an internship an unpaid position?"

"Initially, but I plan to quickly prove my worth and earn a paying journalist position. Beck, I didn't go to college. I have no real-world job skills. This is the best I can do."

"So it's got to be the ghost wolf?"

"I've put a lot of time into it already. I need to do it in a manner in which the humans won't ever believe the wolf is a real, living creature. Maybe some figment drunk hunters are conjuring? Like Fenrir reimagined in their wildest nightmares?"

"That's an interesting angle."

"I promise no one will ever know it's you."

"Especially your family?"

"Deal." She slid into the truck, and when Beck leaned up she bent to meet his kiss. He hadn't pulled on a jacket. She pulled off a long strand of pink hair from his sweater.

He took it from her. "I'm fascinated about the faery in you. Promise you'll tell me about that next time we meet?"

She nodded. "Tomorrow night. I'll make steak."

"Woman, you spoil me."

"It's all part of my devious plan."

"To make me like you?"

She nodded and kissed him.

Dessert was chocolate cake drizzled with caramel. Beck ate all three pieces Daisy offered him. The mood felt much lighter this time around. He didn't plan to suddenly bolt for the door. Spending time with Daisy did distract him if he allowed it. So he did.

"Leave the dishes," she said, grabbing his hand and leading him to the couch. "So how is your shop coming?" she asked as he sat beside her. "Didn't you say you wanted to open it to the public?"

"For as many cars as I have to work on just by word of mouth, it'll be another year before I can consider opening to the public. It's nice work. Keeps me busy."

"When you're not chasing after hunters? How do you feel today? Still weak from the shift?"

"Nope, I'm at one hundred percent. It's only immediately after the shift that I'm weak."

"Well, I hope it doesn't get worse. Do you want me to ask my mom about faery bargains? It worries me that you didn't have to repay the faery who gave you this ability."

"I don't want you to worry about me, Daisy." He kissed her again because he didn't want to get into all that was wrong in his life. Seeking her heat, he pulled her onto his lap. "Let's talk about you," he suggested. "You said you'd tell me about your faery side. So can you shift to wolf or faery? Or is it a combination thing?"

"It's an either/or thing. Wolf shift, or faery shift. I prefer being wolf. But lately things have been complicated."

"Like how?"

Daisy shifted on the couch to sit with her knees drawn up to her chest. She wrapped her arms about her legs. He sensed her closing up, much like he had just done, so he slid closer and tilted his head onto her shoulder. She smelled warm and homey, like the chocolate cake she'd made for dessert. Sexy.

"Tell me?" he said and toyed with a curl of her hair.

She slid her hand up around his neck and pushed her fingers into his hair. This comfortable embrace felt like perfect Saturday afternoons and summer nights that he never wanted to end. And if she would confide in him, that would mean so much.

"It's all screwed up," she said. "My shifting. I should have control of it. Should be able to shift like my brother Blade does. He can shift to vampire with wings. It's the most incredible thing to see."

"A vampire with wings? Can he fly like that?"

Daisy nodded. "Add in the fangs, and he's a threat every man should take seriously."

"Not someone I want to mess with."

"For sure. I'd take on my father before Blade any day. Trust me on that one." She tightened her grip about her legs. "But me. Lately I try to shift to faery and I might get a wing out, but then—and this is so embarrassing—my wolf tail pops out. And I can't seem to control it. I go for werewolf and it happens for a while, but then it's like the faery doesn't want the wolf out so it comes over me. And vice versa. If I'm flying around with wings, suddenly the wolf wants out. Have you ever dropped from in the air, shifting as you fell, to land in a sprawl on the ground as a wolf?"

"Ouch."

"Yes. And embarrassing. That's why I haven't told anyone in my family. You can't tell anyone this, Beck."

The desperation in her voice made him ache for her.

"I won't. But would it help if you could talk to someone in the know?"

"Who?"

"Your mother is faery."

"But not wolf. And since she's lived in the mortal realm for so long—since before my birth—she's not up on all stuff Faery."

"Isn't there something like faery witch doctors?"

"Faery healers? Sure, but I don't know of any in the area. Oh, Beck."

He put an arm around her shoulders, granting her a closeness he sensed she needed. "Maybe it's just growing pains?"

"I don't know. That should have happened a long time ago at puberty. I'm a grown woman. I should have this all figured out by now. I can't talk to my mom about it, or my dad."

"What about Blade? If he's the same as you…"

"I don't know. Blade and I are close. I am with all my brothers. But it feels kind of squicky to me to ask any of them about this problem."

"It's not like you're asking them about sex, right?"

She smiled. "No. And I don't know why I should feel this way. As a girl who grew up in a household full of men, I've seen more naked penis than I probably should have for a lifetime. My family is into the natural state."

"Interesting. Do you think there's any way I can help you?"

"You didn't want me to worry about you, and I certainly don't want you to worry about me. I have to figure this out on my own. But thanks for asking. It means a lot. I'm glad I told you this. Did you feel relieved when I saw you shift from the ghost wolf?"

"I did. So if I asked you to show me your wings, would that be a no-go?"

"That would involve me taking off my shirt."

"Ah." He slid his palm down her arm, the thick sweater loose and warm. Turning his head, he kissed her at the base of her ear and she squirmed closer. "And what is it I've heard about faeries and their wings?"

Daisy nuzzled in and kissed him. "They help us to fly, silly."

"Right, but I thought there was something about wings and sex?"

She took his hand and placed it over her chest. His fingers conformed over her small breast, and Daisy sucked in a breath. If he could just hold her like this forever…

"To touch a faery's wings," she whispered, "is a sexual invitation. It would feel as if you were running your fingers over my skin. But the more intimate areas of my skin, if you know what I mean."

Beck nudged his forehead against hers. He breathed

against her lips. "Then when you feel the time is right to show me your wings, I will be honored. And probably horny."

He captured her laugh with a kiss, and they fell backward onto the couch. Daisy stretched out her legs and he fit his hips against hers, lying on top of her but not putting his full weight on her. He lingered in the kiss. She pushed her hands up under his sweater, finding the rigid abs, and walked her fingers over the landscape.

"What are you doing?" he whispered.

"Counting your six-pack."

"All there?"

"I think there could be eight."

Pushing up on one hand, he used his other hand to tug off the sweater and toss it to the table beside the couch. "How's that?"

"Oh, yeah." Daisy pressed her palms to his abdomen and traced the muscles from side to side, then followed the ridges that veed down toward his jeans. He sucked in a breath at the erotic sensation. "I like these ridges," she said. "They are so sexy. Leads my eye toward—"

"Mischief?" he finished.

She tucked a finger behind the waistband of his jeans. "Maybe."

He pushed up her sweater, and Daisy lifted her hips so it would slide up more easily. When the soft red yarn reached just below her breasts, he settled onto her again and followed his curious hands with kisses. Pressing a kiss to her ribs, he placed another higher, and again, a little higher.

Daisy closed her eyes and clutched at his hair. Her body felt taut and warm. She tilted back her shoulders, lifting her breasts higher. Seeking, silently pleading.

"No bra. You make it hard to go slow, Daisy."

"You're doing just fine." He painted his tongue along

the underside of her breasts, and she sucked in a breath. "I like that."

Sliding his hands up under her sweater exposed her nipples to the air. The aureoles tightened. Beck sucked in one hard tip, lazily curling his tongue about it. She tasted like summer, winter and autumn all rolled into one. His knees bracketed her thighs, squeezing her snuggly. The eight-pack she'd counted rubbed her belly and mons, and his erection angled against her body.

She tucked her fingers into his jeans waistband, the tip of her finger skimming his cock head. Beck jerked up. "Whoa!"

"I'm sorry. Are my fingers cold?"

"No, I'm just… You're in a hurry."

"You think so? I just assumed… Well, you're a handsome guy. I'm sure you've had many girlfriends and lovers…"

"Yeah, but Daisy, that's all they've been—lovers. Not worth spending time with and getting to know. I don't put you in the same category as any of the women I've previously seen."

"I'm not sure how to take that."

"It's good. And because you're different, I want this to go slower, but fast enough that I don't injure myself trying to hold back." He slid a hand down her arm and to her wrist. She pulled her fingers from his waistband. "It's going to happen between us. Sooner rather than later. But let's play it cool for tonight. The moon *is* full in three nights."

"That means in two nights," she started, but didn't have to finish.

Beck knew exactly what she was thinking. The nights preceding and following the full moon, the werewolf wanted out. Most werewolves restricted themselves to just the one night of the full moon. When they lived so close to humans, it was dangerous to let their beast out more often than that. And in order to keep back the beast on those two nights, their bodies needed to be sexually sated. So sex was a given.

Beck dipped his head near hers, their cheeks brushing. "So, uh, how about Saturday night?"

He was asking for sex before the full moon. He couldn't bear a refusal, and he knew he was being forward. He adored Daisy. And he needed more of her kisses and her hands and tongue roaming over his skin.

And if he didn't satisfy his wolf's need for sex, the ghost would come out.

"You don't have to get all ghosty on Saturday night?"

He shook his head. "I'll save it for the full moon." He hoped. He kissed her breast, then nuzzled his cheek against her skin and between her breasts. "I'm not trying to push things, Daisy."

"I know that. I think I'm the one who is more eager."

"Trust me, I'm eager." He ground his hips against hers. "I thought you noticed that?"

"I did. Can we play it by ear until then?" she asked.

"Of course."

"I want to see you tomorrow night."

She hadn't refused him. Whew. "How about a little pond hockey?"

"Really? You think you can take me on?"

"It'll be worth the try."

"Then game on. I'll come to your place after supper. I've got a standing dinner with my grandmother."

"Your grandmother is the werewolf married to the vampire, right?"

"Yes, Blu and Creed. Is it all right if I get to your place around eight?"

"I'm not going to get any work done tomorrow because I'll be thinking about you all day."

His kiss was soft, lingering. A perfect end to a perfect evening.

Chapter 11

Moonlight shimmered on the ice-covered pond on which Beck skated back and forth with a shovel, pushing the light snow cover to the banks. Hockey sticks jutted from where he had jammed the handles into the snow.

Daisy settled onto a snowbank, wiggling her hips to form a seat in the moldable snow, and laced up her ice skates. Within minutes she landed on the ice, hockey sticks in hand.

"You got a puck?" she asked as Beck stabbed the shovel into a snowbank.

He pulled out a thick black rubber disk from his pocket and tossed it onto the ice. His grin curled deliciously. "I'll take it easy on you."

"If that's the way you want to play it. I sure as hell am not a duster," she said, using the term players called one who spent all his time on the bench. She tossed him a hockey stick; he caught it in a gloved hand. "I did grow up with four younger brothers. I would have worn my hockey skates, but they're in Dad's shop for a good sharpening. These will serve."

Her figure skates glinting with flashes of the moonlight, she performed a graceful spin on the rough surface. Growing up in Minnesota made it natural for a girl to take to the ice in the winter, no matter her breed. Daisy could probably skate better than she could fly. She preferred that method to travel, that was for sure.

"Where are the goals?" she asked.

Beck pointed to a nook he'd carved out of the snow in the bank just behind him, and then to a thicket of dried weeds at pond center, around which the ice had grown. Without warning, he took off, stick to the puck, blades shaving the ice.

"Boys," she muttered. "Gotta be careful, Daisy. Don't show him up. Too much."

Yet she could not allow him to win. Such benevolence would screw with the very fiber of her existence.

Going after the puck, Daisy easily stole it away with a sweep of her stick. She made a long shot and landed the goal.

"I let you have that one." Beck skated around her casually, his body leaning into the curve. He wore but a sweater, jeans and gloves. His muscled thighs swept him across the ice like a pro. Claiming the puck from the snowy goal, he shot it toward her.

Daisy returned it to him. They skated, zigzagging toward the goal in the center of the pond. When they neared the thicket of weeds, Daisy swerved in front of Beck, claiming the puck, and deftly backhanded another goal.

"Stop letting me win," she said over her shoulder as he retrieved the puck.

"Deal."

This time the steal was a little harder, but Daisy was not beyond some body checking to get the prize. Slamming her body against Beck's, she knocked him off balance, and his stick arm wavered. She made another shot, achieving the goal.

"Hat trick!" she announced.

Beck's smirk had disappeared. Daisy thought he might have even growled. About time. She craved a challenge.

Skates cutting the ice, they dashed across the surface jockeying for the puck. Daisy kept her body tight and her center low to increase her speed and make herself a smaller target. Beck's body nudged hers, but she sensed he still wasn't giving it his all. If he knew how many bruises she'd collected battling her brothers in a Saint-Pierre family game, he wouldn't be so gentle.

She liked that he respected her. But he was still going down.

"You've got the moves." Beck managed to finagle the puck away from her. "I'd hate to see you with the hockey skates."

She checked him again, but he swung his stick and slammed it onto the ice, cutting in on the puck. With a flick of his wrist, he made the goal in the weeds.

"Score!" He circled the goal with arms raised triumphantly.

Yeah, boys always liked to make sure everyone knew when they'd done something like make a goal. Or beat their sister at chess. Or managed to win a four-legged race through the forest. Yes, wolves could stand on their back legs and punch the air with a triumphant forepaw.

Daisy shook her head and chuckled. "I'm ahead by two."

"Yeah?" Beck skated beside her, guiding the puck with his stick. "Let's make it interesting."

"What do you have in mind?"

"Next one to score a goal gets a kiss from the other."

Sounded like a win-win situation to her. But when challenged, she took it seriously.

Dashing in for the steal, Daisy commandeered the puck momentarily. Beck shoved her hard, jockeying for the puck. He sliced it away from her. She kept on him, skates spitting up ice in her wake and arms pumping to gain on him. She checked him with a body slam, and he returned the shove. Hard. But it didn't set her off balance.

Thrilled he was finally giving her his all, Daisy chased him with her stick gliding near his. He slapped the puck back and forth, and she slid in for the steal, and with a shift of her hip, bumped his thigh. Racing toward the goal, she felt him on her, his stick in her peripheral view.

Smiling at the brisk kiss of winter against her face, and the thrill of the moment, Daisy flicked the stick. Beck slid in and blocked the puck from what should have been a winning glide across the ice toward the goal.

He shifted position, facing her, their sticks to either side of the puck. Heartbeat racing, Daisy growled defiantly yet playfully.

"Is that so?" he said on a light tone. "I don't think so, Saint-Pierre. This goal's mine."

He slipped the curve of his stick against the puck, and Daisy shoved him hard. His stick left the ice. Daisy commandeered the puck and made a long shot for the goal in the snowbank. The puck slammed into the snow, wedging in deeply.

"Yes!" Time for the winner's dance. Daisy wiggled her hips and skated backward, shifting her shoulders in a victory shimmy. "Oh, yeah, I am so good. I win. I win."

"Competitive much?"

"Always have been. Always will be."

"I think I like you better when you're flirting awkwardly with me."

"Sore loser."

Beck skated up to her, a darkness falling across his eyes. He looked like one of those imposing goalies that any player should fear and back down from. Standing straight from her silly dance, Daisy's mouth fell open. She wasn't sure what he was thinking, what to say to him. He didn't look too happy.

Just when an apology tickled her tongue, Beck slammed into her body, gripped the back of her kitty-eared cap and pressed his winter-iced lips against hers.

His breath hushed coolly against hers. Daisy's hockey stick clattered onto the ice. She moved up onto her ice skates' toe picks to stand a little taller and keep the exhilarating kiss.

Her arms falling slack she went with the *being held* feeling. Crushed against him by his powerful embrace, she wanted to take what he gave. And his kiss was delicious. Urgent and hot. His tongue traced her teeth, her lips, her tongue. It was a slow, sensual glide that stirred every portion of her being to a jittery spill of desire. Her nipples hardened beneath the thick knit sweater, and her fingers curled within the mittens she wore.

If every game ended in such a reward, she'd sign on with the NHL tomorrow.

"You win," he said against her mouth.

"I most certainly do. Screw the game. I want more."

She tugged him back down for another kiss. Picking her up, Beck glided toward the snowbank where he'd carved out the goal and, tilting forward, he deposited Daisy onto the shoveled heap. He went down with her, jamming his knees into the snowpack on either side of her legs. Biting off his gloves one by one, he dropped them onto the snow.

His warm hands bracketed her cool cheeks as he lifted her up for another kiss. This one wasn't going to let her win. She felt as if he were controlling her, and it felt...awesome.

"Wanna play another round?" he asked.

"Of pond hockey?" She tapped his mouth. His lips were burnished red from the chill and their kisses. "That's up to you. Would you rather slap sticks or swap spit?"

"Both sound appealing."

"Really?"

He waited for her to pout, and so she did. And then he tugged her upright and pulled her across the ice, collecting the sticks as he did. "Game over! I'm all for warming up inside with a pink puck bunny."

"Dude, I am no man's puck bunny. They're the silly bits of fluff who hang on the players in hopes of getting lucky."

"So you're saying you don't want to get lucky with me?"

She considered it. "Puck bunny it is."

* * *

Daisy raced through the living room and dodged the ottoman, where a patchwork quilt lay strewn. She giggled and headed toward the kitchen. But her plan of evasion was thwarted when Beck slipped around the opposite side of the kitchen and met her near the dining table.

She shrieked playfully as he swept her into his arms and carried her over to the couch. He dropped her onto the plush couch piled with pillows, and she landed on the softness but didn't expect the handsome wolf to follow so closely.

He crouched over her, hands near her shoulders and knees bracketing her legs. "I win."

She supposed he did deserve some small win after she had just kicked his ass at pond hockey. "Deal. You win one silly puck bunny." She scooched up to sit and brushed her hair aside from her face. "Well, not so vapid. Much smarter, I hope. But I suppose being a puck bunny is all about what's on the outside, isn't it?"

"No way. I don't want anyone looking at you."

"So you'll take the tomboy over the bunny?"

"I'll take Daisy Blu, the gorgeous wolf who is not afraid to be herself." He pulled her onto his lap, and she snuggled against his insane heat. "Wanna snuggle?"

"You are a man who knows how to please a woman."

Chapter 12

"The only place is town that sells custom-made shell cartridges is now closed," Sunday said as she strode around the side of the F-150, tugging up her overall straps on each shoulder.

"So whoever made the glass shot probably got it in the Twin Cities."

"Or could have ordered it online," she suggested. "What you're dealing with is custom-made. I'm guessing its origin is paranormal, not human-made. I mean, if the pellets were glass filled with silver?" Sunday shook her head.

Beck rubbed the grease smear on her cheek. "Thanks, Sunday. I appreciate you looking into that for me. You heading home?"

"Yep. It is the night before the full moon." She winked, and strode into the back room that was more a storage for everything Beck couldn't find a place for than a neat employee lounge.

Sunday, the familiar, and her husband, Dean Maverick, the werewolf. How those two ever got together was beyond Beck. But they'd been together a long time, so it proved that opposites really could attract.

And he certainly didn't need reminding that it was the night before the full moon. His breed, for reasons beyond him, needed sexual fulfillment the night before and after the full moon. Well, they didn't *need* it. If they did not respond to the carnal pull, their werewolf would come out. Nothing wrong with that. Only, living so close to humans, the werewolves tended to let their wild side out one day a month—on the full moon. Otherwise they risked too much if ever seen.

Perhaps mating with Daisy tonight would bring them closer. He hoped to have sex with her, but he seriously did not want to push. They both needed sex tonight, but just because they did didn't mean they had to take it from one another. He didn't want to do anything to screw up this new relationship.

Nor did he want to bring the wrath of Malakai Saint-Pierre knocking on his door.

Beck blew out a breath. "I'll take things as they want to go tonight. Let her call the shots." He grinned to think about the shots that woman had taken last night.

Playing hockey with Daisy had been a thrill and a surprise. The chick was competitive. And a great player. She was no puck bunny, but he wondered if she'd be okay with the term puck faery?

The idea of giving over some of his control to a woman was novel, but it didn't feel entirely out of left field.

He headed into the garage office, where he kept a computer. He'd search for silver sales in Minneapolis and St. Paul. He had no idea how to track down this hunter, but he wasn't about to stop until he'd found him and made him pay for tearing his family apart.

Daisy set aside the log she'd printed out from the paranormal forum. She'd had the idea to go in as someone looking to hunt werewolves, and who was looking for the best weapon. She'd gotten all sorts of replies, but no silver shot in glass capsules. Yet. Beck had thought it was advanced technology. Maybe Stryke could help. He knew enough about most things that he may have an idea regarding a lead.

She couldn't think about work right now. It was date

night. With the one man she couldn't stop thinking about. Dreaming about. Wanting to kiss, touch and…

"Have sex with," she said, and rubbed her palms together in expectation. "I am so ready for you, Beck. I hope you're ready for me."

She sorted through the clothing on the steel bar suspended from the high ceiling. Her grandmother had offered to let her go through her closet yesterday during dinner, but Daisy had been in Blu's closet before. It looked like some kind of costume warehouse for every mood, color and emotion a woman could ever have. That chick had the clothes.

"Grandma is so spoiled." She trailed her fingers down her few pieces of clothing. Guess that was possible when Blu's husband was a nine-hundred-year-plus vampire who had acquired a vast fortune over his centuries.

Growing up in her family, Daisy had learned the value of taking care of one's things and not needing something just because a person wanted it. She had a few things she adored, and the rest were functional for when she worked on a sculpture or was out reporting. Sure, she was set for life thanks to her father's investments in her name, but…

"I have to show him I can take care of myself."

Her fingers trailed over the soft red sweater that featured a narrow black marabou tuft around the V collar. It was angora, and she loved wearing it without a bra, feeling the übersoft fabric caress her skin. It was the sexiest thing she owned.

"Perfect."

A pair of black leggings and some black riding boots with skull-studded metal buckles at the knees finished the look. Casual yet sensual.

Beck liked her this way? Not all dolled up like a puck bunny? She'd bought that mostly. But she still sensed he wouldn't mind if she showed him her softer side.

"Do I have a soft side?"

Panic rushed heat into her chest, but she quelled the sudden anxiety by pressing a palm over her heart.

"We'll find out tonight."

Already her inner wolf squirmed in anticipation. Her faery half could care less. This night before the full moon, the werewolf wanted release. So part of her pranced about in an attempt to ramp up her adrenaline, get her to answer the feral call, while another part looked forward to quelling the werewolf the only way it could—with touch, taste and erotic connection.

She needed sex until she was sated. If she'd had a boyfriend who did not know she was werewolf, then he'd always marveled at her incredible horniness and was raring to please her. If no boyfriend, she was not beyond a one-night stand, but she generally drove into the city to find someone she would never again see. It was her nature. She needed to answer this call.

And tonight was going to be perfect. Or she hoped, very close to something wonderful.

Beck assumed Daisy would have eaten by the time she arrived. He set out some wine but wasn't sure what else he should provide. He scanned his cupboards. Ripple chips or cheese crackers sounded wrong. And the tin of BBQ-coated almonds was so not romantic. He supposed cheese and fruit would have been appropriate to set the mood, but he wasn't that talented of a grocery shopper.

Cheese crackers it was.

A clench in his gut suddenly bent him before the kitchen sink. He gripped the stainless steel and closed his eyes, fighting the odd wave of what didn't feel painful, but what was beyond the usual *let me out* pangs he got from his werewolf.

He felt his bones shift slightly and shook his head. "No. Not tonight." While normally he felt the urge to shift the night preceding the full moon, he could always control it. This was insistent. "What the hell?"

If he shifted against his will, that would be a new one. And dangerous. He didn't want to shift to the ghost wolf when Daisy was around.

The twinge of whatever it was subsided with a tug down his spine. Beck straightened and flexed his fingers in and out of fists. "Whew!" Exhaling, he prayed he could keep it under control.

The doorbell rang. He slapped a palm to his bare chest. He'd been in the middle of dressing when it had occurred to him he might need to entertain the woman and had gone in search of wine.

Halfway to the door, the werewolf again gripped his insides and demanded release. Beck slammed a palm to the front door and yowled. He must fight the twist inside his body. He dropped to his knees. His hand began to shift and he frantically shook it, forcing it back into human form.

Again the doorbell rang, followed by a knock. "Beck?"

"Daisy." He gripped the doorknob. The wolf that wanted release suddenly fought against the *were* that he was, the man who needed sensual touch—hell, sex—to tame that wolf. Drawing in a breath through his nose, he smelled the sweet pink faery wolf on the other side of the door. He got a hard-on like that. "Ah, shit."

The door opened against his back. He sat on the floor, legs bent and toes digging into the rug. His senses were dialed to ultraalert, and Daisy's sweetness spilled across his skin like a summer breeze warming his flesh and stirring him to a moan. A wanting, needy moan.

What the hell? He couldn't act like this in front of her. He did not want to scare her, or allow her to think he was some kind of freak. She had to leave.

He slapped his hand against the door, closing it. But she was already inside. Standing there in some thigh-hugging black pants. Metal skulls stared at him from the tops of her leather boots. And up over her winter coat, he eyed the pretty pink waves spilling to her elbows like a treat. Kitty ears capped her head. Those silly pom-poms at the ends of the strings looked like a toy he needed to bat at.

Yeah, to play with the kitty. Mmm...

"Beck, what's wrong?"

"Daisy, I'm sorry." He yelped as an insistent punch to his libido goaded him to jump up, grab her and push her against the wall. "I— This is not right. Something is happening. I'm not sure I can control it."

"Is it the ghost wolf?"

He shook his head. The last thing he wanted was to be in this position before a woman. Unsure, unstable and out of control.

"Do you feel the need to shift?"

He shook his head adamantly.

"Yes?"

"Yes. And no. It wants...you."

She pulled the kitty cap from her head and knelt before him. "*It* does?"

He closed his eyes, biting his lip. Not this way. He didn't want the first time with Daisy to be like this. It couldn't be. He'd never forgive himself.

She pressed a palm to his cheek. The sensation of her slightly cool skin to his heated face shocked an erotic zing from there directly to his cock. The main shaft tightened against his jeans.

"Sex?" she whispered.

Ah hell.

Chapter 13

He was suffering. Daisy had seen the same signs with her brothers at times on the night before the full moon when they'd been younger and had been trying to discern the whole *should I shift* or *should I seek a sex partner* thing.

Beck's skin was so hot. His chest glimmered with perspiration. He pushed her hand away and snarled at her. Was he fighting the shift, or fighting the urge to take her in a loveless quick means of satisfying his driving needs?

While the idea of sex without emotion did not appeal at all, Daisy had come here knowing it wasn't going to be a gushy love-filled event. Love wasn't even in the equation yet.

Okay, so it was. Like was the ultimate goal. And she was on a straight path to liking Beckett Severo.

But desire was the issue right now. And her wolf responded to his panting need to repress his desires with her own delicious tangle of desires. Ah, the tangle she had wanted. She wanted Beck. She wanted sex, plain and simple. She simply…wanted.

She pulled off her coat and pushed it aside.

"You can't stay," he said through a tight jaw. "It can't be this way, Daisy. It's not right."

"Beck, your wolf needs to be sated."

His mouth stretched taut. She smoothed a hand down his chest, glancing over his tight pectorals and to his ridged abdomen. Inside, her wolf stirred, hungry yet patient, if only she would serve it the sensual treats it craved.

"Daisy, please."

She wanted to lean forward and lick his fevered skin, trace her tongue over the ridges of muscles that hardened his frame as if a suit of armor. She wanted to go on the wild ride this uncertain moment promised.

"I want you, Beck. I need this. Don't you desire me?"

"Ah, fuck."

She leaned in closer to his face. Musk and male aroused every nerve ending on her body. Her nipples hardened. Aware her soft sweater brushed against his skin, she leaned in closer and her breasts snugged his chest.

He gripped her hair, holding her back, yet with his other hand he pulled her forward by the hip.

"This excites me. You excite me," she whispered near his ear, then dashed her tongue along his lobe and sucked it into her mouth. "I'm a big girl. I can handle a horny were-wolf. You want to try me?"

"Daisy—but it won't be right."

"Who's to say what is right or wrong? We both want something from the other. We do love each other. Do you love me?"

He nodded fervently. "The easy part, right?"

"Right. No like yet."

His hips bucked up against her as she squatted upon his thighs. He clutched her sweater. "So soft," he muttered. "And red. Oh, Daisy…"

"Let's do this," she said. "Fast, furious, and don't stop until we're both satisfied. Yes?"

"You're not going to go away, are you?" He pushed his hands up under her sweater and palmed her breasts. With a moan, he squeezed her nipples.

"Oh, hell no," she said. "And you don't want me to leave, either. Do you?"

He shook his head frantically.

"Let's make this right. There's no other man I'd rather be with right now than you."

"Same. I...I want you, Daisy. Beyond my werewolf's needs. I swear."

"I know that. So let's get it on."

Daisy thrust her breasts forward, giving him what he wanted, and greedily taking the exquisite pleasure of his touch. She tugged off her shirt, and Beck hissed at the sight of her bare skin. He braced an arm across her back as he pushed her down onto the rug before the door and bent his head to her breasts. Laving at her nipples, one and then the other, he slicked them with his hot tongue. Suckling them hard and then kissing and licking all over her breasts. She squirmed under his ministrations, and pulled him closer with fingers through his hair.

"Not on the floor," he suddenly said, and lifted her with one arm.

Daisy wrapped herself about Beck's torso and kissed him aside the neck as he marched down the hallway. He panted heavily. Still fighting the shift, surely. She wanted to tame him, yet at the same time, keep him wild.

The bedroom was dark, save a beam of moonlight that sifted through the sliding glass doors on the opposite end. A patchwork quilt and mounds of pillows lured them toward the king-size bed. It looked so inviting that Daisy jumped from his arms and sat on the edge of the bed, then fell backward against the pillows.

"Come here, wild one," she said, crooking a finger at him.

"You are..." He shook his head as he approached, unzipping his jeans. "Much wilder than me. Beneath your bookish exterior..."

"You did want me to flirt with you."

"That I did."

He dove for her, landing on all fours above her, which

made her giggle. He cupped one of her breasts and gave it a quick lick before moving up to kiss her neck, and up under her chin until finally his mouth landed on hers, and he groaned into her as he ground his hips against hers.

His erection rubbed against her mons, and with a wiggle of her hips, Daisy positioned herself to feel the hard rod against her sensitive apex.

"Oh, yeah." Threading her fingers into his hair, she took his rough and wanting kiss. Everything about his urgency excited her, made her want to rush to the finish line right along with him. As if they tracked the forest on four paws, she would run with this wolf through the night. "Condom?" she suddenly thought to ask.

He nodded and from a drawer beside the bed pulled out a crinkly package and set it on the pillow.

"Now that's sexy." She slid a hand down his hard abs and farther, over his jeans to cup his erection. It was wide and so hard. "Another stick for this puck bunny to handle."

"Woman, you touch it, you can't put it back on the shelf and walk away."

"Oh, I won't."

Daisy toed off her boots, and they dropped to the hardwood floor with a double *clunk*. Beck reached for his fly, but she stopped him. "Let me."

He hovered above her, in a plank position, allowing her to shove the jeans down his hips. His penis sprang out and landed on her thigh, the hot, wide head of it flaming her skin. She gripped it firmly, and his moan played a wanting melody above her thundering heartbeats.

Hips rocking, he slid his cock up and down in her grasp.

"You're so hard, Beck," she said with admiration. "I can't wait to feel you inside me."

"Not until you're ready." He tugged down her leggings, and she shimmied to wiggle them off. Now they were both naked, and their skin put off intangible steam.

Beck bent to kiss her breasts, gently, pulling at the nipple and then letting it spring from his mouth to cool in the air that tightened the ruched tip to a diamond.

His explorations journeyed south, his kisses marking her belly and navel, and moving lower, licking and tasting and kissing until his nose tickled along her mons.

"Pink here, too," he said in amazement.

"My hair color *is* natural," she said, following with a giggle. "Mmm..." She gripped his hair loosely as he bowed to kiss along her folds. Head falling back against the pillows, she surrendered to whatever he wished to do. "Yes, do that, you big sexy werewolf."

Spreading out her arms across the pillows, she closed her eyes and fell into the giddy, tingly sensations that coiled up her spine and through her being with every lash of Beck's expertly placed tongue. He tended her on the outside for a bit, and then dove into her, thrusting his tongue as deeply as he could and challenging her need to lay back and experience when all she wanted to do was answer back with equal zeal.

He suckled her and teased at her clit, tendering it carefully even though they were both frenzied by the moon. The innate need to connect, to become one with another. To satisfy the carnal within that would otherwise set free their werewolves.

Shoulders pressing into the pillows, Daisy felt the orgasm swirl within her core. She didn't want to fight it, and wouldn't. "Oh, yes!"

Hips bucking as her lover kissed her deeply, Daisy soared into the climax. Beck withdrew to allow her to ride the bliss. Yet he maintained contact, his forefinger gently tracing over her humming clit, while his kisses again moved up her belly and to her breasts. And when his tongue lashed her nipple, the subsiding orgasm swelled and she cried out at the bonus climax.

"Wild wolf," he murmured. "I love the sound of your pleasure. Let me hear it again." He teased a little firmer over her swollen clit, and Daisy's panting breaths increased. "Will you come for me again?"

"Of course I will. But…ohmygodess."

She wanted to ask *what about you?* But the climax hummed too close. And she knew he would get his rewards soon enough. Releasing her voice again, Daisy's body quivered beneath her masterful new lover, a willing recipient of all he wanted her to have.

Holding Daisy in his arms as her body shivered beneath him was amazing. Beck had forgotten about the inner pull to shift. The sex was working. He'd been unsure, had wanted to push her away because he wanted this to be right. But her suggestion that this crazy joining may be right had been on target.

Her sinuous body stretched out alongside his on the bed. Small breasts hugged his chest as she kissed his neck, placing snowflakes here, then there, then moving lower. If she went down on him, he'd lose it too quickly. Every atom in his body was ready to explode. He needed to take his time.

When her fingers wrapped around his cock and slid lower to squeeze at the base, he released a heavy breath. Just what he needed. The woman was well-informed about tending a man's hard-on. He wasn't going to question it, and in fact, he could only applaud. For the moment, the urgency to come had subsided. But not completely. He walked a line between flame and volcanic lava flow. He just had to balance a little longer…

Daisy slicked her fingers between her legs, wetting them, and then slid them in a coil up and down his rod. "You're nice and thick," she purred. "I want you inside me. But first I want to play with you. You like this?"

Her hand had moved up to squeeze under the crown

of his cock, where it was supersensitive. Beck's ability to put two words together ceased. Instead he groaned and gripped her hair. When her tongue lashed the head of him, he thought he saw stars, but that was just because he'd squeezed his eyes so tightly he'd captured the moonlight against his irises.

"Daisy…"

She laved up and down his length, slowly, then a little faster, then licking again at that sensitive underside of his crown. She knew exactly how to ignite every pleasure receptor. His inner wolf danced, tamed and unwilling to shift.

He swore and gripped a pillow as her mouth encompassed him as deeply as she could manage. Hips wanting to thrust, he fought to sustain the crazyhummingwant vibes. Right there. Everything hummed just at the surface.

When she reached up and claimed the foil condom packet, he could only groan as he felt her expertly slip the tight sheath over his pulsing cock. Just one more squeeze…

Beck came forcefully. Even as he rode the pleasure, she mounted him.

"Yes," she whispered, and then she settled onto him, sheathing him deeply within the heat of her body, the exquisite, tight walls that hugged and squeezed him. "Again," she commanded.

And with but a few thrusts, she milked him to a shouting orgasm that bucked his hips up and bounced her upon his loins. She rode him until they both cried out with pleasure. His faery wolf collapsed to his side and, legs tangled together, they faced one another with a smile.

He nudged his toes over her ankle bone, teasing at the smoothness. So soft, her skin. "I like your feet."

"Should I be worried you have some weird fetish?"

"I don't know. I just like touching them."

"Works for me."

"I'm thirsty," she said.

"There's wine in the kitchen. I'll be right back." Beck rose and, his hard cock bobbing, wandered across the room. He pulled off the condom and veered toward the bathroom first.

"Nice ass," she commented.

Daisy scampered out to the kitchen and found her naked lover waiting with a glass of wine in hand. He was munching some orange-colored crackers that looked not at all appealing.

The sex had been great. It had fired her adrenaline and stirred up her wild need for more. And what an incredible specimen with whom to get her sex on. She dragged her clawed fingers up his thigh and pressed her belly against his hard, sweat-sheened abs.

Beck tilted the glass toward her lips. Crisp, cool wine slid down her throat. Her lover's hand tweaked her nipple. She grabbed the glass from him and finished the wine before setting it in the sink, then wrapping her legs about his hips and kissing him deeply.

"You taste like winter spiked with frozen grapes," she said to him. "You know winter is my favorite time of year?"

"Really?" He shifted to lean against the counter, and his erection bobbed against the underside of her thigh, teasing, yet it was just nice being held in his arms. "I grabbed another condom when I was in the bathroom. Want to wrestle in the snow?"

"Naked?"

"I'll keep you warm." He waggled his brows. "We can take a hot shower after."

Daisy dropped to her feet, grabbed his hand and headed for the sliding glass doors that opened to the backyard. The bite of cold January air chilled her skin, and the perspiration beading in her hair may have frozen instantly.

She whooped and danced from foot to foot on the snow-covered back porch. Beck whisked her into his arms and jumped, landing them in a soft snowbank on their sides. They sunk into the soft snow, and he tugged her up to sit on top of him.

"It really is cold out here," she said.

"You'll get used to it. Our wolves would love it."

"Yeah, but we're trying to keep the wolves away tonight, remember?" She circled his erection, which was still hard despite the cold. "Hand me that condom." He did, and she rolled it over the thick head of his cock and down the shaft. She didn't wait for his response as she slid onto his erection, hugging him deep within her.

"You feel so good," he crooned. "I could stay inside you forever."

"We'll end up in a puddle," she teased.

He gripped her hips and moved her up and down his cock. "You're the prettiest wolf in the woods. Faery, too."

"Leave the faery out of it," she gasped. "Or she might try to intrude."

"Really?"

"Beck, please." He could never understand how difficult it was for her when her sides constantly battled for the lead.

"Okay, no more talking because I gotta…" And instead of a cry of climax, as her lover achieved orgasm beneath her, he broke into an ecstatic howl.

Beck carried her inside, tracking snow and water across the living room floor. He didn't set her down until they'd hit the shower and the hot water thawed their icy skin. He kissed her until she thought the only way she could ever survive was through his breath.

Flicking off the water, Beck reached outside the stall and grabbed a big purple towel and handed it to Daisy.

"Wait." She spread the towel wide to reveal the Minnesota Vikings logo that sported a viking head replete with gold, braided locks and purple helmet. "I don't know about this. Seems blasphemous."

"What?"

"Dude, I'm Packers all the way."

"You're a cheesehead?" His abs tensed as he ran a palm over his wet hair. "That's just wrong. Seriously?"

"We so kicked the Vikings' asses this season."

"Oh, no, no, no. This changes everything." He crossed his arms, hair dripping down onto her as they stood in the shower. "If you're a Wisconsin fan, then I don't think I can love you anymore."

Daisy shrugged and handed him the towel. "Easy come, easy go." She stepped out, dripping wet, and performed a hip wiggle. "We're still going to kick your ass in play-offs."

She was grabbed from behind and tossed over his shoulder. "We'll see about that. Play-offs begin right now."

He headed into the bedroom and tossed her onto the bed, wet and giggling. An hour later, the twosome lay in a tangle of sheets. The score? A tie.

"I think I'm sated," she said against his mouth. He kissed her nose, her eyelids, her cheek, her earlobe. "What about you?"

"Oh, yeah. The werewolf will rest peacefully tonight. But I need to ask."

"Yeah?"

"Who's your favorite hockey team?"

"Minnesota Wild, of course."

He hugged her. "Whew. I think I can still love you."

Denton Marx strode the snow-packed yard back and forth, his eyes avoiding the figment that paced so close, yet was unaware of his presence. It had been months. He could not bear to know she was still trapped in the strange middlewhere of nothingness she had once told him about. The Edge. It was a place of unknown horrors inaccessible to him because it was in an entirely different dimension.

He had but one final ingredient he required to prepare the allbeast spell. And though he was not a witch, he knew he could concoct the spell. It simply required following the instructions he'd found in Sencha's grimoire.

He sighed and stopped pacing. She stood there, head bowed and long dark hair tangled about her face. He'd not looked into her eyes. Did not want to, for if he did her expression would eviscerate him.

She was lost. He must rescue her.

No matter the cost.

Chapter 14

They had agreed they would go to different locations to-night. Each werewolf had his or her turf. And as much as Daisy wanted to spend all her time with Beck, joining him in werewolf form could wait. Because as werewolves, they would be compelled to mate. And mating in that form would bond them. For life.

It was a big commitment to make, though the idea of bonding with Beck was appealing. That man was perfection. Daisy had only dated humans and one werewolf. And surprise! That one werewolf, Ryan Addison, had decided to come out to his pack as gay the day after their date.

She really knew how to pick them. Either that, or she turned men gay. Urg.

So she'd only had sex with humans. What Beck brought to the table that humans could not was stamina and a crazy sexy charm that oozed from his every pore. That smile of his! And a certain intimacy that she suspected only came when having sex with her breed. Their senses were heightened; every touch, smell and sound orchestrated their making love.

Not that they'd made love. Last night had been sex. Great sex. And she couldn't wait to do it with Beck again.

She was genuinely starting to like the guy.

"Daisy, you going out soon?"

She'd gone to her parents' house tonight. Theirs was the safest land for shifting. And if she happened upon another werewolf, Daisy knew they'd be family.

"Yes. You going to bed soon, Mom?"

Rissa looked over her shoulder as she strode up the stairs

to the bedroom, her cotton-candy-white hair fluffed effort-lessly. "You don't want me to answer that, sweetie." And she strode onward.

Daisy blushed.

The Saint-Pierre children had grown up knowing their parents were crazy for one another and had sex. A lot. They were never blatant, but it was obvious that their dad could never get enough of their mother. And on a night when Malakai Saint-Pierre shifted to werewolf? The sex must be interesting.

Daisy quickly erased that thought. She didn't want to know what it was like for her parents.

On the other hand, she had the wings and the faery dust like her mother. Whatever she could glean about a faery's sex habits with a werewolf could only prove helpful to her should she finally master her wings and want to get it on with Beck in that form.

Outside, a wolf howl perked up Daisy's ears. She'd seen Trouble and Stryke go out earlier. They'd been arguing even as they'd been pulling off their shirts. The fur would fly tonight, but in a playful, brotherly way.

Tugging off her shirt and wandering outside to the deck where years ago their father had built an outdoor clothes cubby for the family to leave their things, Daisy shivered. Her breath fogged before her.

"I wish Beck was here." She rubbed her arms, recalling the sexy heat from their rollicks in the snow.

"Tomorrow." She'd see him again.

Beck's massive ghost werewolf shifted painfully back to *were* form. When normally his muscles reveled in the luxurious stretch and return to human form, it felt as if the ghost wolf had torn his muscles beyond repair, and now they shrank to a ragged mass that pulsed weakly beneath his skin.

He slapped his biceps and thighs to get the blood flowing. His feet ached, and the bones felt as if they'd not aligned and reformed properly as he stepped awkwardly to the tree stump that housed his clothing. He grabbed the folded clothes and then noticed his fingers and nails were bloody.

"What the hell?" He sniffed the blood. It wasn't his own. And it didn't have the gamey feral scent of an animal. "What have I done?"

These modern snowshoes formed from ultra-lightweight metal and straps were far superior to the clunky wooden shoes Denton had used at home.

Home.

He paused in the forest, sighing. Home seemed so far away. Across an ocean, yes. But as well, across centuries. He preferred his time. It was simpler. Safer. A man could barter for things as opposed to being required to always carry a shard of plastic in his pocket. Money was hard to come by without a job, and he wasn't exactly employable. Nor could he devote time to a job.

His job was tracking the werewolf. And these tracks he followed, while large, were yet too small.

He wanted the big white one.

Slipping off her welding mask, Daisy then pulled off the leather apron and shook out her sweaty hair. The creative bug had bit hard after returning this morning from her parents' home. She'd figured a way to do the tail of the sculpture and had been going at it since. She glanced to the clock in the kitchen.

"Six already? I missed lunch. Supper time!"

Some leftover chicken sat in the fridge. But first a shower. Flicking on the TV on the way to the bathroom, Daisy paused by the bathroom door when she heard the news anchor talking about a wounded hunter. She rushed back to the living room, climbed over the back of the couch and grabbed the remote to turn up the volume.

The segment flashed to a reporter interviewing a man sitting in a hospital room. A doctor stood off to the side. The hunter's face had a slash across the cheek and had just been stitched up. Stunned, he didn't know what had hit him. They'd been wolf hunting when all of a sudden, a big white creature growled and he saw the claws and felt the blood. He ran like hell, initially thinking it had been a bear. Until he'd looked back and had seen the manlike wolf.

"The ghost wolf strikes again," the reporter announced with mock dramatics. "Only now it's getting deadly. Will the citizens of Tangle Lake continue to be frightened by the growing danger, or will they band together to hunt what has become an increased threat?"

Daisy gripped her throat, feeling a sickening bubble rise. "They're going to hunt the ghost wolf? Beck couldn't have hurt that hunter. Would he?"

Beck only wanted to scare the hunters. But he'd said the ghost wolf was hard to control. Getting stronger. She'd seen evidence of that the other night when he'd wanted her so desperately.

The phone rang, and she jumped. Another ring rushed her to the kitchen counter to answer the cell phone. "Yes?"

"Daisy, did you see the news?"

"Beck, what happened?"

"I don't know. I came out of the shift with blood on my hands. I've been sitting in the forest half the day. I didn't want to go home. I hurt that man, Daisy. I…"

"Come over here, Beck."

"Yes. I need…"

He needed to talk, and he needed her to hold him. But he couldn't verbalize it. He must be scared as hell that he had committed such an act.

"Come over, Beck. I'll make us something to eat and we can talk."

Chapter 15

Beck raised his hand to rap on Daisy's door, but paused.

"I shouldn't have come here." He turned his back to the door, then turned to face it again. "I need to see her."

He risked pulling her deeper into the weirdness of what he had become. And what had he become? Some kind of monster? Had he really hurt that hunter last night? Oftentimes he could remember snippets of things his werewolf had done. It was a form of self-preservation that he could not recall hunting small animals and eating them, wasn't it?

But last night? He could recall nothing.

And that scared him. And made him feel like he wasn't in control of the situation. He couldn't be weak now. He'd begun something that required follow through. He had to find the man who had killed his father.

But running into Daisy's arms wouldn't do that for him. It would only...

"Feel good."

He touched the door. Images of Daisy in his arms, kissing him, her bare skin against his, were so sweet. He needed sweet right now. Something soft and pink in his life to counter the dark and unsure.

The door opened to a bright smile and gorgeous pink hair. "I thought that was you. You are all kinds of sexy-smelling, you know that?"

She grabbed his hand and led him inside. Beck reluctantly closed the door. And when Daisy turned to kiss him, he kissed her back, but his body wouldn't completely surrender and allow him that treat. The ghost wolf yet hummed within him. And it wanted out. But since he'd sated his desire to run free last night, he was hoping it would be easier to control tonight.

"And you smell like...motor oil?" he tried.

"Sorry. Just got done working with the bike chains. Taking the grease off them. I haven't had time to shower since you called. I popped some enchiladas in the oven, and they should be done in ten minutes. Do you mind if I shower quickly?"

"I like you smelling like motor oil or Mexican food." He pulled her in for a hug. Her arms wrapping about his torso worked like some kind of therapy he hadn't known he needed. Beck buried his face in her pixy flame hair. Her body melding against his was insanely luxurious. It was everything the ghost wolf was not. Sweet, soft and so giving. Not dangerous. Loving.

"Tell me about last night?" Her bright violet eyes blinked up at him.

Raking his fingers through his hair, Beck walked over to the couch with Daisy attached to him, her legs about his hips. He never wanted to stop touching her. She kept his wolf tamed, and he desperately needed that right now.

Sitting, he curled her around to sit with her back against his chest and her bare feet propped on the coffee table. He wrapped his arms around her, bumping his fists together over her stomach.

"I don't remember anything," he confessed.

"Nothing?" She tilted a look back at him, her eyelashes dusting his cheek. "Is that weird for you? I mean, I can usually recall bits and pieces from my werewolf's adventures."

"I can, too. But since I've been shifting to the ghost wolf...nothing."

"I think you should give this gift back to the sidhe who

granted it to you. It seems as though it's getting stronger."
She turned on his lap and met his gaze. "More powerful?"

He hated to admit it, but he was losing control of it. He
must be if he'd attacked a hunter.

"He was okay though, right?" he asked. "The guy on
the news?"

"I think so. Looked like he'd had stitches. Do you always get that close to them?"

"I don't think so. I just scare them. They run. My werewolf feels some sort of triumph. Everything is good."

"Except not anymore."

He bowed his forehead to her shoulder. She stroked his
cheek. The tenderness shamed his inner wolf, yet his *were*
tilted closer to her.

"Daisy, you're so good to me. I feel safe with you. I know
that sounds weird, coming from a guy."

"I understand. It's become something you hadn't expected. Bigger."

He nodded.

Turning on his lap, she dipped her forehead to his and
bracketed his face with her warm palms. A few breaths.
The touch of her mouth against his wasn't quite a kiss, but
so much more. An understanding. The silence was comforting, because it was accompanied by the calm pulse of
her heartbeats.

"Will you talk to the faery who did this to you?" she
asked.

Beck sighed. "I can't. It's not finished yet."

"When will it be finished? When the ghost wolf has
killed?"

"You know I don't want that."

"You obviously can't control it. Whether or not you want
it isn't key here. Be smart, Beck."

"I will be. I have to be. But I can't give up looking for
the man who killed my father. I won't. I refuse."

"No, you shouldn't. But maybe you need to make a new plan?"

"Yeah, I don't know." He stroked her hair. "Can we just be together tonight and not talk about the ghost wolf?"

"I thought you wanted to talk about this?"

"I do. We just did. I don't know, Daisy. This is tough for me. I feel like you're pushing me." He leaned forward, catching his elbows on his knees and his forehead against his palms.

"Do you know you can trust me to tell me anything?"

He nodded and sighed. "I don't trust easily, Daisy."

She nuzzled her nose along his jaw and up to his earlobe, and whispered, "Trust me."

"I do trust you. But I don't want you to get hurt by trusting me."

"That's up to me to decide whether or not I want to trust you. And you know that I do."

Something dinged in the kitchen, and Daisy jumped off his lap and skipped toward the oven. "Supper's ready!"

After supper Daisy excused herself to take a shower, because even if Beck didn't mind the motor oil that smelled as if she'd dipped the tips of her hair in it, she did. She was just rinsing off when the shower curtain slid on the metal bar and Beck stepped into the tub, naked.

He moaned near her ear and tugged her against his body, sliding his hand down her slick belly to land his fingers at the apex of her thighs. "Now you smell like candy. Makes me want to eat you up, but you fed me so much."

"I do like to cook. My one feminine grace."

"You are all woman, Daisy."

His fingers worked lazily at her clit, and she jutted back her hips and shifted her feet wider to allow him access. She slapped her palms to the wet tile wall. His other hand cupped her breast, massaging, softly tweaking and squeezing. She wiggled against his hard cock, until it nuzzled between her thighs.

"That's nice," she said. "Slow like that."

"I want you facing me. Turn and sit on that ledge."

The ledge at the back of the tub where she usually propped her head when bathing was just wide enough to sit on comfortably without slipping on the slick surface. Daisy barely got situated when Beck knelt beneath the shower stream and bowed his head to her. He licked his way down to her folds and danced the tip of his hot tongue teasingly, then made his movements more promising, and finally, focused.

She slid a leg over his shoulder and gripped his wet hair. Sucking in her lower lip, she closed her eyes and took what he gave.

Beck rolled to his side and stroked his fingers down Daisy's back. She cooed a murmuring noise that sounded exactly how he felt. Satisfied. Exhausted. Extremely blissed out.

Pale morning light shimmered on her skin. The delicate hairs lifted in the wake of his strokes, then settled. Scents of the candy shampoo, remnants of the sugar cookies they'd eaten for dessert and the erotic aroma of her sex curled in his nostrils.

He had never been happier.

Yet he felt guilty for it. Had he a right to such happiness when his mother was alone and pregnant? When innocent wolves continued to be slaughtered for sport by idiot mortal hunters? When his father's death was yet unavenged?

No. But he wanted to steal a few more moments to himself. Be greedy and bask in Daisy Blu. He had to. He needed this quiet sanctity with her. Because it was a warm respite amidst the darkness that had haunted him lately.

He closed his eyes and held his hand millimeters above her skin. The heat from her rose, pleading him closer.

"You are like no other woman," he said.

She turned to face him. "I hope not."

He chuckled. "You have rammed into me, punched me and kicked my ass on the ice. You cook like freakin' Julia Child. You wear grease smears like some kind of Alexander McQueen fashion statement. Your hair always smells like my favorite childhood memory of candy binges on Halloween night. And...you kiss like you mean it."

She kissed him. Firmly. Intently. "I meant that." Another perfect kiss. "And that one, too."

"I like you, Daisy Blu," he whispered.

It was the truth. And it was real. He liked spending time with her, talking to her, listening to her, just being with her. Definitely stronger than love.

"I like you, too, Beckett Severo. And what are we going to do about that?"

"Do we have to do something about it?" He kissed the tip of her nose. "Let's just go with the like. Take it for what it is, and enjoy it."

"Goddess, but I like you." She nuzzled her head against his collarbone and spread an arm across his torso, finding her place, legs curled up to her stomach, against him. "Do you think it was just the whole moon thing? Us needing one another, and being there for one another, that makes us feel this way?"

This thing he felt for Daisy ran deep within him. And it had been brewing since the first time she'd bumped into him in the forest.

"Do *you* think it's that?" he asked.

She shook her head. "No. This is real. I want it to be real."

"It is, my pink faery wolf."

Closing her eyes, she landed a kiss on his mouth with precision. "One question."

"Shoot."

"Who is Alexander McQueen?"

Beck smirked. "He's some designer guy whom Sunday is always going on about."

"Sunday talks about fashion?"

"She has a serious fetish for all the fashion shows. Plays them all the time when she's working in the shop. She'll talk my head off about sparkly shoes."

"Seriously? Sunday, the one chick who may be more of a tomboy than me?"

"Oh, hell. I did not tell you this."

"Oh, yes, you did. I so have to tease her—"

He kissed her hard enough to steal her words. "You'll go to your grave with that info, or Sunday will never forgive me. Promise."

She sighed. "Fine. But only because I don't want you to get beat on by a girl."

"You're the only girl allowed to beat on me."

She punched his arm gently. He faked a wounded grimace.

Beck smoothed his hand over her back, tracing down the curve of her spine and the fall of her hair. "Show me your wings?"

Her lips parted. She exhaled.

"I mean, if you want to," he said. "What you told me about having trouble shifting… If it's a problem…"

"It could be. If I bring out my wings, the wolf might take over. But I want to show you. Now that we've declared mutual like for one another, you need to know all of me."

She sat up and scooched to the end of the bed, but turned as he leaned up on an elbow. "Promise you won't laugh if it goes wonky?"

"Daisy, the only thing that could ever make me laugh at you is the fact that you are a cheesehead."

"And I have the foam cheese hat to prove it," she said proudly, pointing to a shelf below the clothes rack where, indeed, a bright orange wedge of foam cheese had been tucked. "We are so going to a game together some time. My team will kick your team's ass."

"If that's the way you want to play it. Wings, lover. Stop stalling."

"I've never shown anyone but my family my wings."

"Really? Not even…?"

"Other lovers? Beck, I've only had human lovers. I would never reveal my true nature to them."

"No, that wouldn't be smart." He sat up against the pillows and scruffed fingers through his hair. "I suppose it's not like you can walk down Main Street with them out. Kind of like our werewolves."

"Exactly. I only use my wings when I'm in the forest on my parents' property and feel like flying. But then, I usually get small."

"You can get tiny?" He held up his fingers in a guesstimate of her size.

"About twice the length of your hand," she said. "You've never seen a faery small before?"

He shook his head. "Werewolves and vampires. That's it for my experience with the paranormal breeds. Oh, and a demon one time. My father pointed him out to me. I've led a sheltered life, Daisy. And it's not like Minnesota is spilling over with all sorts."

"You just need to know where to look. All breeds are everywhere."

"Maybe I've never wanted to look."

"Yeah. I get that about you. You've been protected by your family."

"Says the princess whose dad stalks her lovers."

"Touché."

* * *

Knees bent, Daisy sat back on her haunches and shimmied her shoulders. Dare she?

She wanted to share herself with Beck, but the wings
thing was intimate—beyond getting naked and having sex.
Never had she shown her human lovers her wings. They
hadn't been aware she was anything but a chick with pink
hair. And they had surely suspected the pink had come from
a salon. It was never wise to bring up the fact that she was
an entirely different breed than human. Secrecy was her
best means to survival.

But secrets weren't necessary with Beck. Heck, he'd
shown her his deepest secret with the ghost wolf, albeit accidentally. So she would give him this. Because she wanted
to, and because she wanted to take their intimacy to the
next level.

He liked her. And it felt wondrous.

Fingers crossed the wolf wouldn't horn in on the action
and turn her into a freak show.

"All right." Daisy slid off the end of the bed and stood
naked before Beck's ice-blue gaze. "Close your eyes."

He did so.

Daisy sucked in a breath and closed her eyes. Bringing
out her wings was different than shifting to wolf. And she
didn't do it often. When shifting to wolf, she pulled her
focus inward, but her wings required she move part of her
vita outward. Shoulders back and head down, she felt the
tingle along the upper part of her spine. It tweaked painfully, and she winced. Her mother had commented that
she didn't shift to faery often enough; that was the reason
for the pain.

With an inhale and a hopeful wish that things went well,
Daisy sent out her vita in the form of wings behind her
shoulders. And they curled out from her body and unfurled,
stretching out seven feet at their highest.

All faery's wings were different, some shaped as the insects she had seen in the mortal realm, such as the butterfly, cicada or dragonfly. But others were unique, like no insect or creature she had ever seen, and she could only imagine they were common in Faery.

Daisy had never been to Faery. She didn't have the compulsion to visit as her brother Kelyn did.

A sifting of faery dust sparkled in the air about her and landed on the end of the bed and Beck's legs. Another good thing about not shifting to faery often? No constant sweeping up of dust.

"Open your eyes," she whispered.

Beck sat forward, arms resting on his knees as he opened his eyes. He immediately said, "Wow."

Hands to her hips, she twisted side to side. When Beck motioned she spin about, she did so, pausing to look over her shoulder to gauge his reaction.

"Those are incredible. They look like something from a fantasy painting. Pink and silver. Gorgeous."

The filaments on the peaks of her wings curled in appreciation at his admiring tone. Daisy ran her fingers over the edge of one wing, which looked silver under certain lights, and then clear or iridescent in the sunlight. Sheened over in pink, the upper sections resembled an arabesque butterfly wing, and the lower sections were closer to cicada wings. She gave them a flutter, and they dusted Beck's face and arms.

"Mmm…smells like winter."

"You think so?"

"Yes, crisp and fresh. Like an ice-covered meadow I'd like to run through in wolf form. Is this faery dust?" He rubbed his fingers over his forearm to display glinting fingertips.

"If you were vampire," she said, "you'd be high right now."

"I am high on you, Daisy Blu." His grin burst off the scale. "Come here. Can I touch them?"

"At your own risk, lover boy."

"Right, because there's something about touching a faery's wings…"

She straddled his lap and curled one wing forward and around behind Beck's shoulder. He ran his fingers gently along the top of it, and the touch sent shivers through her wings. The veins flashed bright pink briefly before the erotic sensation entered Daisy's pores and scurried over her skin.

"Mmm…" She dipped her head against Beck's. "I can feel that as if you were stroking my skin."

He blew a hot breath over the sheer wing fabric. Again the veins brightened. Daisy moaned as that one moved lower. It was almost as if he'd blown on her loins. She felt his heat there. She'd never gotten intimate with a man while her wings were out. Could this be the start of something new and exciting?

Spreading his palm, he pressed it carefully against her wing, tracing tiny circles along the ridged cartilage that formed the structure.

Daisy pushed a hand over her mons and gasped. Putting pressure against her clit, she arched her back, and her breasts skimmed Beck's chest.

"That really turns you on."

"Oh, Beck, you have no idea. If I would have known, I would have done this sooner…"

"With a human man?"

"Oh, no, never."

She curled her wing along his back, and the heat of his skin permeated her wing. She felt it all over her body.

Beck lashed her breast with his tongue, sucking in the nipple. His hands carefully traced her wings as if he were exploring her skin, and he mined a delicious deep pleasure that Daisy had not before felt. It focused on her core, and yet sent out tendrils to her extremities. It was as if an imminent orgasm wanted to explode at the end of every nerve in her body.

Gripping his hair as he suckled one breast and then the other, Daisy tilted back her head, unable to form words. She surrendered to him. To the heady, overwhelming sensation and flame and cool and giddy and gasping, panting, racing, thundering—

The orgasm struck with surprising force, capturing her body in a glamorous shiver of pleasure. Faery dust glittered out from her pores. Her muscles constricted and danced and then loosened and again tightened. Beck held her across the back as she soared in his arms, her wings spreading wide behind her and shivering in joy.

"Oh, my God, Daisy, you're so gorgeous." A kiss there at the base of her throat, and he laid his head against her skin. "I can feel your pleasure vibrating in your body." He slid his fingers between her legs, and the slip of one of them glancing over her clitoris sparked the orgasm anew. "Come again, faery lover. Mmm, I love to hold you close."

Her body grew liquid within Beck's embrace. The room indeed smelled like winter. Though Daisy had never thought to describe the scent of her dust like that before, it fit. Riding the orgasm, she melted forward onto Beck's strong arms and chest, nestling her head on his shoulder and sighing. Wrapping her legs about his hips, she then curled her wings around to hug them both.

"Thank you," she whispered.

"What for? I like to turn you on, Daisy. It turns me on. That doesn't need any thanks."

"Thanks for being someone I could trust enough to do this with. That meant a lot to me. I've never come like that before. It was amazing."

"I'll say."

All of a sudden, Daisy's body jerked without volition.

Her gut clenched. The tips of her fingers tingled. And she knew what wanted to happen. "Oh, no."

"What is it?"

She ran toward the bathroom. "Don't follow me!" Closing the door, just as her wings folded down, a wolf tail popped out. "Damn it!"

"Daisy?"

She tilted her head against the door, sensing Beck stood just on the other side.

"Your wolf?" he asked carefully.

"Yes. Just uh, give me a minute."

"Take all the time you need. I'm not going anywhere."

She spread her fingers over the door and closed her eyes. Hearing Beck land on the bed and puff up a pillow, she couldn't help but smile. So the worst had happened. Before her lover. He hadn't freaked. And she hadn't freaked. Too much.

Everything was going to be okay with Beck. Whether or not she ever got her faery and wolf to play nice together.

Chapter 16

The phone on the nightstand vibrated. Beck grabbed it. Daisy's phone was encased in hand-tooled brown leather. Probably something her dad had made for her.

She was still in the bathroom. Poor girl. She'd been nervous about showing her wings to him and risking her wolf sneaking out—and it had.

He checked the incoming call info.

"Can't a guy get a break?" he said. "Seriously. The man is stalking me."

The bathroom door opened, and a naked faery wolf without a tail or wings wandered out to the edge of the bed.

"It rang while you were in there." He handed her the phone. "Still ringing."

She kissed him, then answered. "Hey, Daddy."

The dad. That man had impeccably discomforting timing.

Beck sat up, his feet hitting the hardwood floor. At least the old man hadn't intruded on their pairing last night. Or this morning.

"What?" Daisy's fingers flexed near her thigh. She paced beside the bed. "When? How is he? I'll be there as soon as I can get there."

She began collecting her clothing from the floor. Beck sensed her urgency and scented her sudden fear. "Daisy, what is it?"

"It's my brother Stryke. He's been hurt by a hunter. Hit with a silver arrow."

"Ah hell." Beck joined in the clothing search and pulled up his jeans. "Is he okay?"

"Yes, he was just grazed. Mom called in a witch to help him get through the silver poisoning. But I've got to go to my parents' house right now."

She jumped on one foot as she pulled up her jeans and buttoned them. Beck tossed her the sweater he'd pulled off her last night. "Thanks. I'm sorry to leave like this."

"Don't be. Your family needs you. I'd go with you but—"

"But that's okay." They knew Beck would not be welcome in her father's home. "Will you lock up for me? I have to leave right now. But you can stay. Shower. Whatever."

He nodded. "Call me when you get a chance, okay?"

"I will!" she called as she ran for the front door and shoved her bare feet into the pack boots on the rubber tray. "Last night was great! We need to do it again. Er, without the wings and tail fiasco, I mean. Talk to you soon!"

The front door closed. Beck collapsed backward onto the bed and closed his eyes. Last night had been great.

But should he have been out looking for the hunter with the silver arrows instead of here? He might have prevented her brother's injury. Hell, the brother could have been killed.

Arrows? Was that another weapon in the hunter's arsenal, or was there more than one bloodthirsty human wandering the local woods in search of werewolves?

The family had gathered in the Saint-Pierre living room. The vast country cabin featured an open layout, the cathedral ceilings two and a half stories high. The south wall that looked out over the nearby stream was entirely windows. Daisy had spent many a sunny summer afternoon swimming in the stream that boasted a waterfall a half mile west. Now it was iced over until March, or even April.

Stryke lay on the comfy leather couch in wolf form.

Daisy beelined for him and hugged her brother. "Oh, Stryke." She nuzzled her face into his brown variegated fur. He smelled like winter and blood. "I can't believe this happened to you. Is he going to be okay?"

Her mother sat beside her and pulled aside Daisy's hair from her face. "He will be. He just needs to rest. I sent Kelyn to the witch for more wolfsbane. Dez is the keeper of the Book of All Spells and is very wise. I trust her. She said we need to keep feeding it to Stryke to counteract the poison."

"Wolfsbane? Isn't that dangerous to us?"

"If used incorrectly. In the right dose," her mother explained, "it can heal. I don't want any of my children going into the forest anymore."

Daisy cast her eyes over Trouble and Blade, who sat on the other couch. Trouble's fist bounced on his jittering knee, contained anger tightened his jaw. Blade's silence was always stunningly chilling. Her father stood in the kitchen, arms crossed high upon his chest.

"That's an impossible request, Rissa," Malakai said. "If they stick to my land, they'll be safe. Why was Stryke out on public land anyway?"

Trouble tilted his head back against the couch, looking toward the ceiling. "He was wasted."

"Since when does Stryke drink?" Daisy asked. He was the cool, calm and collected brother. The wise one the other brothers always went to for advice. "Blade?"

The darkest of the family closed his eyes and shook his head.

"It's a woman," Trouble offered. "She was snarking about him to her friends. He's been really down."

"Idiot," Kai muttered. Then he looked directly at Daisy. "Daisy Blu. Outside. Now."

"But I want to sit with Stryke." She leaned across her

brother's body and nuzzled her face against one of his soft tufted ears.

Kai strode toward the side door. "I won't repeat myself."

Feeling resentment at her father's command, Daisy reluctantly rose and wandered out behind him. Since she'd left the family home years ago, she'd expected more independence. It seemed her father would never grasp the concept that he could no longer tell his daughter how to live her life.

The formidable werewolf wore a flannel shirt and jeans. He'd strode out barefoot onto the heated concrete sidewalk that led from the house to his workshop. It was a great place to return to while still in wolf form to warm the chilled footpads.

Kai paced a few lengths, then turned on Daisy. "I thought I told you to stay the hell away from Beckett Severo?"

Daisy cringed from his tone.

"I can smell him all over you."

Shoot. Should have showered before she'd come here. Big mistake.

Her father stepped closer, using the intimidation tactic that he often used with his sons. She'd never garnered harsh words from him. Had always been his little girl. Could do anything and get away with it.

And she wasn't about to stop.

"You can't tell me who I can see, Daddy. I'm a grown woman. I have relationships. I—" She wouldn't go so far as to say she had sex with men. He knew that. "I wish you'd respect my privacy and my need to make my own life."

"There is no privacy within the pack."

"There should be! How's a girl to ever find a boyfriend if she's always got her father breathing down her neck?"

"I don't do that!"

"Yeah? Well, you're doing it now. And besides, Beck is a good man."

"Who sneers at the idea of a pack. He may be good—

hell, I respected his father. The boy came from good stock—but he's not right for you, Daisy."

"I'm not going to listen to this. You're spoiling everything. I came here to support Stryke, and now you're making this about me."

"I'm…" Kai blew out a breath, jammed his hands at his hips and looked aside. "You're right. We need to focus on Stryke and making sure he heals. We'll talk about this later."

"I'm not going to be here later."

Daisy marched back into the house. But once in the kitchen, her bravery waned. Tears spilled down her cheeks as she neared the hallway. From behind she felt Blade's arm slip around her shoulder, and he led her outside through the front door and pulled her into his embrace.

Blade was the second-oldest of the brothers, but so different from his siblings in his darkness and utter stillness. He moved like a shadow, and most paranormals feared him without even knowing him. His vampire was wild yet controlled, a fierce warrior. He'd suffered for his vampire's hunger. And he had the scars to prove it.

But he'd ever been gentle with her, his older sister. And she and him were close because they were each part faery. Yet Blade had mastered his faery side beyond Daisy's expectations for her own faery.

"Why the tears?" he asked.

"Oh, Blade, sometimes Daddy can be such a hard-ass."

"It's because of the guy I smell all over you, isn't it?"

"Seriously? I should have showered before coming here."

She hugged her brother, who stood in a shirt and jeans, no shoes, despite the below-zero weather. His black hair, which was so black it gleamed blue in the pale daylight, spilled across her cheek.

"It's Beckett Severo," she confessed to him. "He's not in a pack, and that is driving Daddy crazy. Blade, I think

I'm falling in love with him. Well, I'm already in love with him. But I just stumbled into serious like, too."

"Like," he muttered. Blade knew Daisy's definition of love and like were very different things. "Really?"

"Yes, I like everything about him. And while it should be fun and exciting and silly and sexy, Daddy is making it so not-fun, and he's ruining it."

Her brother kissed the top of her head. "I'm pretty sure that's what fathers are supposed to do. How about the men who believe they've the worth to woo their daughters? But did you ever think maybe Dad does it because he wants to challenge Beck?"

"I don't understand."

"If the Severo man can stand up to Malakai Saint-Pierre for you, then he'd be a worthy wolf. I'm guessing that's in Dad's thought process."

"Yeah? Well, he needs to stop it and let me have some fun. It's not like I'm picking a mate."

"You're not?"

"No. I don't know. No. I don't think Beck has that in mind, either."

"Then you should ask him. Because if you don't, Dad will. Or maybe your brothers need to ask him what his intentions are?"

"Blade, no. Stay out of my love life, will you? Why does this have to be so difficult? Just let me have this with Beck."

She pushed past him to head back into the house, but his final words reached her.

"Sometimes family can be a bitch, Daisy Blu."

Beck strolled into the small pawn shop off of Lake Street in Minneapolis. He'd begun to search for silver dealers, and after seeing just how many in the Twin Cities did sell, he decided to try a different tact.

A gruff, leather-clad, bandanna-wearing shop owner

strode out from the back room. The beaded fringe before the door clattered and slid over his shoulders. He looked the classic bearded, motorcycle-riding bit of well-worn human who probably worshipped Lynyrd Skynyrd and never met a beer he didn't like.

Thinking about the band rushed a sudden and over-whelming heat to Beck's heart. He gripped his chest, so visceral the feeling was as it quivered the muscles in his jaws and tugged at the corners of his eyes.

His father had listened to the '70s rock band all the time. Severo had been what this man was before him now. Easy, laid-back, seasoned and worldly-wise.

"Help you, son?"

What Beck wouldn't give for one more moment standing before his father, waiting to hear whatever it was he wanted to say to him. Whether it was to suggest he buy land in the country instead of getting a house in town, or to tell him about the time when he'd had to escape a vampire tribe that had kept him and his parents captive, only to then witness the hunters slay his parents.

His father had been the strongest man Beck had ever known. Physically and mentally.

"Boy?"

"Uh." Beck shook off the memories that threatened to release tears. "I'm looking for some silver. The purest stuff you've got."

"All sold out. Don't get a lot of it lately. Silver is trading at a prime price."

"Actually, I'm trying to find someone who may have bought some from here and altered it for a shotgun shell or an arrow."

"Why? You a cop? You don't look like a cop."

Beck raked his fingers through his tousled hair. "I'm not a cop. I'm just trying to solve a puzzle. Do you get a lot of hunter types in here looking for silver?"

"What would a hunter do with silver? Unless he's hunting werewolves, eh?" The man chuckled, and shrugged off the joke as he walked around behind the glass counter and slid aside a velvet tray filled with gold rings. "You going werewolf hunting, boy?"

"I can't honestly tell if you're joshing me or if you're serious. Do you believe in werewolves, mister?"

"If you watch the news, you would. You hear about that big white wolf monster that's stalking the hunters?"

"The ghost wolf. I think it's the other way around. The hunters are going after the wolves. The ghost wolf is trying to protect his own."

"Aren't you all save-the-wolves?"

Beck's eyes landed a bumper sticker under the counter glass that touted *Will hunt for fur*. He realized that this man would probably shoot a wolf if he had the chance. His hackles tightened, but he gritted his jaw so he wouldn't growl.

The man shook his head. "I'm just having fun with you, boy. But no. No one looking to make silver bullets."

Beck pulled out the tissue he'd tucked into a pocket and spread it on the counter. "You ever see anything like this?"

The man bent to study the glass bead, then grabbed a jeweler's loop to give it a closer inspection. "Is that silver *inside* crystal?"

"Glass. The glass shatters on impact, and the silver leaks out."

The man straightened. Now his look grew hard, and Beck scented an edge of fear. "I think you should leave, boy."

"Does that mean you have seen it before?"

"It means I don't entertain idiots who think to hunt non-existent creatures. I suppose you're packing a stake for Dracula, too?"

Beck swept up the tissue and backed away. "Thanks for the help. Sorry to have bothered you."

* * *

Denton proved a better aim with a bow and arrow than the modern rifle he'd attempted to use previously. Though the rifle had served him a kill, it hadn't been the breed of wolf the spell required. And that other wolf had been there. Snarled and snapped at him. He'd decided to let the dead one lie. He couldn't use it.

It had been the first time Denton had killed for a reason beyond to bring food to the table. And he wasn't much of a hunter, which explained his thin frame. But he'd made five kills in the months he'd been in this horrible time.

"Only one left."

He eyed the arrow, which had a glass point filled with silver. He'd gotten it one hundred years from now. But he only needed it to work once, in this year, and finally he could concoct the allbeast spell.

Chapter 17

Daisy finally cleaned up a photograph using Photoshop. The white wolf stood on powerful hind legs. Its head was ruffled with thick white fur. Ebony talons scythed the air. Its eyes glowed red.

She couldn't publish this photo. It exposed her lover for a monster.

But not publishing it would compromise her chances at winning the internship. This was truly a prize-winning photo. Dare she? Did she really need it? Maybe journalism wasn't her thing?

She needed this internship to finally prove her independence to her father.

The day had been long and cold. Icy rain slicked the tarmac. Yes, he lived in Minnesota. Cold was a natural state six months out of the year. Why hadn't his parents moved to Florida to raise him? He could seriously work the beach-bum vibe.

A stop for groceries on the way home was necessary, but Beck wasn't feeling motivated after the shop owner's rude treatment. Though he felt deserving of it. How to ask around about silver bullets without sounding like a complete wacko?

The blinking blue neon sign outside the Blue Bass bar—the last dive bar before Burnham—called to him. A shot of whiskey to warm his bones sounded more interesting than squeezing oranges in the produce section.

Inside the small bar paneled in wood timbers and blinking madly with various beer signs hung all over the walls, a few men played a game of pool under the watchful milky eye of the bar's mascot, a stuffed blue bass. One man sat at the bar, his head bowed and long black hair concealing his face.

An old-timer sporting a white beard to his belly and commandeering the table next to the men's room waved to him. Beck nodded in acknowledgment—the guy was here every time he stopped in—and ordered a whiskey. He asked the bartender to pour the old man another of whatever he was drinking. He'd never spoken to him, hadn't a clue who he was, what he did or where he lived. Didn't matter.

The first swallow of whiskey burned sweetly. Beck pressed the shot glass to his forehead and closed his eyes. The sounds of pool balls clacking battled with the cheesy country tune that proclaimed cowboys the best rides.

Beck laughed to himself, thinking that women should really give werewolves a try if they were looking for a wild ride. Then again, best keep all the wild goodness away from the mortal females. They wouldn't know how to handle him.

Hell, what was he thinking? He'd dated many a mortal woman. They could handle him in *were* shape just fine.

Daisy had been his first wolf. And it had been a risky pairing. Normally packs protected their females as if they were gold in Fort Knox. The only wolves allowed to sniff around them were fellow pack members, or wolves from neighboring packs. But if Beck knew correctly, Daisy's pack was just her family. So she would have to seek a wolf elsewhere to mate and marry. Naturally, her father, the pack principal, would insist she marry another pack wolf. It could prove a good alliance for the two packs. Hell, the whole lone wolf thing was a real stigma to packs.

One of the men at the pool table whooped triumphantly.

He bounced back and forth on his feet as if a prize fighter. He was wearing—a leather skirt? With a plaid sweater that stretched across his physique. And combat boots. Yikes.

Beck shook his head and noticed the other two players shook off the winner's antics and approached the bar. One was tall, thin and had messy blond hair. His face was angular and alien. He looked down his nose at Beck.

The other revealed short hair shaved to his scalp when he pushed back a hoodie. Sleeves covered his hands to midfinger. He also glanced at Beck, while the other, the one still cheering his win, bounced around as he racked the balls.

"Trouble!" the one closest to Beck called. "We get it. You won."

The bouncing winner wandered up to the bar next to the one who had spoken. The twosome exchanged looks. The winner asked, affronted, "What, man?"

The one in the hoodie nodded toward Beck.

An uneasy creep tightened at the back of Beck's neck. Then he scented them.

Ah hell.

"This guy smell familiar to you?" the one in the hoodie asked his cohort.

Now the dark-haired one, who had been sitting at the bar, lifted his head, tilting it as he observed the one in the skirt walk up to Beck and make a show of sniffing the air.

"Well, I'll be," Trouble, the skirted one, said. "You Beckett?"

Yeah, this felt fifty ways of wrong. Beck pushed the empty shot glass toward the back of the bar and turned to offer his hand to the man, who stood about as tall as he did, yet his shoulders were a bit broader and his wild eyes gave him a menacing edge that Beck sensed he was going to learn a lot more about. Like it or not.

"Beckett Severo," he said.

Trouble didn't shake his hand. And then Beck realized

who he was. Who all four men were. But before he could speak, Trouble's fist connected with his jaw, knocking him off the stool and grasping for hold on the brass rail edging the bar.

He'd felt the Saint-Pierre power punch before. Daisy's right hook had nothing on this guy.

"This is the one who has been nosing around Daisy Blu," the hooded one said. "I could smell you on her the other day when she came to see me."

Beck winced and shook his head. His jaw might have dislocated with that punch. "Visited you? Are you Stryke? The one who got hit by the silver arrow?"

"What the hell are you doing with my sister, eh?" Trouble punched him in the gut.

Beck caught his elbows against the bar. Now Stryke and the blond moved around to stand beside Trouble. Without looking over his shoulder, he sensed the dark one at the bar remained sitting.

"Take it outside," the bartender ordered. "Unless you're willing to pay for the damages. Could use some new decor."

Trouble gripped Beck by the scruff of his neck and shoved him toward the back door, which opened out to a small parking lot, glazed over from the icy rain that had stopped when Beck had entered the bar.

Beck eyed his truck, parked across the street. He was grabbed from behind, an arm hooking around his neck. Punishing knuckles met his kidney in a bile-stirring introduction. They'd paired up, the sneaky Saint-Pierres. And he was going down. He staggered forward, swallowing his bile. Shit, they could punch.

But he wasn't in the mood for running with his tail between his legs. He had worse things with which to deal. And these boys had better learn he was not a wolf to mess with.

Righting, and turning to face the trio—the dark one

with the long hair had leaned against the trunk of the bartender's black SUV, arms crossed over his chest—Beck thrust up his fists.

"Listen, guys, I don't want to start anything with Daisy's brothers. But I sure as hell am not going to stand here and let you beat me to a pulp."

He swung for Trouble, catching him on the jaw.

Shaking it off as if a nuisance, Trouble bounced back and forth on his combat boots as if a prize fighter. The ice gave him little challenge. "A love tap? Is that all you got, lone wolf?"

Beck swung again, this time pounding his fist into Trouble's gut. The wily wolf huffed out his breath, caught Beck at the nape of the neck and, with a twist, slammed the side of his head against a nearby car trunk.

Face to metal scoured pain through Beck's skull. His nose dripped out blood. He didn't want to do this. And oh, yes, the ghost wolf inside him wanted to do this.

Swinging around, he thought to punch the crazy wolf in the face, but instead one of the others caught his fist, smiled and delivered a high kick that doubled him at the gut. Bent over, he felt the new wolf's fist at his jaw.

"Good one, Stryke!" Trouble called. The wolf still bounced at the periphery of Beck's vision. "Hey, lone wolf, take it easy on Stryke. He's still healing from the hunter's arrow. Almost killed him, that asshole."

Turning, Beck gripped Stryke by the shirt and shoved him against a pickup cab. "You see the hunter who shot you?"

"Dude, I was on four legs at the time."

"Yeah, but you have his scent, right? I need to find that hunter."

"You talk too much." Stryke swung up a fist, which Beck blocked with his forearm.

The two tussled, throwing punches and dodging a few

swings. The guy was fast on his feet, but his punches didn't pack the power that his brother Trouble's did. Just when Beck thought he had the guy, he swung high, and Stryke's boot caught him in the gut. Damn, he'd gone for the kidney again. These boys did not fight fair.

Spinning around, Beck's eyes fell across the crazy one who was clapping and cheering for his brother. Still, the tall dark one stood off by a pickup box. Beck decided to stay away from him. The less he had to face, the better. And the blond one? Where was—

An iron fist crushed Beck's jaw. His feet left the ground. His body soared high, and he landed on top of a Camaro hood. Blackness toyed with his consciousness.

"Kelyn, that is the only punch you get," Trouble reprimanded the blond one. "You'll waste the guy before we've had our fun."

As Beck's body slid from the hood, he matched gazes with the tall, lithe one who'd just punched his brains into next week. A violet eye winked at him. The faery of the bunch. Beck's boots slid on the ice, and he went down.

Trouble looked over Beck, sprawled in a prone position. "That's our bro, Kelyn. Feel like your brains are oozing out your nose right now?"

Beck swore. He'd never think faeries a bunch of pussies again.

"Yep, he's a one-punch deal," Trouble said. "But you're still conscious, so we'll give you points for that. Come on, lone wolf, we're just getting started."

Beck clasped the proffered hand, and Trouble tugged him up to his feet. He winced and stumbled forward, but knowing the enemies stood close, didn't focus on the pain. Instead, he just needed to survive this.

Whatever the hell *this* was. They were having too much fun working him over. Because he was screwing their sister? Good reason. He couldn't argue that.

"If you think you're going to scare me away from Daisy—" Beck spat blood to the side "—you're going to have to try harder."

Trouble whistled and bounced high, stomping the ground in his macabre glee. "Oh, I'll bring it! Hold him, Stryke."

Beck swung at Stryke and managed a punishing blow to his gut. Stryke spat aside blood, grinned, then lunged, slipping an arm behind Beck's neck and his arms to get him in a shoulder pin. As he struggled against the wolf, he felt Trouble's boot hit his cheek. His skin broke. Blood spilled down his face.

"You think you have a right to move in on our sister?" Trouble asked. "Wolves who don't run with a pack shouldn't be so bold, don't you know that?"

Beck shoved Stryke backward against a truck. The wolf chuffed out a breath. Arms still wrenched back, and Beck rolled forward, flipping Stryke over his head. The two brothers collided and went down.

"Good one," Trouble groaned from the ground. He shoved his brother off him. "Kelyn, let's end this."

"Ah, shit." Beck turned but didn't have time to register more than a fist aimed between his eyes. Blackness won over the pain. Beck dropped to the icy pavement.

Trouble bounced up to his feet, but a groan struck from his aching side.

Blade, hands in his pockets, strolled over to the fallen wolf and knelt over him. "This wolf can certainly take some punishment."

"That he can." Trouble pounded a fist into his opposite palm. "I like him."

Blade stood, nodding agreement. With a whistle from Trouble, the brothers gathered. They performed a group fist bump over Beck's prone body.

"Let's get the hell out of here before the owner calls the cops," Kelyn suggested.

"Right." Trouble wandered off toward the parked vehicles. "Stryke, grab the loner."

"What? I thought I was the one recovering here?"

With some grumbling about always having to clean up the mess, Stryke bent and managed to hoist Beck's body over a shoulder. "Where's his car?"

Blade pointed down the street, and the brothers found the truck. It was unlocked, fortunately for Beck. Trouble would not have paused before smashing out the window with a fist.

Stryke laid him across the front seat, and Beck stirred from his blackout.

"He must really love her," Stryke muttered.

"Yeah, that's what I was thinking, too, when he stood up to us. Poor guy." Trouble toed Beck's foot out of the way so he could close the door. "We were just playing with you, lone wolf. It's the big guy you should be worried about. That would be our dad, Malakai Saint-Pierre."

"Bring it," Beck muttered. Then he passed out again.

Trouble and Stryke laughed. Kelyn shook his head, muttering about pussy wolves.

And Blade had already wandered off, blending into the night.

Beck woke shivering. He sat up on the front seat of his truck. The windows were iced over, but daylight glinted in the rearview mirror.

How had he—?

Opening his mouth to yawn, he winced and swore. Rubbing his hand carefully along his jaw, he wondered if it was broken. It should have healed from the beating he'd taken last night. If it hadn't been for—

"That damned faery."

The brothers must have scraped him off the ice and tossed him in his truck. A surprising courtesy. He shuffled in his front jeans pocket for the keys and turned on the ignition, flipping the heat onto high. Collapsing back across the seat, he pushed his hands over his scalp.

They'd been toying with him last night. Maybe. Probably. But those punches hadn't been a tease.

"Daisy's brothers."

And yet one of them had said something about watching out for the dad. And Beck had idiotically said something like "bring it." Oh, foolish lone wolf.

He groaned and sensed the pain shifting from his back to his side. Some well-aimed kidney kicks. He lifted his shirt and saw the mottled maroon-and-green bruising. When it took longer than six to eight hours for a werewolf to heal, then he'd really taken a beating.

He wondered if the dad wasn't on his way to finish the job right now. Maybe Malakai Saint-Pierre was standing outside the truck, waiting for Beck to wake up?

Sniffing the air, Beck didn't sense anyone in the vicinity. He was alone. Beaten. And freezing his ass off. It was going to take the heater a while to warm up.

Pulling himself upright, he let out a groan and shuffled behind the steering wheel. While good sense told him to drive home and sleep off the pain, all his heart wanted to do was turn toward town and knock on Daisy's door.

Chapter 18

"Come in," Daisy said to the sad-faced werewolf standing in her doorway. She winced. His jaw was bruised green with spots of violet, and he clutched his ribs. "I heard about what happened."

"Yeah? Did your brothers call to report the gory details as soon as they'd finished working me over?"

"Aw, they didn't mean it. They were just love taps." Daisy forced the words out even while she was torn apart inside. Damn, Trouble. Her brother could never let anything be.

"Love?" Beck paused in the living room as she coaxed him toward the bed. "If that was a love tap, I don't ever want your faery brother to love, adore or otherwise even like me. The man left a permanent impression of his knuckles on my kidney."

Indeed, her brother Kelyn may look like the weakest of the Saint-Pierre brothers, but he was the secret deadly weapon. Why had Trouble allowed him to participate? He knew Kelyn's strength was deadly. That was so wrong.

"Come here. Let me take a look at the damage. Sometimes Kelyn doesn't know his own strength."

"You think?" Beck dutifully followed and sat on the end of her bed. "They all had their go at me. Except the one." He lifted his arms as she pulled the blue sweater over his head. His ribs were mottled and green. He was healing, but still sore, for sure. "The tall dark one stood back and watched."

"Blade only raises his fists for one reason."

"What's that? To maim?"

"To kill."

She met his wondering brow with a shrug. She wasn't about to explain the dark stuff Blade had already experienced in his short lifetime. Gliding her fingers down his chest, she stopped when he winced. "That does not look good. Kelyn?"

He nodded as he lay back on the bed. "Got me twice." He slid a hand over hers as she unbuttoned his jeans. "Really?"

"I want to make you comfortable. Loosen your clothes a bit."

"You going to work some faery healing on me?"

The thought to try hadn't occurred to her. Though certainly if her faery were stronger, she could do it. And oh, did she want to make it all better for him right now. "Uh, I could try?"

"Anything that involves you putting your hands on me is okay by me."

"My mother has been trying to teach me healing since I was a little girl. If I can tap into my faery side, I can draw up my vita to heal yours. It's just—well, I explained how my faery and wolf battle. You've seen the results. And I haven't practiced much. Do you trust me?"

"Of course I do. And if it doesn't work, who am I to argue with a faery wolf putting her hands on me, eh?"

He stroked the ends of her hair that dangled over his chest. The man's arctic eyes tempted her forward to kiss him. Softly. She didn't want to put too much pressure where her brothers' fists had likely pummeled. She hated that her brothers had done this to Beck, but she understood it had been their means of checking him out. Beckett Severo had been weighed and measured and, thankfully, had not come up wanting in her brothers' opinions.

That was the real reason she wasn't railing at the Saint-Pierre boys' cruel treatment of her lover. Trouble had even said he liked the guy. Seriously. He'd said he respected Beck for standing up to them and taking his punches like a man. But none of them had thought their opinion would change their father's mind about Beck.

"That feels so good." He kissed her gently, then closed his eyes as she floated kisses down his chin and neck. "You know they had the courtesy to stick me in my truck and not leave me lying in the icy parking lot all night?"

"That's my brothers for you. Strange kindness." She dashed her tongue down the center of his chest, and he moaned.

"Is that how the healing works?"

"No, I'm just getting you warmed up."

"Ah. Well then, proceed as slowly as you like."

She straddled his thighs and spread out her arms. Much as she preferred her wolf half, her faery half did have some useful skills. For Beck's sake, she hoped to tap into them. Focusing inward, she summoned her wings. They unfurled with a whoosh of wintery chill and a flutter of faery dust that settled with a glint onto Beck's chest.

"I like your wings," he said. "You know a guy could have all kinds of fantasies involving them?"

"Keep a few in mind, big boy."

She clapped her hands together before her, rubbing her palms rapidly to warm her skin. Slowly she began to pull her palms apart, focusing her thoughts inward to the vita that raced through her system. Every molecule in her being and in the world responded to her thoughts. She felt the stirring between her palms.

A spark of violet faery magic grew within her hands and stranded in pink, blue and emerald that glittered with faery dust. Daisy knew it was her very life essence. As it manifested, it sputtered and disappeared, raining faery dust over Beck's abs.

"Give me a minute to warm up," she said. "I've got it in me. I can do this."

If she had spent more time nurturing her faery half this would be a breeze, but she'd never thought anything about being faery was useful. Or comfortable. What girl could slap a hockey stick and make the goal with the impediment of wings slowing her down? Or trying to keep the wings from getting singed while welding metal? Not going to happen.

Though she did like having her wings out for a good stretch. And to give it a moment's thought, wings made her feel...pretty. More womanly.

Hmm...maybe she needed to devote more focus to her faery.

Again the green and violet strands formed between her palms. Daisy rushed both palms to Beck's ribs, where Kelyn had gotten him in the kidneys with his iron fist.

Beck moaned and tilted his head to see what she was doing.

"Lay back. Take it in," she directed. "This may not last long."

"It feels cool, and I can feel it...inside. As if it's wrapping about my kidney. Wow." He closed his eyes and laid back. "Crazy."

Crazy, indeed. That she was even managing this giddied Daisy's hopes, and she got so excited she lost her concentration, and the healing vita poufed out again.

But with Beck's eyes closed, he didn't immediately notice. Curling forward a wing, she brushed it over her lover's face, drawing his smile widely.

Beck sucked in a breath. "Oh, yeah. I...I think you did it."

"Of course I did." She smiled and sighed. Well, he had been close to fully healed before she'd gotten to him. But she may have helped a bit.

She strolled her hands, now coated with faery dust, across his skin and up toward his collarbone where the bruise had receded. Gliding down his chest, she roamed over his hard curves, pausing when she felt the tenderness of damage beneath her delving touch. It was an intuitive feeling that her mother had taught her to utilize. She wanted to be able to kiss the pain away, to protect her lover from all hurts.

She wondered if faery healing could help a man's grief?

Hands gliding down his stomach, she curved them over his hip.

"Doesn't feel cool anymore," he murmured.

"That was all the healing vita I could manage. Now, for your lovely parting gift."

"My—wha?"

"Pants off," she whispered.

"I don't think they got me below the belt," he muttered.

"Really? You don't want me to even have a look?"

Beck quickly shimmied down his jeans and kicked off his shoes, and the whole tangle landed on the floor at the base of the bed.

"Thought so," she said.

She glided her hands down his hips and over his boxer shorts. Black with tiny white skulls on them. Cute. His erection bobbed against her palm. She gave it a firm squeeze.

"Please?" her werewolf lover asked.

Daisy's wings swept forward over Beck's chest and up along his face. It felt as though he was being touched by the wind and snow and summer all at the same time. The faery wolf settled onto his cock, welcoming him inside her depths and rocking a slow yet insistent rhythm. She felt so good. There were no words to describe being inside her. *Hot. Awesome. Wondrous. Sticky.* All insignificant.

He turned his face into one of her wings and breathed in deeply, then licked the delicate wing. She even tasted sweet. He'd fallen into some kind of wonderland, and he wanted that damned white rabbit to catch him. Here was home. She felt so right.

"Oh!"

Daisy's body jerked above him. Suddenly his cock slapped against his belly. She stumbled off him and dropped off the bed and to the floor. The wings disappeared.

"Shit," she muttered. "Not again."

"Daisy!"

Daisy's wolf whined and scampered out of the bedroom area, toenails clicking across the hardwood. She crept around to the other side of the couch. A few miserable whines struck Beck right in the heart.

He caught his palms against his forehead. "Poor girl. She's having as much trouble shifting as I…"

He blew out a breath. He couldn't speak it out loud, but he knew how Daisy felt. Because he was struggling with his own shifting troubles. Troubles he had brought upon himself. And now that the sidhe gift had begun to take its toll on him, he wasn't sure how to stop it, or change it, or make it drain him less.

He was destined to move forward, even if it killed him. And it likely would.

Maybe Daisy's suggestion that he talk to the faery who had given him the ghost wolf was worth a try. But could he stop being the ghost wolf before he'd finished what he set out to do?

What did he really intend for the ghost wolf to do? Scare the local hunters out of ever hunting wolves again? Kill the hunter who had killed his father?

He knew that answer, and while he hated claiming it, he knew he had to. He wanted the hunter dead. An eye for an eye. Wasn't that only fair?

Yet instinctually, Beck knew his father would never be proud of such an action.

"Beck?"

Sitting up, he spied Daisy's crop of pink hair pop up from behind the couch. He pulled on his jeans then padded over to the couch. Pulling his naked faery wolf into his arms, he sat with her wrapped up against his chest. Kissing her hair, he held her and didn't speak. Words weren't necessary. He'd just witnessed her greatest challenge, and he felt sure she was embarrassed, frustrated and probably even angry with herself for allowing him to see it.

He bent to whisper at her ear, "Nothing will ever make me stop liking you, Daisy Blu."

Beck held her on the couch for the longest time. Daisy was glad he didn't talk, save to whisper that he liked her. She liked him, too. This romance had developed into serious like. And she'd once again revealed the most devastating part of her life to him, and he had merely wrapped her in his arms and told her he liked her.

Like was so much better than love. Because they both knew love was a part of it. They'd fallen into each other and genuinely enjoyed being there. She just wished there was a way to figure out what the heck was up with her. Beck wouldn't have answers, but it felt as if she'd released a heavy weight from her soul now that he was in on her secret.

"I'll get it figured out," she muttered, turning on his lap to sit forward and clasping his hands over her stomach. "Wolf or faery? Seems like I can't be both."

"If you had to choose," he asked softly, "which would it be?"

She shrugged. "My family is mostly wolves. Yet my mother is faery. I have always favored my wolf. To be honest, the faery half of me has always felt so...feminine."

"Your wings are crazy gorgeous. What's wrong with being feminine?"

"Nothing. But you should have noticed by now that it doesn't come naturally to me."

He stroked the side of her feet. She remembered he liked to touch them. "You're not a tomboy."

"You don't think so? Even after I kicked your ass at pond hockey?"

"You're a chick who happens to play hockey well. And who enjoys working with a welding torch. Why do pink bows and silly high shoes have to define you as feminine?"

She shrugged. "Never thought of it that way before. But I'm going to pick wolf, if I have a choice between the two."

"I'd miss your wings. And your healing. That is an incredible skill. Could you really give that up?"

"Don't fool yourself. I barely healed you. Your body was already well on its way to healing."

"You helped."

She turned and brushed at the faery dust on his biceps. "You feeling better?"

"One hundred percent."

"So tell me how it's going with your ghost wolf?"

"It's about as good as your shifting situation. Honestly? I get weaker every time I shift, Daisy. I don't think I can do it for much longer."

"Then stop."

"I intend to. But I still haven't done what I set out to do. My search for the hunter with the silver bullets is turning up a dead end."

"Stryke was hit by a silver-tipped arrow. Do you think it could be the same hunter?"

"Possible. I can hope it's only one man we have to worry about. I'm not sure what to do, Daisy. What would you do, as a journalist?"

She tilted her head back against his shoulder. "I am an aspiring journalist. This story about the ghost wolf is my first big investigation."

"And look, you've discovered the truth behind it."

"Right, but I can't tell anyone. Do you know how that drives me bonkers?"

"You want to tell people about me?"

"As a journalist? Hell yes. I'm sure this story could win me the internship. But as your lover and fellow werewolf? Heck no. This is your secret, and a secret the whole werewolf community needs to guard."

"I'm sorry to have put you in this position."

"Don't be. Beck, what you're doing is awesome. You've scared the shit out of the hunters."

"Yeah, but for how long? The ghost wolf hurt someone, Daisy. I don't think it'll be long before they come after me with pitchforks and silver bullets. And after that, who's to say the gray wolf population won't again feel the threat? And what about Stryke? He was almost killed. I think I've screwed this up, big-time."

"No. Let's think about this." She stroked her hands along his thighs. "I agree that the ghost wolf needs to pull back for a while until things calm down."

"But what if I can't? Daisy, at night…"

"What is it?"

"It's like the ghost wolf pulls at me if I even see moonlight. I've drawn all the curtains in my house."

"That's weird."

"And you saw how I was the other night when you came over to my house."

"Horny as heck."

Beck sighed and hugged her to him. "I don't want to hurt anyone else. I can't. My father would have never wanted that."

She kissed his knuckles. "I think your father would be proud to see what you've accomplished."

"I'm not so sure he would approve of the means to what I've done."

"The faery bargain?"

He nodded.

"Yeah, that worries me still."

"That makes two of us. I'm worried about your faery situation. I'm worried about mine. When did life become so full of worries? I'm too young for this crap."

He stood and padded over to the bed to retrieve the rest of his clothes. Daisy popped up her head and leaned on the back of the couch, watching him dress.

"If you go to the faery to ask about giving the ghost wolf back," she said, "I'd go with you. Maybe…"

"Maybe the faery would know how to help you?"

She nodded, glanced aside.

"Sounds like a plan. But I've got some work to do before then. If you don't have any ideas on how to track the hunter, then I've got to rack my brain and come up with something. I wish your brother could help me, but I asked him last night if he recognized the hunter, and he was more interested in putting bruises on me."

"How could he know anything if he was in wolf shape?"

"Exactly. But he might remember his scent."

She followed him across the living room, naked. When he paused before the front door, she wrapped her arms around him from behind. She wanted to ask what he would do when he finally did find the hunter, but she wasn't sure she wanted to hear the answer.

"Should I tread carefully around town now in fear of your father?" he asked.

"I'll have a talk with him."

"You shouldn't have to, Daisy."

"Yeah, but we are a couple, right? I mean, I want us to be."

He turned and kissed her forehead. "You're my sexy faery wolf. But that goes against everything dear old dad wants for you. And you know I don't want to make trouble."

"Kind of late to consider the ramifications, don't you think? I don't want us to end, Beck."

"Neither do I. I guess I'll have to figure a way into your father's good graces."

"Let's just play it by ear for now. My dad is not part of this relationship."

"I don't want to sneak around. Your brothers have already given me a warning."

"It wasn't a warning so much as they weighed and measured you. And do you know? Trouble actually said he likes you."

"He did? Wait. That's like friend like. Not the kind of like we have?"

"Right. My brothers approved of you, but they don't get a vote where my dad is concerned." She kissed him.

"I've never had brothers, so I can't imagine. But maybe soon, eh?"

"What do you mean?"

"Uh…" He stroked her cheek and shrugged. "My mom is pregnant."

"Really? That's amazing."

"She was going to tell my dad on the night he died."

"Oh, my goddess. Beck, I'm so sorry. You two have been through so much."

"I'm a survivor."

"How is your mom doing?"

"She's much better lately." He kissed her again. "I'm hoping for a brother, but Mom said she wants a girl. Ivan Drake has been visiting her, and I think that's helping her a lot."

"I'm glad. It's got to be hard being alone and pregnant."

"Which reminds me, I think I'll stop by my mom's today and give her a hug."

Daisy wrapped her arms about Beck. "I hate to give you up."

"How about sharing me?"

"I can do that."

Chapter 19

"Hey, Mom."

Beck kissed his mother and noted she was wearing a soft floral perfume. Her long brown hair was pulled up into a neat bun with a few curly strands hanging down around her face. And her smile remained even after she'd acknowledged him.

"Feeling good?" he asked.

Bella led him into the kitchen, where it smelled like brownies. "I'm feeling great, Beck. I even guessed you'd be around today, so I made you brownies."

"Heloise's recipe?"

"You know it."

The former maid had died while serving his parents—killed by vamps—but Bella always made her brownie recipe in honor of the woman whom she and Severo had loved as if a family member.

Beck had to use a fork to dig into a brownie heaped with cream cheese frosting and served on a plate because it was cut so big. Man, this was heaven. And if his mom had brought these brownies to the ice festival, she would have had to charge double what the others had charged—and would have made a fortune.

"How's the baby? Have you been in to see the doctor?"

"Ivan is taking me next week."

Beck nodded, but kept a comment to himself. So how close were Ivan and his mother getting? Because Ivan was married to a witch, had been for decades. He didn't want to bring the two together that much.

"I know what you're thinking," Bella said.

The twinkle she'd always had in her eye had returned. That set down Beck's shoulders even more. His mom was doing much better.

"Ivan is a friend. And Dez stopped by yesterday to help me make these brownies. The two of them have been what I've needed to…you know, take a step toward the future, is the best way to describe it."

His mother's sigh was evidence that she would always hold Severo in her heart. Hell, it had only been three months since his father's death. It was going to take a while for them both to get over his loss. Did they even have to get over it? And really, who decided how long the grieving process should be, or what, exactly, it entailed? He'd grieved already and was moving on. And now that his mother seemed to be heading toward the future, he could relax and know she would be all right.

"How are you doing, sweetie? Is the shop ready for opening?"

"I'm in no rush to open it to the public."

"No rush, or no energy? Beck, now, I know I'm the last person to be telling you what to do—"

"You're my mom. You sort of have that right," he said through a mouthful of brownie.

"Right. But lately, I've been—you know."

He rubbed her arm. "Understandable."

"Thanks. But I'm surfacing from the depression. Every day feels brighter and more promising. Yet I wonder if you've gotten stuck lately?"

"Stuck? No, I'm just taking my time with the shop."

"I'm not talking about the shop. Have you talked to anyone about losing your dad? Beyond me?"

Beck's stomach clenched. He pushed the plate across the counter. "Dad's gone. There's nothing more to say."

"He'll never be gone, Beck. We both hold him in our hearts."

Beck lifted his chin. He had to stay strong for his mother. "Yeah. You're right. He's in my heart. So do you think I could get a couple of these brownies to take with me?"

Bella smoothed her palm over his forearm. "Have you visited his grave?"

They'd buried his father out at the back of their property beneath the willow tree Severo would often sit under when in wolf form. An escape from the world, he'd once explained to Beck about the spot. But as well, a connection to the earth, the very universe that grounded him and brought him peace.

"It's just ashes and bones in the ground, Mom. Dad's spirit is long gone from this realm."

Saying it released a tear down Beck's cheek, which he hastily swiped away. That was a lie. Severo's spirit remained within him. He hoped forever.

"It's getting late." He stood abruptly and turned toward the foyer. "I'm going to get some more things from Dad's shop."

"I'll cut up some treats to take home with you."

"Thanks!"

He rushed to the shop and closed the door behind him, leaning against the steel surface and sniffing away the tears. "Damn it."

He'd anticipated some random feelings when coming here, but he'd expected them to be over his mother and her sorrow. But Bella seemed to be improving. And here he stood, crying?

He hadn't cried at the funeral. He had shed copious tears as he'd knelt in the snowy forest over his father's dying wolf. So why now? Tears would not bring back the dead, nor could the dead know he was heartbroken without him.

Beck slapped a palm over his chest. Heartbroken?

No, he was— It certainly felt as if something inside him had been broken. Cracked open. But *heartbroken* was a stupid word. It was something lovers felt after breaking it off. The heart didn't really break. It just felt like that sometimes.

But if he admitted it to himself, his heart had been torn apart and pried wide open by his father's death. And it hurt in ways he couldn't explain.

New tears spilled down Beck's cheeks. He slid down against the door and squatted, catching his forehead against his palms. Angry with himself for such a weak display, he slammed a fist behind him, punching the steel door. He swore and punched the door again. Turning and standing, he pummeled the door with both fists, over and over, jaws gritted and muscles tense. He shouted, releasing foul oaths he'd never speak in front of others.

And then he pressed his forehead to the cool steel where his knuckles had carved in dents. An exhale climbed from his being, slowly, resolutely. Lungs panting and body shaking, he no longer shed tears. But his heart felt hot and heavy, oozing with something he had only felt that night of his father's death.

Very well. His heart was broken.

And within him stirred the ghost wolf. The part of him that knew how to manifest his pain. It howled and clawed. His biceps flexed, tingling with the urge to shift.

Beck twisted his head to eye the door at the back of the shop, placed there as an exit into the night for the werewolf. He pulled off his sweater, and even as his arms began to lengthen and shift, he toed off his boots and shuffled out of his pants.

The door swung open as the werewolf's howl greeted the cold, winter twilight.

* * *

Bella had listened to the sounds echoing out from behind the steel door of her late husband's shop. Her son hurt. And he didn't know how to let go of that pain.

Beck's howls brought tears to her eyes. And then she could only hope that perhaps by beating his anger out on something like a steel door, it could begin to help him heal.

Now she saw him dash across the yard in werewolf shape. Yet—that wasn't Beck. What was that creature?

She raced to the patio door and pressed a hand to the glass. The werewolf loping off behind the hedge was taller than usual and sleek. Less fur covered his body than a normal werewolf. He was pale, almost ghostlike.

"White?"

That wasn't Beck. When he shifted, he took on much the same fur color as his father's dark brown, yet with some blond shades mixed in.

As the werewolf howled and dropped to all fours to race across the vast meadow behind the house, Bella clutched a hand to her throat. She'd seen the news stories. Could it be? Her son? But how?

"Oh, my God, Beck, what have you done?"

Early morning woke Beck with a freezing clutch at his skin. He came alert abruptly and looked about. He was lying on his parents' snow-covered patio deck before the tarp-covered pool. Naked.

He immediately checked his hands. No blood.

He lashed his tongue around inside his mouth. Didn't taste any blood—a sure sign his werewolf had been successful on the hunt.

Glancing to the patio door, he looked for movement. His mother slept late. A vampire thing.

Stepping quickly toward the back door, he found a shop towel to wipe off the melting snow and dirt, and then dressed. He'd leave, and call his mom later. She shouldn't question his shifting and going out for a run. He did it often. They owned a vast parcel of land, and it was safe here. His werewolf always stayed on the property.

Opening the shop door, Beck was startled by his mother, standing in a long red velvet robe that caressed her swollen belly. Her hair was down, and her eyes were puffy. She hadn't slept.

"We need to talk," she said, and turned to stride into the living room.

Chapter 20

The morning was too bright. And oddly warm. Daisy dashed across the street in a long pink sweater and some brown leggings. Her rubber-soled riding boots splashed in the slush. Yes, slush in mid-January. The sun was bright and the weatherman had promised forties, if only for the day. Wonders did not cease.

The Panera restaurant was a favorite meeting spot for her and Stryke, who waved her to the table where he sat. The only one in the family who didn't do coffee, he sipped a huge cup of chai latte. He splayed his hand over the plates already sitting on the table.

"You ordered for me?" She sat and immediately forked into the egg-and-steak breakfast platter. It was hot, and the tomatoes tasted summer fresh. "Have I told you lately I love you, brother?"

"Not often enough. Beautiful day, isn't it?"

"Yep. But I suspect that is not the reason you called this morning meeting."

"I just wanted to see my big sister. Does everything have to have a reason?"

"Probably not. And most especially not with you. I'm sorry, Stryke. You're right. We haven't had a good talk in a while." She slid a hand over his and rubbed his wrist. "So how are you healing?"

"Truth? I feel great." He rubbed his shoulder where the arrow had skimmed him while in wolf shape. "That witch's spell herb stuff worked like a charm. There's not even a scar. Wolfsbane. Whoda thought? Almost believed I was going to bite the big one."

"You're tough. All the Saint-Pierre men are."

"As well as the women." He winked.

"You know it. Though the fact that there's a hunter out there with silver bullets and arrows disturbs the hell out of me and—" Daisy shoved in a fork loaded with egg to keep from finishing that sentence.

"You and Beckett?" Stryke prompted. He set down the chai and rapped his knuckles on the table. He wore a platinum ring on his thumb, fashioned by their father.

"I thought you guys approved of him," she defended.

"Trouble liking the lone wolf is not the mark of approval earned, Daisy Blu."

"Oh, please." She rolled her eyes at her brother's pompous assumptions about Beck. "He's the first decent wolf I've ever dated."

"He is also packless."

"He's kind and caring."

"I sure as hell hope you haven't bonded with him."

Eyes flashing wide, she met her brother's discerning brown gaze. "That's none of your business, Stryke."

"Daisy." He leaned across the table. His voice lowered, and his stare intensified. "Don't be stupid about this. Sure, you can date the guy and piss off Dad all you like. But you know bonding with another wolf is serious shit."

"I know." She set down her fork and leaned forward to clasp Stryke's hands. "Don't worry. We're just having fun. Dating and, you know, doing stuff like playing a little one-on-one pond hockey. I like the guy, okay?"

"Yeah, well, we all know what 'like' means to you."

"Because it means the same to you."

They'd shared their ideas of love and like a few summers ago, after Stryke's first devastating breakup with a human woman who had moved to New York for her career.

How he had wanted to follow her, but family compelled him even more.

"And since you're in like," Stryke said sharply, "pretty soon you won't be able to resist the urge to bond."

"Like you would know. You've never bonded with anyone."

"And I don't intend to until I find the one. Someone in a pack, whom my family approves of, and who will give me children and—"

"Really? Stryke, you're not making an order. Bonding with someone you love is a real thing. You don't do it to please anyone but yourself and that person. You make it sound so clinical. Like it's been written down in some rule book, and you have to check off all the right boxes before it can happen."

"Maybe that's the way it's supposed to be. Daisy, the pack has rules."

"I know. But how's a lone wolf like Beckett Severo ever supposed to find someone to bond with if he isn't allowed to date within packs?"

"That's his problem, not yours."

Daisy stabbed her fork at the thinly sliced steak. "I can't believe you're being like this. You're always the one to see both sides and weigh things rationally."

He sat back and rubbed a palm over his close-cropped hair. Daisy liked that he kept it shaved a quarter inch to his scalp. His eyes were so bold and bright, so telling, and nothing should distract from her brother's appeal.

He was being anything but appealing right now.

"Much as you may not believe it," he said, "I am standing on middle ground. Good for you that you've found someone you enjoy spending time with. I mean, it's difficult for us—our breed—in the mortal realm. Much more so for us males." He lowered his voice, his eyes taking in the half-filled dining room. "It's not like the female werewolf population is vibrant up here in this neck of the woods."

"You need to go to Europe. I hear the werechicks are abundant over there."

"Is that so? Werechicks?" He winked and sipped his chai. "We are heading to Paris next summer for Kambriel's wedding." He shook his head and chuckled. "Can you imagine me falling in love with a fancy Parisian werewolf? That's never going to happen."

"Why not? You think the wolves in Paris are too good for you? I think you're too good for them. You're a wolf out of place, Stryke. A renaissance man stuck in the land of ten thousand flannel shirts. I know you'd fit in well in Europe."

"Just because I don't wear flannel like the rest of the population doesn't mean I don't fit in."

"Sure." But she really wanted to see her brother flourish, and to find that woman he dreamed about. "We'll leave it for the trip, eh?"

He tipped his latte to her, then sipped. Suddenly Stryke sat straight. His chin lifted as he sniffed the air. He set down the cup without a sound.

"What is it?" she asked.

Staying her curiosity with a subtle lift of his forefinger, he slowly turned about, taking in the patrons sitting nearby. The restaurant was peopled with all sorts, including a few hunters in flannel and orange vests who had stopped for a fuel break during the morning hunt.

"He's here," Stryke said. "Call your boyfriend."

"What? Who's here?"

"The hunter who almost killed me. The one with the silver arrows. I can smell him."

Beck got the call from Daisy just as he was trying to avoid talking to his mother about what she had seen last night. His cell phone jangled. Bella glared that motherly "don't you dare" look at him.

Beck put up his hands, signaling he'd let the call go to voice mail.

"Are you the ghost wolf?" Bella asked.

"Mom, I don't know what you think you saw, but it was definitely not that." He hated lying to her. But she didn't need that kind of angst right now. "The snow was blowing last night. I'm sure your vision was blurred."

"I have excellent vision," she snapped. "And I know what I saw. That werewolf was not you."

"So maybe there was another wolf around the house last night? I should go take a look around. Make sure everything is secure—"

"Beckett Severo, stop lying to me!"

Beck's phone rang again. He clenched a fist near his hip pocket.

"Answer it!" Bella entreated.

He dug out the phone, saw it was from Daisy and answered. "Hey, I'm at my mom's right now. Can I call you back?"

"I don't want to bother you, Beck, but I'm with Stryke, and he's one-hundred-percent sure we're sitting in the restaurant with the hunter who has been using the silver in his ammunition."

"Does your brother recognize his scent?"

"Yes. We're at Panera. Can you get here fast?"

"Yes. Uh…" Bella silently waited for his attention. "Yes. Ten minutes. Don't let him get away."

"He just sat down. You've got maybe twenty minutes at most."

"Thanks." He shoved his phone into a pocket and grabbed his coat from the rack by the door. "Mom, we're going to have to take a rain check on this conversation."

Shuffling around to block his path, Bella flattened her back against the front door. "What was that about?"

"It's Daisy. She's...." Beck exhaled. "She thinks she's found the hunter who killed Dad."

Bella's jaw dropped open. Her hand went instinctively to her belly, smoothing across the swollen signal of life beneath the red robe. In an instant, his mother was reduced from a confident woman to a frail, needy girl who just needed to be protected from all the bad things the world put before her.

He pulled her in for a hug. But if he didn't move now, he may lose this only chance. "I have to go."

She gripped his coat. "What are you going to do if it is him?"

Beck ground his jaw tightly.

"Don't you dare, Beckett Severo. Your father would never—"

"You know I would never hurt another man, Mom."

"Do I? Beck, if you are the ghost wolf—what I saw on the news the other night..."

He hugged her because he didn't know what else to do to quell her fears. Because her fears were real. And even he wasn't sure what the ghost wolf would do to the hunter.

"I can handle this," he said. He would have to handle it. "But I have to hurry. I'll call you later."

"No, I'll stop by your place," she called as he dashed outside into the daylight.

"Mom, don't do that! It could be dangerous."

He thought she said, "Danger doesn't frighten me."

Beck shook his head as he fired up the engine. His mother had been fearless when his father was alive. It was the vampire in her. It had emboldened a woman who had once been merely mortal, a website designer and dancer who hadn't asked to get involved in the realm of all she had once believed fantasy. Love had changed her life irrevocably.

He could completely understand that emotional power now.

"Too many people could get hurt," he muttered as the truck spun out of the driveway. "Have to stop this now."

Fifteen minutes later Beck spied Daisy in the Panera parking lot, walking alongside the brother with the short hair. Stryke, the one who had been hit with the hunter's arrow yet had recovered well enough to deliver him some punishing blows in the bar.

Beck touched his ribs over the kidney and muttered, "Damn faery."

Clad in a pink sweater darker than her hair, and knee-high brown riding boots, Daisy waved to him, pointing north with a mittened hand.

He drove up alongside the siblings, rolling down his window. Stryke ran around to the passenger side and hopped into the truck.

"He just left," Daisy said.

"Drive," Stryke said. "I've got his scent, but now that he's in a vehicle he'll be harder to track. Step on it!"

Beck leaned out the window and kissed Daisy. "Thanks. I'll be back for you."

"I'm good. I'll head home. You two do what you need to do."

"Right," Stryke directed as they pulled out of the parking lot. "He's headed south, out of town."

Beck followed directions, his fingers clenched about the steering wheel. His senses were so heightened, he couldn't get Daisy's smell out of his brain. And combined with Stryke's subtle aftershave, he had to lean his head out the window and suck in the brisk air.

"Chill," Stryke directed. "You're on edge, man. I can

feel your need to shift. Relax. We'll get him. We just need to follow him, discover where he lives."

Beck could indeed feel the shift. It stirred in his fingers and felt as if his gut muscles were being stretched up and down. The last thing he wanted to do was reveal what he was to Daisy's brother. That would end any possible relationship with the sister right there. And he didn't want to hurt the guy.

"I can't let him wander out to harm another wolf," Beck argued. "We've got to stop him now."

He stepped on the gas, tracking the hunter's car only four car lengths behind.

"I want to get the bastard as much as you do, but we have to think about this." Stryke rubbed his hands together.

"You called me. I have to assume you wanted to go after the man as much as I do."

"Yes, but to track him. Get a bead on him. There has to be a better way. A way that involves more than you leaping in to break his neck. You need numbers."

"Numbers?"

"More wolves."

"Why? To give that asshole more targets?"

"If you think some big white ghost wolf is scaring hunters, what do you think a whole pack would do?"

"Yeah well, I'm fresh out of a pack."

"I've noticed." Stryke rapped the car door with his knuckles. "My brothers will help."

Beck winced.

"Dude, you want to date my sister? You'd better get tight with her brothers."

Right. But getting tight might involve shifting, and that way was too dangerous. And if not that, Beck wasn't sure how many more beatings he could take from the quartet.

Once out of city limits, the hunter's truck pulled off the

road and drove up a private driveway. Beck pulled over to the side of the road and parked.

"I can do this myself." He pulled the key out of the ignition and grabbed the door handle.

Stryke's fist twisted his jaw sharply to the left. Beck shook his head. "What. The. Hell?"

"I've thought about it. We do this with my brothers or not at all."

Beck rubbed his jaw, unsure if the bone had cracked, but he wouldn't be surprised if it had. "Fuck."

"Look, that's the only option I'm giving you. Otherwise I knock out your lights, drive you back to town and leave you to sleep it off in the cold again."

"I can take you."

"You want to try?"

They were wasting time. Likely they'd parked before the hunter's land. Beck needed to track the hunter into the woods.

"Call them," Beck said. "But if they're not here in ten minutes, I'm going to track him down on my own."

"We've got time," Stryke said as he pulled out his phone. "Look."

Beck saw a single headlight zigzagging at the back part of the land.

"He's on a snowmobile," Stryke said. "I'm sure he's got traps to check and other shit. We'll find him. Hey, Trouble! Gather the troops. I found the hunter who sliced me."

Chapter 21

Daisy slowed on her walk toward home. A brown Mercedes seemed to be following her. She dared a look over her shoulder. The woman behind the wheel waved and pulled over to the curb. A smiling chestnut-haired woman got out, tucking a scarf about her neck. "Are you Daisy?"

"Uh, yeah?" She thought she recognized the woman, but with the scarf over her hair and the winter coat tugged up around her neck, she couldn't be sure.

"I couldn't let him leave like that. So quick. And without an explanation. I need to talk to you," she said, and held out a gloved hand to shake. "I think we can help one another."

Daisy tugged off her mitten and shook the woman's hand. "And you are?"

"I'm Belladonna. Beck's mom."

Beck drove around the posted private-property signs, heading south along the forest edge. He didn't want to have to deal with trespassing issues.

Thing was, he knew this land. Or knew about it. It was a mysterious piece of property that had oftentimes sat vacant over the years. Rumors in Burnham told that it had been owned for centuries by the same family. Family members came and went, some taking up residence, others living off-site, yet keeping the property tidy until the next willing family member decided to occupy the spot.

Beck hadn't heard that a new resident had moved in. In fact, his wolf had, on occasion, gone sniffing around the boarded-up house. But the smoke wafting from the chimney proved someone was living there now.

"There's Trouble," Stryke said, pointing out a black Ford pickup truck. "Blade and Kelyn are with him, too."

Beck pulled off the gravel road onto an old trail that hadn't been used for years, to judge from the tangled and rusted barbed-wire fencing. There were no private-property signs, so both guessed this would be a good spot.

"Still got him in your nose?" Beck asked as they got out to meet the brothers.

"Barely. We'll have Kelyn track him from the air. Kelyn!"

"The air?"

Beck shook his head, but followed Stryke over to the brothers, who got out of the truck. When he saw Trouble marching toward him with a focused look in his dark eyes, Beck flinched. And then he took the punch to his gut like a trooper.

"Good to see you again, lone wolf," Trouble said, retracting his fist. "Stryke says you've spotted the hunter who tried to take him out?"

Straightening from the less-than-friendly punch, Beck nodded. "Could be the same hunter who killed my father."

"Well then, we're on it." Trouble gathered the brothers around. No skirt today, just leather pants, a turtleneck and a vest that looked like real fur—but really? "What's the plan, Stryke?"

"Kelyn needs to fly high and track him from the air. I'm losing his scent," Stryke explained, "so we need to hurry. Let's walk in a ways in *were* form and shift far from the road. Beck, follow us. You cool with that?"

"So long as we're not standing around. Let's go." Beck strode forth.

Trouble wandered out to lead, along with Stryke.

The quiet dark one, Blade, took up the rear, and Kelyn was nowhere to be seen. Until Beck noticed the fall of faery dust on the trail ahead of him. He tilted his head back and saw the bird-size figure soaring through the treetops.

"Kelyn will find him," Stryke called back.

They tracked deep into the forest, where the thick pine trees brushed Beck's face with fragrant yet scratchy needles. The ground was packed with snow and layers of brown pine needles. He noted the lingering scent of rabbits, squirrels and deer.

The faery flew back and near Trouble's head where, Beck assumed, the brothers were somehow communicating. When Trouble pulled off his shirt and kicked off his boots, the others followed suit, save for Blade.

Time for the shift. Beck stripped down, tossing his clothes near the base of the same tree as the brothers had. That they'd not beaten him bloody yet was a good sign. But they had no stake in finding the hunter because of Severo's death. They were here because of Stryke.

The brothers shifted while Beck struggled to control his inner wolf's need to shift to werewolf. They weren't going werewolf right now. Wolves on four legs would serve this mission much better by providing stealth and a smaller target.

But the ghost wolf wanted out.

Trouble's wolf was black dusted with white around his maw. The cocky fighter howled as he dropped to all fours. Stryke, a brown wolf, wandered up beside the punch-happy brother. Blade—he didn't see him anywhere.

Snow began to sift down in thick white flakes. Beck felt the coolness on his face and used that to concentrate on shifting to four legs.

The brothers had loped on ahead.

The faery buzzed about Beck's head. He swatted at it, then slammed a shifting palm against the birch trunk. "Fuck" was his last human utterance as the ghost wolf took control.

* * *

Daisy warmed up hot chocolate for Bella and was thrilled to find a few unbroken almond biscotti in the cupboard. The vampiress sat silently watching as Daisy went about the motions of preparing hospitality. Daisy had spent a lot of time with her grandfather Creed, so she wasn't leery around vampires, nor did she fear them. They were just another breed that occupied the vast and wonderful world.

Yet Bella had been a mortal until she was bitten in her twenties. Daisy couldn't imagine what it must be like to have known one life, then to be thrust into another life that was so different. Drinking and eating food one day, and then to survive on blood the next? It sounded almost as complicated as trying to balance one's wolf with one's faery.

As she set the steaming chocolate and a plate of cookies before Bella, Daisy realized her faux pas.

"I'm sorry. You probably don't eat."

Bella turned the mug around and gripped the handle. "I like to taste things." She sipped the hot chocolate. "Ohmygoodness." Her eyes brightened, and her cheeks grew noticeably rosier. "This is mead."

"Beck likes it, too." Daisy sipped from a mug that declared her a bookworm.

"My son does love his sweets. This must be how you won his heart."

Daisy didn't know what to say to that. Because really?

"Oh, I'm sorry," Bella suddenly said. "I'm sure it was more than a sip of chocolate that turned Beckett's eyes onto you." She sighed and drew her gaze gently over Daisy's face. "You seem like a nice girl. Your hair is pink, though." Bella sipped again, quickly.

"It's natural. I'm half faery on my mom's side."

"Oh, that's right. She's so pretty, your mother. Married Casanova, eh?"

"I hadn't thought anyone called my father that anymore."

"Sorry. It's what I remember the women used to whisper about Malakai Saint-Pierre."

Indeed, her father had been the area's resident Casanova before her birth. But no more. Her mom and dad were solid.

"Are all your siblings like you?" Bella asked. "Half werewolf and half faery?"

Daisy laid out the details on the family genetics, and Bella consumed the whole mug of hot chocolate and a few nibbles of biscotti. "I like your son a lot, Mrs. Severo," Daisy offered. "He's kind and funny and, well, he is so honorable."

"He takes after his father," Bella said. She looked aside, catching her chin in hand. Her thoughts were probably on her late husband, Daisy decided, and she didn't know what to say. But after a few seconds, Bella returned with a smile. "I hope the next is a girl." She smoothed a hand over her belly.

"Beck told me he's going to be a big brother. If you ever need anything, you must let me know."

"Thank you, Daisy. What I need is to know if Beck has spoken to you about his father."

"Like how?"

Bella shook her head, bewildered. "I don't think he's talked to anyone about Severo's death. He certainly hasn't with me. And I think he's holding it all inside. And now I've learned about… Uh, have you heard the news on TV about the ghost wolf?"

"He told you?"

"I figured it out. So you know that's what Beck is? Whew. I was pretty sure he had told you, but just now I had a moment where I wasn't sure if I should say anything."

"I saw him shift," Daisy offered. "I was in the woods one night he was out. So you've only seen the news reports?"

"Actually, I saw him last night. And he didn't look as

his werewolf normally does. Has he talked to you about that? Daisy, I'm at a loss." The woman's eyes glossed, and her hands shook as she pushed the mug away. "I need to know my son is okay."

"He believes he has it under control, but I'm not so sure about that." She clasped Bella's hand. "I want him to stop being the ghost wolf."

"Me, too. But how does he do that?"

"Has he told you everything about what he's become?"

Bella shook her head. "I wanted him to talk to me this morning, but then he got a phone call from you and rushed off. Is he going after the hunter?"

"As far as I know, he's just tracking him. The same hunter nearly killed one of my brothers."

"Oh, no. Is he all right?"

"Stryke is great thanks to a little witch magic from Desideriel Merovech."

"Ah, she and her husband, Ivan Drake, are good friends of mine. Your brother is one lucky wolf to be under Dez's care. But tell me, Daisy, what do you know about this beast that my son has become?"

Beck wasn't a beast, but Daisy knew that the ghost wolf looked like it to most. And if the ghost wolf had a mind of its own that could control Beck, then surely it was a beast that needed to be stopped before it went too far.

"He went to a faery for the gift of the ghost wolf. I think he needs to return to that same faery to get rid of it."

"Then why doesn't he do it? Oh." Bella dropped Daisy's hand and pressed her palms to her face. "I don't know why I didn't see the obvious until now. He wants to avenge his father's death."

Daisy nodded. "I think so."

"I don't want to lose another family member." Bella's voice trembled. "I can't. I don't know how I'd survive—"

Daisy clasped her hand. "We won't let that happen. It's going to be all right. I'll do anything I can to make it so."

"Can you get him to talk to the faery?" Bella asked.

Daisy nodded, though she wasn't sure she had such persuasive powers over Beck. She didn't want to trick him or force him to do something that she felt was best for him. He had to do whatever he felt was right for him. But revenge wouldn't be right for anyone.

"Do you love my son?" Bella asked.

"Love?" It was more on the lines of serious like. But Daisy thought to keep the explanation of her scale of emotional commitment to herself. So she simply nodded.

"Then for the sake of your futures," Bella said, "we need to stop the ghost wolf."

Chapter 22

Denton Marx stood in a snowy clearing, a leather-bound pair of binoculars dangling about his neck. At the sight of the wolf pack charging toward him, he turned to race back toward the snowmobile he'd parked near a ravine. Hasty bootsteps kicked up snow in his wake.

One wolf, the darkest in color, split off and headed toward the snowmobile, while the other herded him away from the escape vehicle.

Yet from out of the forest emerged a creature that surprised even the wolves. The black-and-white wolf, getting ready to lunge for Denton, suddenly startled. Tail curling down and between its legs, it lowered its head and looked around behind it. Its brother backed away, growling, showing its teeth to the ghost wolf.

Denton, scared but fiercely determined not to lose the opportunity he'd waited weeks for, hissed as the two wolves suddenly began to shift to larger forms.

"About time," he said. "I knew I'd see this sooner or later. Just one silver bullet should do the job nicely. And then, finally, I can free Sencha."

Overhead, a darting birdlike creature gave the hunter little worry. He didn't remark on the creature's wings or the sprinkling of dust that sifted down to blend into the snow's glinting surface. Yet higher flew a dark shadow with a vast wingspread.

What the hell?

Marx needed a weapon. He raced for the snowmobile, a

fascinating contraption that he favored over a horse as conveyance in this deep snow. Behind him the shifted werewolves growled at the approaching white beast. It was two heads higher than them and did not slow its approach.

The black-and-white werewolf lunged for the white, ghostly wolf. Not slowing, the ghost wolf slapped the nuisance out of its path.

Shaking and determined, Denton eyed his bow and arrows strapped to the back of the snowmobile. The shotgun was tucked in a knapsack. Just twenty more strides…

Leaping, the ghost wolf passed him and landed on the snowpack before the snowmobile. The force of the creature's landing pushed the snowmobile over the ravine's edge, and it tumbled down forty feet to an iced-over stream edged with boulders frosted in thick snowfall.

Denton swore and turned to face the monstrous creature that loomed over him. He'd stood up to a vampire, a demon, a snake shifter and more. He would not back down now. He'd invested too much. Claws slashed the air before him and—

Suddenly the werewolves snarled into a tangle, attacking the ghost wolf. Crawling toward the ravine, Denton wanted to slip away from the danger. He wasn't armed. But he wouldn't miss this for the world. Real werewolves going at one another. If he could just kill one of them…

But it was over too quickly. One of the werewolves yelped, having taken a brutal slap of claws to its back. The ghost wolf stepped away, and then raced off toward the forest.

In but a blink the two remaining werewolves shifted to their wolf state and wandered over to the ravine's edge.

"No!" Denton cried. He clung to the edge, thankful he'd worn the rusted cleats he'd found in the shed on his boots, which kept him from falling.

The pack growled, showing him their teeth. One lunged

for him, snapping warningly. Denton felt as if they were merely trying to scare him.

Stupid wolves.

They turned and raced off, leaving him dangling over the ravine even as the great winged creature circled overhead.

Beck arrived at the site where they'd shed their clothing and shifted, coming out of the ghost wolf with the agonizing twist at his spine and muscles that had accompanied the shift this past week. As if it wanted to cling to its werewolf shape and never release him.

He landed on the ground on all fours and grabbed his jeans. Behind him, he sensed the faery change shape, coming to full size. A glance over his shoulder revealed Kelyn, fully clothed—how did he manage that?—standing with hands to his hips.

"Don't say anything," Beck barked as he pulled up his jeans. A wave of dizziness wobbled him over the snowy surface.

"What's to say?" Kelyn offered with a chuff. "You...all right?"

"Of course!"

The brothers arrived as a pack and shifted up to *were* shape. Something dropped down from the treetops with a flap of wings. Without bothering to grab clothing, Trouble stalked up to Beck and slammed his hand beneath his jaw, shoving him against a birch tree. "What the hell?"

Beck eyed the bleeding cuts slashed into his shoulder. From the ghost wolf.

"Give him some room, Trouble," the faery insisted. He kicked the snow and turned to retrieve his brother's pants. He tossed them to Trouble. "Get dressed."

Trouble shoved Beck hard against the throat, but backed off, taking his brother's offering and pacing away. His back was marred with three long slashes. He slapped his shoulder. "Damn, that hurt!"

"You're the ghost wolf?" Stryke said as he pulled a sweater over his head. "Why didn't you say something, man? It would have been good to have some advance warning."

"I hadn't meant to shift like that," Beck defended. He stumbled on nothing more than the snow, but caught himself by balancing his arms out to his sides. He shook out his left foot until he felt the bones snap into place. Damn, that was just wrong. "It's getting out of control. But it doesn't matter right now. The hunter is on foot. We have to go after him."

"The hunter will keep," Stryke said. "But you are another issue. Who did this to you?"

"It's faery magic," Kelyn offered. The blond one drew his violet gaze across Beck's face. "I can sense it."

When Beck made to argue, he was stopped with a challenging lift of Kelyn's chin. If the faery could sense the origins of his ghost wolf, perhaps *he* could help him? No. He didn't know where he stood with the brothers. And wherever that had been, his stance had just gotten worse.

"Did Daisy do this for you?" Trouble asked, stomping back over as he pulled his fur vest on. "I didn't think she could do stuff like that."

"Daisy did not—"

"It takes great faery magic to accomplish something like the ghost wolf," Kelyn said. "And you can't control it?" The brother shook his head and wandered off to where Blade, the dark, silent one—how had he gotten dressed so quickly?—ventured toward the parked vehicles.

"This is not good," Stryke said. "The hunter has seen us shift."

"He already knew," Kelyn called back.

"What?" both Stryke and Trouble asked. They rushed to catch up to Kelyn and Blade.

"I heard him say 'it's about time' while I was hovering overhead. The man knows what he's hunting," Kelyn said. "The question is, *how* does he know, and why the hunt?"

"To bag a werewolf," Trouble offered. "Idiot humans don't need any better reason than that. But now..." He glanced over a shoulder at Beck. "I bet that hunter's sights have been set higher. Fuck, man, you pack a punch as that creature. Excellent challenge, I must say. You got me good."

"I wasn't trying to get you, good or otherwise." Beck started down the trail toward the vehicles behind the brothers. "I wanted to get that bastard."

"You pushed his weapons out of the way," Kelyn said. "You saved my brothers."

Beck waved that suggestion off with a dismissive gesture. They'd fucked this one up, and now the hunter would not stop until he'd gotten his prey.

Back at the trucks, Beck jumped into his and fired up the engine.

"Where you headed?" Trouble asked.

He didn't reply. He'd had enough of the group approach.

"You can't do this on your own, man!" Trouble called.

The dark one shook his head and said, "Let him go."

And with that, Beck drove off. He avoided driving by the hunter's property again. The man wouldn't have returned home yet with his snowmobile a loss. He'd have to walk. Might make it back by nightfall.

And by nightfall Beck hoped to return.

Daisy had just arrived at Beck's house to find he wasn't home. She and Bella had decided the gentle approach to getting Beck to return to the faery might work.

Just when she thought to hop in her car and call a brother to see if they were still out hunting, or possibly had stopped for a drink afterward, Beck's truck pulled up the driveway.

She laughed at herself for thinking her brothers would

have a drink with Beck. Beck would probably suspect they were greasing him up for the slaughter. Her brothers meant well. And the fact they'd gone to help Beck look for the hunter only proved that. They'd accepted him in their own way.

How to adjust her father's attitude about the lone wolf?

Beck charged out of his truck toward where she stood at the front door. Daisy sensed the anger wavering off him like steam after a shower. She stepped down onto the shoveled sidewalk because it felt wrong to stand on the step, higher than him. She wanted to show him respect, an innate wolf quality.

"What are you doing here, Daisy?" he asked as he walked by her and shoved the key into the door lock.

No hello kiss? No hug?

Though she wore a winter coat and her kitty-eared cap and gloves, Daisy rubbed her arms. She wasn't cold, just...

"What did I do?" she asked. "Beck, are you mad at me?"

Shoving the front door open, he turned and slid his eyes over her face. Just when she thought he would soften and pull her in for that hug and kiss, he gritted his jaws.

"Didn't it go well with my brothers?"

"They let the hunter go."

"What?"

"Your brothers..." He fisted the air. "I don't want to talk about it. I'm...not in the best mood. I think you should leave."

"But, Beck—"

"Daisy." He grabbed her by her shoulders as a father would a child. "Don't you understand how dangerous it is for you to be around me? I don't want to hurt you."

"Yes, but—what happened with my brothers? Tell me."

Jaw tight, he finally blew out a breath and confessed, "They saw me shift to the ghost wolf."

"Shit."

"They took it well enough, but damn it, the hunter got away. They wouldn't let me go after him."

"Or were they protecting a human from a ghost wolf who might kill it?"

He squeezed her arms tightly. Grimaced. Then let her go. "Right. You would think that."

"Beck, they were saving you from yourself. You can't continue to shift to the ghost wolf—"

"Leave," he insisted.

His tone was curt. Final. So he was in a bad mood and didn't want to talk? She could stand up to a grumpy man any day.

But when he turned to show her his teeth, canines down, Daisy stumbled backward, stepping off the sidewalk onto the snowy bank. She almost toppled, but caught herself.

"Go!" he said. "Get the hell away from me!"

With no words to reply, Daisy rushed to her car and got inside. Heartbeat frantic, she fumbled to turn the key in the ignition. Beck stood on the steps watching as she backed out the driveway. And only when she turned onto the main road did she see his front door close.

"He may be a lone wolf, but he sure likes to work the alpha vibes," she muttered. "Stupid, angry wolf."

Intellectually she knew he probably needed time alone to work off some steam, to come down from the weirdness she suspected the ghost wolf worked on him every time he shifted. He had a lot to deal with. The hunter who had killed his father was out there, and he had been close enough to...

Would he have killed the hunter had her brothers not been there to stop him?

Daisy shook her head, not wanting to believe Beck capable of murder.

But it wasn't Beck she had to worry about. It was the ghost wolf.

Malakai Saint-Pierre dialed up his son Stryke because he knew he had plans to meet Daisy this morning. It was evening, but she hadn't been at her place. "Stryke? Your mom wanted me to pick up some things at the store, so I stopped by to look in on Daisy. She's not home. You see her today?"

"Uh, this morning for breakfast?"

That was a strange kind of nonanswer that had ended on a questioning tone. What was the kid hiding? Stryke was the siblings' confidante, and he was damned good at keeping secrets. "So where is she now?"

"I uh…haven't any idea, Dad."

Evasive? Hmm…Kai could always tell when his children were hiding something, or trying to protect one another. Which they'd managed with flair while growing up. And just because they were adults now didn't mean they'd stopped the group protection ploys.

"You sure you haven't the tiniest guess at where your sister could be?"

"Nope."

"Fine. Talk to you later, Stryke."

Kai hung up and swung the car around at the corner. He had a damned good idea where to find his daughter.

He'd hated treating Daisy like that. The moment her car had reached the end of his driveway, Beck had wanted to rush out and chase after her, beg her to forgive him and give him a second chance.

But he wasn't stupid. The last thing he wanted was to hurt Daisy. And right now, he was so wound up in trying *not* to shift to the ghost wolf that it was all he could do to keep it back.

So Beck had gone out back, just off the snow-covered patio where he'd laid out stones last summer to form another patio around a fire pit. A punching bag hung from the oak tree, and he pummeled it with his fists. Stripped to the waist, he worked so furiously that the sweat didn't have time to freeze.

He beat the bag soundly, kicking it, imagining it as the hunter. So long as he kept physical, moving his body, engaging his muscles and mind, the ghost wolf kept back, seeming satisfied with this workout.

His father had helped him hang this punching bag. Severo had been the first to try it out, giving it a good kick and then remarking that he was getting too old for the physical stuff.

Beck had laughed and clapped his father across the back. He was stronger than his son, but Severo did like to spend most of his time hanging around Bella. He would have been proud to know his wife was carrying his second child.

Another punch set the chain jangling as the bag bounced in the air and fell heavily. The solid oak branch creaked.

What would he do with a little brother? Or sister? How would that child's life be affected, growing up without a father? It didn't seem fair. It wasn't fair. And Beck certainly had no idea how to lead someone younger, to show them a good example and raise them right.

Maybe his mom could find a new husband? No. He didn't want that for the family, or for Mom. She would mourn Severo for a long time, he suspected. As would he.

Because he did mourn. He felt his father's loss in his gut, and his head, and his broken heart.

"Not broken," he muttered as he delivered a punishing kick to the bag. "Can't be. I won't let it be!"

So maybe he hadn't moved through the grief as he'd convinced himself he had. Screw it. He was tough. He could handle this. Because he had to. He was the last standing Severo man.

He hadn't heard the approach, but now he smelled the intruder. Beck swung around and charged the man, who stood not ten feet away. He shoved his shoulders and pinned him against a wide oak trunk. Growling and showing his thick canines to the man, Beck didn't even blink when he realized who it was.

Malakai Saint-Pierre smirked, then narrowed his brows. His face changed from the surprise of the attack to a determined expression indicative of a deadly predator.

"Come at me, boy," Kai challenged. "Let's see what you've got."

Chapter 23

Shoving away from the older, stronger wolf, Beck did not stand down. Instead he put up his fists and growled. How dare the man show up at his home—on his private property—without an invite?

He swung a fist. Kai dodged it with a taunting chuckle. So the alpha wolf would laugh at him? Wrong move.

Beck swung a left hook, knowing the man would dodge that, and so caught him in the kidney with a right uppercut.

Kai grunted at the connection. "Good one."

His opponent moved so quickly, Beck could but shuffle on the snow- and ice-packed ground, his boots slipping, but he maintained stance. His adrenaline pumped as he took a fist to the jaw, and another to the gut. Still not as powerful as the faery's punches.

Daisy's father pushed him, and Beck lost footing on an ice slick, landing in a snowbank. He scrambled up, barreling into the other wolf. They both tumbled to the snowy ground, fists finding their mark against tender organs. The Saint-Pierres had admonished and ridiculed him for the last time. Beck's father would have never taken such treatment. He would show Malakai Saint-Pierre who he was dealing with.

They battled it out, crashing into the boxing bag, other times rolling across the snow as fists flew and kicks connected with ribs and shins. Grunts of exertion and huffs of breath leaving pummeled lungs marked the air in puffs of chilled pain.

Beck struggled inside. He didn't want to do this. He fought against the man he should try to impress in order to win a chance to love his daughter. Yet he had already stolen Daisy out from under her father's care, and Kai had every right to come at him with all he had. Which is what he was doing now.

Beck landed on the packed snowbank behind him, gripping his gut. Ab muscles tight and flexing, he pushed off from the low bank, yet couldn't quite stand, landing on his knees before the towering werewolf, who heaved and panted over him.

Depleted, his soul ached more than his muscles ever could. It was too much. He had suffered too much lately.

"I can't do this," Beck sputtered. Blood drooled from his mouth. His jaw had taken a bruising punishment. "Not right. But he would want me to…maybe. I don't know anything anymore. He shouldn't have…"

Beck heaved in a breath, and when he exhaled, he caught his palms on the boot-trampled snow before him. "He shouldn't have left me." His ribs ached with each inhale. But worse, his heart clenched. "I need him. I don't know what to do anymore. I…I can't…"

He was acting foolish before the other wolf. But he couldn't stop the fluid stream of emotion that coiled up from his broken ribs and squeezed about his heart before spilling from his mouth.

"I loved him. I…I want him back."

"Boy, your father was a good man."

Beck nodded, bowing his head, his focus on the man's rubber-soled biker boots. His father had worn the same, yet Severo's boots had been as tattered and worn as the man had been. Beck remembered trying to walk in his father's boots when he'd been a quarter his size, stumbling about in the heavy things until he'd toppled into a graceless sprawl. Severo would pick him up and hold him upside down from his ankles, swinging him until he begged to be tossed onto the sofa in a fit of giggles.

"He was my family," Beck muttered, his bloodied fingers clawing into the snow. "I've known nothing else. I can't accept another family just like that. It wouldn't feel right. Please understand…"

Beck felt Kai slip his fingers through his hair. The man jerked his head back to meet his eyes. "You're like your father, Beckett Severo. And that's something you should be proud of."

And when the wolf should have delivered the final punishing blow to knock Beck out and put him out of him misery, Kai did something strange. He pulled Beck up to his feet and wrapped his arms around him, crushing Beck's face to his chest in a hug.

Beck struggled, but only initially. It was too difficult to fight now. He was exhausted. Emotionally, he was broken. *Heartbroken.* He had only wanted one final hug from his father. And now, he clung to Malakai Saint-Pierre and buried his face against his shirt. He didn't cry. Tears had long left him. But his body shuddered with the pent-up pain and grief that he'd held within for too long.

It flowed out now, shaking his bones in the frigid air and against the man's brawny frame. He couldn't think to push away because this was stupid or nonsensical. He needed this release. So he surrendered to it.

Kai gave the back of Beck's head a firm pat. "Give it time. You'll come through this. I know your father was proud of you, and you won't let him down, will you, boy?"

But he already had.

Pierced through his heart by an intangible silver-tipped arrow, Beck disengaged from Kai. "I think I have let my father down. I've done something terrible."

Beck shoved away and shuffled back to fall against the snowbank that had been beaten down by repeatedly catching his sorry body during the fight. "Mister Saint-Pierre, I have to tell you something."

"Is it about my daughter? I know you're fucking her, boy."

Beck winced.

"Just let me say one thing." Kai leaned in so close that Beck wasn't sure if the man would bite him, punch him or hug him again. "If you marry my daughter, then you'll have no choice but to join our pack."

"I...I..." What? "I don't know what to say to that."

"Just putting it out there." Kai straightened and smacked a bloody fist in his palm. His grin wasn't so much menacing as playful, much like Trouble's teasing I-like-to-beat-you-bloody smile. Like father like son. Or vice versa?

"I've harmed a human," Beck confessed. "I'm sure of it. It was on the news." Sitting there, he caught his head in his palms and pulled at his hair. He looked up suddenly. The urge to spill all was irresistible. "I'm the ghost wolf."

Kai cast him a disbelieving tilt of the head. A what-the-hell look. And then he whistled in appreciation. "Is that so? You've been up to some stuff. How the hell is that possible? What *are* you? I thought you were full-blooded werewolf?"

"I am. I...went to a faery after my father's death. All I could think about was avenging his death."

Kai gripped Beck by the shoulders and yanked him to his feet so he stood toe-to-toe with him. "Idiot."

"I— No, I wanted to help, too. To keep the mortal hunters from going after the wolves. And also, to find the one who killed my father."

"Noble. Idiotic," Kai barked. "Faery magic demands a return boon. What did you promise in exchange for such a monster?"

"I'm not sure. I promised the faery any return favor she should request."

Kai swore under his breath. The big wolf shoved his hands into his front pockets and turned away from Beck,

eyeing the waxing moon framed by spindly birch trees that
edged the iced pond.

"My mother and father," Kai began, "wanted children
so badly they sought a faery's help. You know a werewolf
can't have a vampire's child?" He turned a glance over his
shoulder, and Beck nodded in acknowledgment. "So they
needed some faery magic. But they promised a child in
exchange for that magic. Each of them, on separate occasions, made that bargain with the same faery. My mother
promised her firstborn. My father promised the secondborn.
Each had their own reasons. They had no idea Blu—my
mother—would get pregnant with twins. It's a long story.
Suffice it to say I was born cursed and ended up battling
a faery for my life and my wife, Rissa's, life to fight that
curse. You shouldn't have gone to the sidhe, Beck."

"I was desperate. I knew nothing about faeries save
that they could work remarkable magic. I confess…" Beck
glanced across the ground and swallowed hard.

"What?" Kai asked. "You asked for your father's life
back, yes?"

Beck nodded, ashamed that his desperation had led him
to such a request, but still clutching at the ache in his heart
that had him wishing it could have been accomplished.

"No good magic can bring back the dead," Kai said.
"You should be thankful the faery refused you that request."

"Yes, I know that now. And yet, the hunters are scared
shitless to hunt wolves now."

"They won't be for long. Because you can't be the ghost
wolf forever." Kai turned and approached him. "How long
does it last?"

Beck shrugged. "Not sure. It's…"

He could confess that every time he shifted it was harder,
more painful, and that he suspected it would slowly kill
him. But he wasn't about to succumb to the fear of an unknown future.

"It'll kill you," Kai decided for himself. The man possessed wisdom comparable to Severo's knowledge. Beck respected him for that. "You better fix this, boy. You can love my daughter, and I suspect you might—"

"I do. I mean, we like one another—"

"Yeah? I know about Daisy and her liking men more than loving them. She's particular that way. Well, if it's like, then I won't have you dying on her. Fix this mess, Beckett. Or I'll fix you."

Kai strode off and around the side of the house. Beck heard the truck engine fire up and drive off.

Spitting blood onto the snow, Beck caught his head in his hands. He did want to fix this. And Daisy deserved better. But not until he'd had his showdown with the hunter.

He needed resolution. One way or another.

Malakai and Rissa Saint-Pierre had raised Daisy to be a strong, independent woman who did not require a man to complete her or make her happy. Happiness came from within. If a person couldn't be happy in and of themselves, then how could they ever be happy with another person in their lives?

As well, her parents had taught her that men respected women and never hurt them.

Daisy pushed back her welding mask to rest at the top of her head. She was no longer in the mood for creation. Tugging off her leather gloves, she dropped them on the work bench then turned and leaned against it, her eyes unfocused on the wolf she was crafting from bicycle chains.

Beck had not hurt her last night. Physically, anyway. She even tried to convince herself that he had not hurt her emotionally when he'd literally pushed her away and told her to leave him alone.

She knew he had been trying to protect her from that

ghostly werewolf within him that threatened to take over and destroy whatever was in its path.

Like her?

He worried about hurting her. And that troubled her. She didn't want him to have that worry, and she didn't want to fear him in any way.

Was he struggling with these issues as much as she was? Certainly he must be. He didn't need to worry about her while he was still grieving his father.

Maybe they'd gotten involved too quickly. Perhaps her father was right in an odd, roundabout way, that Beck wasn't the wolf for her.

She shook her head and set the mask aside. She couldn't deny her heart. Because this was the first man she'd actually worried over so much. That had to mean something. Like maybe he was worth the worry.

"He is," she said, shrugging down her suede work overalls.

Beneath, she wore black leggings and a long gray T-shirt. It was chilly in her place today so she wandered toward the bedroom and snagged a soft blue sweater to pull on over the T-shirt, then stepped into the bathroom to splash water on her face. It got sweaty wearing that welding mask.

Someone knocked on the door, and her heartbeats quickened. She knew who it was. She could scent him. But mingled with Beck's woodsy aroma was an out-of-place floral odor. Perfume?

Rushing to open the door, Daisy found a huge bouquet of red roses standing in the opening.

"Beck?"

"I'm back here. Somewhere."

The roses moved forward, and she guided them in toward the kitchen counter. The long-stem roses were already in a vase that Beck set on the counter. There must be three or four dozen, she guessed.

"They're so pretty."

"Better than blue?" He heaved out a sigh and splayed his hands. "I'm sorry about last night, Daisy. I shouldn't have been so quick with you. I—"

She touched the cut above his eye that was almost healed. She hadn't seen it there yesterday.

"Had a little scuffle," he offered in explanation. "Can you forgive me? I don't want you to get hurt."

"I understand. It was the ghost wolf, wasn't it?"

He nodded, shoved his hands in his front pockets and looked aside. Unsure about touching her? Or not wanting to?

Daisy couldn't stand there and let him get by without a kiss. She stepped before him, and with another stroke over the cut, she kissed him. It was an "everything is good between us" kiss. A promise that they were doing the best they could and that whatever roadblocks they encountered, she was in it for the bumpy ride.

His breaths softened and mingled within hers, and she sensed his heartbeat slow. Finally he surrendered to the embrace. Beck's hands glided up her back, pulling her in to meld her body against his. He was so warm despite having come from outside, where the below-zero temps had reduced the city to an icebox.

"From now on, whenever you tell me to leave, I will without question," she said. "I trust you know yourself and the beast within you."

"I hate having to deal with this beast. But the worst is that you have to deal with it."

"Then maybe it's time you did something about it?" Her conversation with Bella Severo popped into her brain. "Find the faery you made the bargain with and reverse it?"

He smirked. "Your father said the same thing."

He turned toward the couch, but she gripped his coat sleeve. "My father? What the heck?"

Beck shrugged off his coat and tossed it over the couch arm, then tugged her onto the couch with him. "Your dad stopped by my place not long after you left last night."

"But—why? And you were…"

"Not in the best mood or form. After you left I went out back to beat on the boxing bag. Tends to tame the ghost wolf when I work up a good sweat."

Daisy couldn't figure out why her father would go to Beck's house. Though he had called her this morning. Said he'd looked for her last night. She'd lied and said she was out shopping. Right. Because she loved to shop. Not.

"Did he know I had been there?"

"Of course. He could smell you."

"So he went to your place looking for me?"

"I guess so. We fought. Then we had a weird talk."

"You fought?" She couldn't believe this. Sitting up on her knees, facing him, her eyes veered to the cut near his eyebrow. "Beck, are you serious? You and my dad were throwing punches?"

"He came up behind me when I was punching the bag. I turned and threw a defensive punch before I knew who it was. Then he challenged me, and I was already worked up and itching to punch something, so…we shoved each other around a bit."

"A bit? You have a cut on your eyebrow that still hasn't healed. My dad is not someone you should mess with. And did you forget the fact that he's my dad?"

"Daisy, it's cool. We…had a moment. It's all good between us now. Mostly."

"What?" Unsure what to do—hug him or nurse him—Daisy couldn't bring herself to touch him. "Beck, you are blowing my mind with this. I so don't understand."

He bowed his head to her shoulder and nudged his nose up against her chin. The touch was so tender, so needy, she tilted her head beside his.

"Your dad knows how I feel about you now," he said, "and I know you're the most important thing in the world to him. His whole family is. He understands I would never do anything to harm them. I told him I was the ghost wolf."

"So you two beat each other up, then you had sharing time? I don't even know what to say to that. I can't believe Dad didn't mention anything when he called this morning."

"We came to a sort of gentleman's agreement to tolerate one another. At least, that's what I took away from it. Your dad is a good man. I respect him, Daisy."

"I know you do. I just didn't think I'd ever hear about the two of you hugging."

"I didn't say we hugged. Did I say that?"

"No, but your defensiveness makes me think that maybe you did." She smiled and kissed him quickly.

Whatever had gone on between the two, she was pleased Beck was in one piece. And only slightly wounded. Her father had certainly restrained himself.

"I was thinking of going out for a run this afternoon," she offered, thinking a change of subject was due. "It's so cold today. No one is out and about. But my wolf loves running over the crisp, iced snow."

"I can get behind that. And then we'll come back and warm up afterward."

"With hot chocolate," she agreed.

He kissed her cheek. "And sex."

"That's the best motivation I've heard for making the run short."

He stood and pulled her up into his embrace. "We could skip the run. Stay inside and make love all day."

That sounded even better. But if she got him out of the house on a run, there was a good chance they could go looking for the faery.

"To be honest, I could really use a run," she said. "It'll make coming in to warm up all the more fun. Yes?"

He kissed her in answer.

Chapter 24

"Mmm, my gorgeous werewolf."

A pale faery fluttered above the snow, her body draped with sheer fabric. Dozens of winged insects resembling white moths lazily waved their wings from within her finely braided yet flowing hair.

After Daisy and Beck had gone for a run in wolf form, they'd shifted back near a maple tree where they'd left their clothes, dressed, and then Daisy had suggested Beck try to call out the faery. A few kisses, a little snuggling and a pouty big-eyed plead had done the trick.

Beck hadn't spoken, but instead had closed his eyes and summoned the faery he'd called to after his father's death. And she had appeared quickly, in a burst of frost and sultry giggles. And white moths.

"Why have you come back to me, Beckett Severo?" the white faery cooed. "Are you not pleased with the gift I bestowed upon you for nothing more than the promise of a favor returned?"

Daisy lingered behind Beck, fascinated to look upon the gorgeous faery. Her wings had never looked so stunning. It was as if the white faery's wings were liquid and run through with rainbows flowing through her veins as the wings shifted slowly through the air. And even though the thermometer hadn't topped the freezing point, she looked a porcelain princess, alive with life.

"I am thankful for the gift you gave me," Beck said. "The ghost wolf has been successful in pressing back the hunters. The gray wolves in the area feel a safety that they haven't known since before the hunting ban was lifted."

"And were you able to achieve your foremost goal?" the faery asked. She hadn't regarded Daisy yet. Her violet eyes took in Beck as if she admired his strength and courage. And perhaps more than that.

"I know where the hunter who killed my father lives."

"Though your goal was not stated, I could read it in your soul, Beckett Severo. The ghost wolf must end the hunter's life," the faery stated.

"No," Daisy blurted out.

The moths about the faery's hair suddenly swirled into an angry tornado and aimed toward Daisy. She cringed behind Beck's broad shoulder.

With a sweep of a hand over her head, the faery calmed the raging insects that must be a part of her very being. "Do not listen to the half-breed whose curse will not allow her to decide whether she is wolf or faery," she said on an obvious sneer. "My brave warrior werewolf has not yet completed his task. Therefore I cannot request a return boon until you have."

She thought Daisy couldn't decide whether to be wolf or faery. What curse? That didn't make sense. Her father had been the one born with a faery curse upon his head.

"What do you mean by that?" Daisy asked. "I'm sorry, Beck, but I have to know if she senses something about me."

"Yes, I'd like to know, too." He clasped her hand and squeezed reassuringly. "Daisy is having, er, troubles with shifting."

"She was supposed to be born either wolf or faery. She must choose," the faery said curtly. "As simple as that."

"How do you know that?" Daisy asked. "I have brothers who are half-breeds. I've always thought—"

"As the firstborn child of Malakai Saint-Pierre, you shoulder remnants of the curse cast upon him by Ooghna.

Your father was not to fall in love with a faery, or he would ransom his heart."

"But the curse was broken when my father killed Ooghna."

The faery snarled at Daisy, revealing pointed teeth. Perhaps she had known the warrior Ooghna, who had once been the Unseelie king's champion.

"Malakai Saint-Pierre murdered the warrior Ooghna. You are meant to be only wolf or only faery, but the curse lingers. Until you make a choice, you will ever struggle between the two."

"So it's as easy as that?" Beck asked. "She simply decides whether she wants to be one or the other?"

The faery nodded. "I thought you called me to discuss you? I do not owe this one any more than what I have revealed."

"I thank you," Daisy rushed out, knowing one should always appease the sidhe. "You've been a tremendous help. And you're right. We called you because Beck is suffering."

"I wouldn't say suffering. As I've said, I appreciate the gift. The ghost wolf is becoming difficult to control," Beck said. "I want to return the power to you, if I may. I don't want the beast to harm innocents."

"Is that so?" The faery's wings flitted back and forth before Beck and Daisy as she considered the wolf's request. "I see no malice in harming humans who claim murder as their goal."

"I do," Beck said. "As a creature of this realm, I cannot justify harming innocents."

"The hunter was not innocent."

"The humans are acting on morals that have been bred into them. Yes, it is a fear-based reaction to want to murder a wolf, but I don't think the ghost wolf can ever change that. And so…I've had a change of heart."

Drawing up her chin, the faery looked down her nose

at the werewolf. "What would you give me in return for such a boon?"

"I, uh…"

Daisy placed her other hand over her and Beck's clasped hands. The faery noted their handhold, and again the moths showed their dismay. Daisy dropped his hand. Best tread carefully around this one.

"What would you ask of me?" Beck said.

"I'll take something that is important to you. Your wolf."

"No," Beck answered hastily. "I— No. You mean I would become merely human? Is that even possible?"

"Everything is possible."

"I suppose it is in Faery. But…my wolf. It's what I am. Is there something else? Anything?"

The faery sighed heavily and the moths swirled toward Beck, circling his head testily. Daisy could smell their spring scent, like raindrops on new moss. Only when one of the creatures dashed before her face, cutting her skin with a wing, did she step back and behind Beck again.

"Mind your place," the faery admonished Daisy. And to Beck she said, "The only other option is to take your firstborn."

"My— But I'm not even married."

"You will marry her," the faery said with bored assertion. "And you will have children. Most likely half-breeds, if she chooses her sidhe nature. Always a boon in Faery, mind you. Those are the two options I will give you to, in turn, remove the power of the ghost wolf from your frustratingly moral soul."

Beck glanced down to Daisy. He looked into her for the answer. But what did she know? And what right had she to tell him what was worthy of a trade? They were to be married? If so, then she would never hand over her firstborn. But the faery couldn't possibly predict their future when their relationship was yet so new.

"I've always said making the wrong decision is more fun." He shook his head and regarded the faery. "But no. I'd never sacrifice my child."

"Then your wolf it is," the faery said with delight.

"No! I refuse to sacrifice what I am. I just…can't. I guess that means I'll have to deal with the ghost wolf on my own."

"Do not ever seek me again, werewolf," the faery said. "When you have finished what the ghost wolf desires, then I shall return for my favor."

Sweeping her wings forward once, the faery dispersed into thousands of white moths and soared away above the naked treetops.

"I'm sorry." Beck pulled Daisy against him.

"I'll be fine. We're going to be fine."

A kiss to her nose was warm in the icy air and made her smile. "I'll just have to live with this curse."

"No, you don't. Didn't you hear what she said? She can't ask for a return favor until you've completed your task. So don't ever kill the hunter, Beck. It's as easy as choosing to forgive."

He opened his mouth to reply, but only shook his head.

"Yes, forgive," she repeated.

"It's not as easy as you make it sound, Daisy. If I don't kill the hunter, the ghost wolf will kill me."

Sliding an arm around her waist, he walked her back to the truck parked on the gravel road outside the forest.

Once inside, the engine running and the seat warmers cranked to high, Beck leaned over and kissed Daisy. "What are you going to choose?"

"What do you mean— Oh. You think she was right?"

"I have to believe she has some means to foretell things about us. And it makes sense. If your dad was cursed, you could carry remnants of that curse within you."

Daisy nodded. "I don't know. It's a weird thing to consider. One or the other? I'm wolf *and* faery. There are parts of my parents in me that I wouldn't want to sacrifice over the other."

"You did tell me you favor your wolf."

"I always have. But to think about giving up any part of me?" Daisy sighed.

"Maybe you should talk to your mother about it? She might be able to confirm what this one said. At the very least, you need to tell her about you carrying the remnants of the curse."

Weird how their lives had been so entwined with their parents'. Beck's mother coming to her to help her son. Her father going to Beck and possibly forming some kind of truce. And Beck suggesting she seek her mother's help.

Family truly was the foundation of everything that made life worth living.

"I'm glad you said you wouldn't give up your firstborn," she said as Beck turned onto the road and flicked on the headlights. The twin lights beamed through falling snow.

"How could I?"

"My grandparents both agreed to such a bargain."

"Your father told me."

"People do what they must when they are desperate."

"Then I guess I'm not desperate."

"What about giving up your wolf? That sounds worse."

"Don't worry. I'll always be wolf." He tugged her hand to his lap and gave it a squeeze. "And I will like you if you are a wolf. And I will like you if you are faery."

She forced a smile. To make such a decision felt too ominous to think about. She just wanted to return home with Beck, strip away her clothes and make love with him until the sun woke them both.

Mugs bearing the dregs of their hot drinks imbued the air with sweet traces of chocolate. The mugs had been sitting on the nearby nightstand untended for over an hour. Some things were far better to pursue than chocolate.

Daisy rolled over and straddled Beck, knees on either side of his hips. He lay with his head off the pillow, eyes closed, mouth reddened from their long and erotic kissing session. She had come with him only kissing her lips and sucking her nipples.

Now it was her turn to bring him to the edge. Gripping his erection, hot and stiff in her fingers, she rubbed it against her moist folds, seeking to glide it over her clit, which yet pulsed from the delicious orgasm.

Her lover moaned and tilted his hips upward. She used both hands on him, one cupping his thick head, the other gliding up and down the shaft, twisting lightly, then pausing on the sweet spot just below the ridged head of it. That made him hiss and beg. "Please, Daisy."

With a wiggle of her hips, she slid down and took him in her mouth. One hand still held firmly the base of his majestic penis. She loved the thickness of him, the feel of his skin as she laved over it, tasting and teasing. His scrotum was tight against his body, and she sensed he was nearing release.

And Daisy realized that all her life she had strived to compete with men, to win, to prove herself better. She thrived by taking control, owning the win.

Yet now, with Beck literally at her command, she only wished to make him feel as amazing as it felt for her to be loved by him. (Make that liked by him.) She didn't need to best him. She wanted to share life with him.

Lashing her tongue over his cock, she sucked it in and served him the ultimate release.

The waning moon was framed in the window. They lay on their sides, content and basking in the cool light.

"I don't want to compete with you," Daisy said.

"Why not?" he asked with gasping breaths.

"I don't need to. I feel better standing on equal ground with you."

"I like the sound of that. But I'll still let you win at hockey."

She punched him gently and he overreacted, splaying out his arms and groaning. "First she gives me pleasure, then she beats me. I can't win!"

"You've won me. The punches are just a bonus, wolf boy." Daisy nuzzled her face against his neck and took in his heat and the aroma of his bliss. "You know what else I'm thinking about?"

"How many ways you can get your brothers to torment me?"

"I would choose my wolf," she whispered. "Because I feel most connected to my wolf."

"Your wolf is beautiful. So is your faery. Give it more thought. Don't rush into anything. I'll support you no matter what your decision. I love you, Daisy Blu. And that's beyond like in my world."

Chapter 25

"Wow." Daisy's mom, Rissa, curled up her legs on the leather couch that looked out over the backyard and the iced stream. Snowflakes fell like down from an open pillow, dusting the world with peaceful, glinting whiteness. "How long have you been having this problem, sweetie?"

"A few years. It's been mostly a nuisance, but lately the wolf insists on taking over my faery. And vice versa."

"I'm so sorry." Rissa stroked Daisy's hair, imbuing it with a faint trail of faery dust. "I wish you would have told me sooner."

"You know how I am."

"You tend to think something will go away if you just ignore it. Like that time you spilled paint on my sofa and turned the cushion upside down."

"Will you ever let that one go, Mom?"

Rissa laughed. "I guess not. Sorry. I've always thought of your wolf as one of the boys."

"Probably because I am one of the boys."

"You've had difficulty honoring your feminine side, sweetie. Your faery is the wise, gentle, healing and nurturing part of you. I so wanted you to excel with your healing studies, but you were more interested in playing with the boys." Rissa sighed.

"Did I have a choice?"

"Probably not. You know, when you were a baby your sidhe side was prominent, you flew all the time."

"I did?"

Rissa laughed. "Kai was always yelling to me, 'She's in the rafters again!'"

Daisy peered up at the rafters. She only remembered Kelyn fleeing for the wide beams when his brothers tried to gang up on him. Really? She'd flown a lot as a baby?

Her mother nodded. "I couldn't let you outside without a tether."

"You put a leash on me? I so don't remember any of this."

"Yes, well, when the boys came along you got competitive. You forgot the freedom of flight and dropped to earth, choosing to throw mud pies and race through the forest, and chumming around with your father all the time. You wanted to win his time. And you did."

"Wow. No wonder my faery feels so alien. I'm sorry, Mom."

"Nothing to apologize for. You're a bright, beautiful woman. I'm proud of the woman you have become."

"But apparently I'm not completely grown into myself." Daisy exhaled. "I've been so worried about trying to get a job lately, to prove to Dad that I am capable and don't need his help, when all my life it's all that I've done. Depend on him. And now this thing with Beck. Of course Dad would feel protective. Oh, Mom."

"Oh, sweetie, your father will survive this love affair just fine. You do what makes your heart happy. And your wolf. So the faery you spoke to with Beck said you have to choose. As simple as that? Choosing?"

"I guess so. But does it sound right to you?"

"I've grown distant from Faery. Haven't been there since before I met your father. It sounds possible. I mean, that you carried remnants of Kai's curse with you. I'm so sorry about that."

"Don't worry about it, Mom. I'm sure it wasn't something that Dad could control. Besides, he broke the curse and won you. So it's all good."

"What does Beck say about it? You two are lovers, yes?"

"Yes. I adore him. He says he'll like me if I'm wolf or faery."

"Well, he should. My daughter is a very likable woman. So it's that serious, then? Like?"

Daisy nodded, a big grin filling her heart. "He's the one. I'm sure of it. But don't worry, we haven't bonded with our werewolves. Dad would freak, I know."

"I don't know. Kai's bark is much worse than his bite. You know that very well."

"Yes, and he did talk to Beck. He said Dad seemed okay with it all. But I'm thinking maybe Beck's head was spinning from one of Daddy's punches, and he probably misunderstood."

"Allow your father to surprise you."

"Fine. But now I have a lot of thinking to do. Because beyond my own problems, there's Beck and his ghost wolf. He needs to give it up before it kills him."

"Could you love him if he was human?" Rissa asked.

Daisy had also explained the faery's offer to take either Beck's wolf or his firstborn.

"I'm sure I could."

"A wolf would suit my daughter better."

"What if I choose faery? Then a human lover should not be so odd. It is only if I choose wolf and Beck sacrifices his that…" She turned to meet her mother's eyes. No words necessary. The two hugged as the snowflakes continued to fall.

"Promise you won't tell Dad about this?"

"Why? Daisy, if you have to choose between being wolf or faery, then we're all going to have to know. Your decision, whether or not you believe it, will affect the whole family."

"I know." Daisy sighed and tilted her head against the back of the sofa. It felt great to finally tell her mom.

But now, the decision of which breed to choose. If it was really possible. "But for right now, let's keep it quiet. Until I decide what to do."

"What's that about not telling your dad?" Kai strolled in.

"Girl stuff," Rissa said quickly.

"I can handle girl stuff."

"No, you can't." Rissa kissed Kai, then turned to Daisy. "Go to Beck. I'll talk to your father."

"Thanks, Mom."

Bella tugged Beck into the kitchen and proceeded to lay out a spread of delicious cookies on the counter before him. As if she needed to bake to survive, Bella kept turning out the goodies.

She poured him a tall glass of milk while he tore into the hot-from-the-oven chocolate chip cookie that oozed out chocolate and was crowded with walnuts. He loved nuts in anything and everything.

"You should start your own business, Mom," he offered between bites of the decadent goodness and sips of cool milk. "I have never tasted cookies so good as yours. Or for that matter, brownies. And the red velvet cake. You could buy that little place on the corner in town that always seems to turn over at least every two years."

"There's a reason businesses don't thrive in that location," she said, sitting on the bar stool beside him. "The land is probably cursed. And bakeries tend to open in the wee morning hours to begin baking for the day. Can you see your late-rising mother managing a 3:00-a.m. wake-up call?"

"Probably not. You could start something new. Midnight Munchies."

Bella nodded. "I kind of like that. Now that you've put the idea in my brain, it'll never go away."

"So how's my little brother doing?"

"You think it'll be a boy?" She smoothed a palm over her belly. "I'd like a girl."

"Whatever it is, we'll love it like crazy." He kissed his mother's cheek and focused back on the cookie. One more bite. He pushed his plate toward the baking sheet, and Bella divvied up two cookies this time. "I think I'm in love, Mom."

"What?" Bella turned on the stool. "Really?"

"It's Daisy Saint-Pierre."

Bella grabbed a cookie and took a quick bite. She cast Beck a worried glance. Or at least, he thought it was worried. "Isn't her father the one who has it in for you?"

"He does, or rather, did. Now I'm not so sure. Well, you know Blu, Daisy's grandma, right?"

Bella nodded. "She's nice, but...loud. Out-there. That werewolf doesn't act her age. Her husband, Creed, is chivalrous, though. Severo looked up to him."

"Daisy has said her dad admired Severo."

Bella slid her hand over his and curled her fingers into a clasp. "None of that matters. What does is how she makes you feel. Do you love her?"

"I do. She's fun and smart. And she likes to feed me. You'll have to get her hot chocolate recipe."

"Yes, hot chocolate," Bella murmured.

"I proposed to her after drinking it."

"You—?"

"Don't worry. I wasn't serious. We were having fun. And fun is what we do. She's not like most of the girlfriends I've had."

"Sexpots?"

"Mother."

"Son, you do have a type. Anything blonde, leggy and willing to moon over you. You can't know how glad I am you never fell in love with any of those choices."

"How do you know I didn't?"

"Beck, really? I'll grant you a man's desire to fulfill certain needs, but you're too smart to give your heart to anyone less than exquisite."

"Daisy is exquisite, pink hair and all. Her mother is faery."

"So…"

"Don't do it, Mom. I can see the wheels turning in your brain. We're just dating."

"Yes, but when a wolf finds the one who makes his heart skip, then you may as well sign on for the long haul. So you could have werewolf faery babies, you know."

Not if he decided to succumb and give up his wolf. Which he'd thought he could never consider. But really? How selfish would he be to keep the ghost wolf and continue to harm innocents?

"Daisy is a half-breed," he said. "I've seen her wings. They're pretty cool. And one of her brothers is full faery. Man, that guy can deliver a punch."

"Don't tell me. Her brothers have roughed you up? Interesting. The family must approve of you."

"Strangest way of granting approval I've ever known. And her dad. He beat the hell out of me— Ah, I shouldn't have told you that."

"But you're okay?"

He nodded and finished the glass of milk. "I gave as good as I got. But get this. Malakai Saint-Pierre actually said if I married his daughter, then I'd have no choice but to join his pack."

"That's about as accepting as I've heard."

"Yeah. I've been wondering if I should give some serious reconsideration to the whole joining a pack thing. But it's a decision that would affect more than just me. If I did, it would involve you, as well."

"Let me tell you a secret." Bella pressed Beck's hand against her lips for a kiss. "Your father and I had discussed joining a pack, or even starting one, when you were growing up. We went back and forth over how it could be good for you."

"Dad considered as much?"

She nodded. "So don't feel as though you owe your dad some sort of unmade promise to never join a pack. He would be proud of you no matter what you do. So long as it doesn't harm others and makes you happy."

Beck tightened his jaw. Harming others. Inside he could feel the ghost wolf twang at his muscles. If he fulfilled his promise to his dying father, he would not stop until the hunter was dead. And Severo would never be proud of him then.

He caught his forehead against his palm.

"Beck? What is it?"

"I miss him," he whispered.

Bella rubbed a hand across his back. The soothing motion made him want to push it all away. He didn't know how to succumb to these emotions, and didn't want to.

Yet he had with Malakai last night. He'd broken down before the mighty wolf. It had felt oddly safe to do so.

But he couldn't allow his mother to see him weak. She was the one who needed the support right now. He turned and hugged her. "We're going to be just fine," he offered. "Pack or no pack. I'll take care of you and my little brother."

"I love you, Beck, but I don't want you to feel as though I am your responsibility now. I'm a big girl. I can do this."

"But you don't have to do this alone. I'll always be here for you. And don't forget that."

"I won't. And guess what? Dez invited me over for a girl's night this weekend, and I'm going. I'm feeling the urge to have a little fun, maybe laugh and gossip with the girls."

"You don't know how good that makes me feel, Mom." He kissed her temple. "One more cookie?"

* * *

Beck recognized the pickup truck in front of the Blue Bass, so he pulled over and wandered inside. Trouble threw darts at the board. Kelyn stood back, arms crossed, obviously losing. His brother made the bull's-eye and thrust up his arms in triumph.

To judge Kelyn's eye roll, he'd probably lived with his brother's antics so long that there was nothing he could do but accept the grandstanding.

Sliding up before the bar, he ordered a shot of whiskey. Beck sensed both brothers got a whiff of his scent. Hell, they'd scented him before he'd even entered the bar. Such casual ignorance of his presence must be an art form.

Beck wrapped his fingers around the shot glass. A dart landed on the bar an inch before the glass. He plucked it out of the varnished wood surface, twisted at the waist and threw. Bull's-eye.

Kelyn's approving nod resounded above Trouble's chuckle. The burly brother slid onto the bar stool next to him. He was wearing some kind of leather skirt again, lace-up biker boots and a puffy winter vest over a sweater. The faery was, oddly, clad in jeans and a ripped T-shirt. No winter coat hanging on the hook near the door, either. Faeries must have excellent control over their body temperature.

"Still swooping my sister?" Trouble asked.

"Swooping?" Beck tilted back the whiskey shot to hide his grin. "Do you really want to know?"

"Nope. Heard my dad paid you a visit. You look all in one piece, so it must have gone well."

"He didn't tell you? I'm his new favorite son."

Trouble laughed and slapped Beck across the back, which burned more than the whiskey. "So how's it going tracking the hunter? If you don't get him, you know my brothers and I will. Right, Kel?"

The faery, who now tossed darts in practice with both hands, nodded.

"Hell, we know where he lives," Trouble said. "Let's go set his house ablaze."

"An eye for an eye isn't going to change things, man. It might even make things worse."

"How?"

"A revenge killing?" Beck reasoned, more with himself. "He only wounded your brother. He murdered my father. But even I can't justify taking a man's life."

"That crazy white werewolf you become would do it."

The man didn't know how right on he was. Beck clenched his fingers over the top of the shot glass. "I can't believe you would seriously consider killing another man."

Trouble leaned his elbows on the bar. "I'm no murderer. But the guy isn't like the usual hunters if he's using silver bullets and arrows. He saw us shift. And Kelyn said he acted as though he'd expected it. The man knows about our breed, Beck. That's not a good thing."

"I agree. But what does he know? And is he hunting werewolves for notches on his shotgun, or does he have another purpose? Is he a werewolf hunter? We need more information on this guy. I don't even know his name."

"I gotcha covered. Kel!"

The faery strode over and sat on the other side of Beck. The bartender placed a tall glass of ice water before him and received an appreciative nod.

"Kelyn looked up the hunter's address online," Trouble said. "What was his name?"

"The land has been owned by the Marx family since the eighteenth century," Kelyn said. "Burnham wasn't even a town back then. But the property has been handed down on paper through the years. Last name listed as owner was a Denton Marx, but I don't think that's a current resident. Denton Marx has no online presence."

"That doesn't mean anything," Beck said. "I just fumbled online for the first time last year to look up info on starting up a garage."

"Yeah, well, as far as I know, whoever is living in the house now doesn't have a job, and may hunt for a living. Probably sells pelts and meat to the locals. I flew over his property and took a look."

"And?" Beck asked. The fact that he was seated between the brothers and neither had tried to rearrange his face was a miracle. Guess he'd won his way into the family's respect.

"There was a deer carcass hanging from a tree. Must have been a fresh kill. Saw a snowmobile that looked like something from another time, and a big shed that I assumed must be where he keeps his weapons and probably a freezer full of game. Some stretched rabbit furs outside the shed, as well. Either he's a pro, or he's so off the grid he lives off the land and is a complete ghost regarding an online presence."

"Sounds like a pro who is obviously looking for bigger game," Trouble said. "Uh, I have to ask… It's about your father, man."

Beck rolled the shot glass between his palms. "Yeah?"

"Was he in werewolf form when he was shot?"

"No, we were both in wolf shape. It was our usual weekend run in the forest. I chased the hunter off, otherwise my guess is he would have stuck around to claim his kill."

"So he didn't see him shift to human form after, uh…?"

"No. My father didn't shift until I'd gotten him to my mother's house. He uh…" Beck swallowed. "He lived that long after taking the bullet."

"Sorry, man," Kelyn offered.

"Yet that hunter used a silver bullet," Trouble said, "so he must have known what he was hunting. Does he think if he takes down a werewolf, it'll stay that shape so he can stuff it and mount it as a prize?"

"Dude." Kelyn shook his head. "That image gives me the heebie-jeebies. And I'm not even wolf."

"Yeah, well, all you gotta worry about," Trouble said, "is getting pinned like a bug by the wings, little brother."

"That is so wrong," Beck said. He managed a smile, and the brothers chuckled. "So what do we do?"

Trouble tilted back a swallow then asked, "Can you control the ghost wolf?"

"It's getting harder every time I shift. I don't trust myself."

"Maybe we can use the ghost wolf to draw out the hunter, then we move in for the coup de grâce."

"The what?" Kelyn asked.

"Hey, it's French. Grandpa taught me." Trouble stood and slammed a couple ten-dollar bills on the bar. "Let's talk about this tomorrow, eh? I've got a date."

Beck gazed down the man's attire.

"What?" Trouble tugged up the waistband of his skirt. "You never seen a guy in a kilt before?"

"Looks like a skirt to me."

Pain reverberated through Beck's jaw as Trouble's fist retracted. The wolf smirked and walked off.

Kelyn chuckled.

Not like he hadn't expected the pain, eh?

Chapter 26

Beck pumped lightly on the brakes as his truck slid toward the stop sign on an icy road. It had rained overnight, freezing the world to a gleaming sheen. He didn't have chains on his tires, but the automatic brake system was reliable. He slid to a stop, then slowly rolled through the intersection toward Daisy's street.

He'd been thinking a lot since leaving his mother's house. Should he sacrifice his werewolf to stop the ghost wolf from killing? It was an extreme sacrifice. But killing someone would be an unthinkable crime.

And to give up his firstborn? No doing. Especially if that child was also Daisy's.

Could the faery really have such knowledge? If she did, then Daisy also had a big decision to make. And Beck thought they could better decide together.

Parking before the three-story brick warehouse, he grabbed his coat, ran up the inner stairs and knocked on Daisy's door.

"Shoot," he muttered. "Should have brought flowers."

The door opened and Daisy jumped into his arms, wrapping her legs about his waist and kissing him hard. Dropping his coat on the floor, Beck walked inside with the faery wolf clinging to him.

She smelled like motor oil again, which meant she must have been working on her sculpture. And beneath the industrial top notes, he sniffed out her softness in a hint of chocolate on her skin and a dash of sweetness in her hair.

Beck kissed from her mouth to her nose, and to her ear, which made her squirm in his arms.

"You always smell like candy."

"You like sweets."

"That I do. Are you working?" he asked.

"Thinking." She nodded toward the work space. "Firing up the welding torch always helps me think."

"I bet I can guess your thoughts."

She dropped down from his hold and kissed his chin. "You probably can."

"I thought I'd come over and we'd think together."

"That's awesome. I can use the extra brain. All right if I shower off the smell of work?"

"Only if I can join you."

After Beck toed off his boots, she led him into the bathroom where they stripped and headed under the steaming shower.

Slicking his hands over her skin, he mapped his desire across her breasts, down her belly and between her legs. She cooed and nudged up on her tiptoes to give him access. He liked the sounds she made when he pleasured her. Coos, moans and outrights gasps that insisted he either go faster or slower, or just that speed. Her pink hair slicked against his chest. She clung to his biceps and rocked her hips while he stroked her to climax.

As her body shuddered against his, he realized he wanted to hold her forever, feeling her pleasure, knowing her joy. And it didn't matter if he was a wolf or human. Her pleasure would always be the same. As would his.

Wouldn't it?

If he were not wolf, he could never bond with Daisy. Perhaps they could bond as werewolves and then he could sacrifice his wolf? What results would come of joining together in the deepest, most meaningful way possible for their breed, and then to walk away from the very nature with which he'd been born?

A hand about his cock twisted firmly. Beck gasped. She jacked him off, and he tilted up her face to kiss her wet lips. The shower spattered their faces, his shoulders, her hand sliding up and down his erection. She went faster, firmer, luring him to an edge he only wanted to jump off if she led him.

He gripped her hand, not stopping her, only following her lead. And he erupted, crying out a throaty surrender that felt so easy, too easy.

Far easier than surrendering his very being.

Still wet from the shower, Daisy's hair dripped onto Beck's shoulders. He sat on the bed against the pillows. She had straddled him and was rocking her hips, taking him deep inside her, in and out, back and forth. He'd slipped away to heaven, or that place called Above. It was all he could do to grip her derriere and guide her, but she didn't need the help. She knew what she was doing.

"I'm choosing wolf," she said. "No question about it."

Beck's eyes flashed open. "What? Oh, Daisy…"

"If I choose wolf, then we can be together as wolves. Assuming you don't sacrifice your wolf to get rid of the ghost wolf."

"I was thinking of doing just…that."

She stopped moving, his cock embedded within her. Pressing her hands aside his cheeks, Daisy studied her lover's arctic eyes. "But if you're no longer wolf…"

"I could still like you. Would you still like me?" He nudged her upward with a thrust of his hips.

Daisy rocked slowly now, aware he was close to climax and wanting to get him there, but this conversation was making her think. Too much. "I would. I…"

What would her father think of her loving a mere

human? And why did she have to think about her family at a time like this?

Increasing her motions, Daisy squeezed her inner muscles about Beck's erection.

"If you were faery," he said, his eyes closed as he rode the pleasure, "a match with a human wouldn't be so odd, would it?"

She shook her head. Faeries in the mortal realm tended to hook up with humans simply because their kind were few and far between, and the appeal of something different, the mortal, was there.

"I don't care what you are," she said. "I just want you, Beck."

Did she? Was she being honest with herself? Why this heavy conversation right now?

Right. Because they'd both intended to discuss this. And it needed to be discussed. Just…

She stopped moving again and bowed her head to Beck's. He hummed deep in his throat and cupped her breasts. "This is good," he said. "Like this. I don't need to come. Just being inside you is right. I could live here, surrounded by you, your beauty and warmth. Your pinkness."

She giggled and kissed his neck. "You're too good to me."

"I want you to feel my love. My like. My want and need for you. It's only growing stronger. I like your independence. I like that you're not afraid to be yourself. You are proudly weird."

"I'll take that. Let's bond," she said suddenly, without thinking through the implications. "Tomorrow night. Let's go out by your place and do it."

"Daisy, you know that means we intend to mate forever?"

She nodded. "Do you want me?"

"Hell yes. But…"

"Don't say anything about family or if it's right or who we'll annoy if we do it. Let's just do this for us. And then whatever comes afterward we'll handle together. Bonded."

"I love you."

She kissed him. And it was a forever kind of kiss that wrapped about his heart and squeezed just firmly enough so that he knew the world and his future would be right. With Daisy Blu.

Beck wandered out of the grocery store, a ten-pack of paper towels hoisted over a shoulder and a heavy tub of kitty litter in the other hand. He set both in his pickup truck box.

He glanced to the man fishing about in his open car trunk, parked next to him and nodded. The guy sported a Vandyke beard to match his brown hair, which was pulled back with a leather tie. A leather coat hung on his thin frame, not a modern style but more fitted. It looked old. But not retro old, more like antiquated. Like something from a different century. Must be one of those role-playing sorts.

When the man's eyes met Beck's, something inside Beck thudded. He clenched his fingers into fists. He recognized him, but…how?

Inside, his muscles stretched along his bones. His heartbeats thundered. And his wolf growled.

And then he guessed. He had not seen the hunter in the restaurant parking lot when Daisy and her brother had called him to track him down. The only moment he'd been close enough to mark the hunter's face was when he'd been wolfed out in the snowy field and had pushed the snowmobile down the ravine.

"It's him," he muttered under his breath.

Stretching his neck and fighting against the wolf that demanded release, Beck stepped around the back of his truck and toward the hunter. "Going out hunting?" he asked, because the man wore a bowie knife strapped at his thigh, above knee-high boots that also looked like something from time past. The knife reeked of animal blood.

Standing but four feet from the man, Beck winced. He forced his hands into his front jeans pockets and yet clenched his fists. Beyond the animal blood he scented the human. He was human, not some unknown breed. But Beck cautioned himself: werewolf hunters often were human.

"Later," the man replied gruffly. He briefly glanced at Beck. His attention was on sorting the contents in his trunk to fit in the bags of groceries. "You a hunter?"

"Not wolves."

The man jutted up his head and arrowed his gaze on Beck, his eyes dark and hollow. "What makes you think I hunt wolves?"

While he spoke English, he possessed a strange accent. Sounded like one of those pompous guys Beck had seen in costume dramas on TV.

"I, uh…was just talking about myself, man," he said. "Everyone in town is a hunter. You hunt deer?"

"Everything," the man said quickly. "Including wolves. I have one more kill, and then I'm finished with this town."

"What's wrong with Burnham?"

"It's not my home," the man said bluntly. Satisfied with how he'd arranged the contents, he closed the trunk.

"So a wolf will be your final kill?" Beck asked.

The man nodded. "Indeed."

"Wolves won't go near humans unless provoked. There's no reason to kill them beyond sport."

"There are many reasons."

"Why don't you enlighten me?"

The man drew his gaze up and down Beck. His hand glanced near the bowie knife, but he didn't touch the weapon.

"You one of those pro-wolf groupies I've heard about on the fancy television? Your DNR says I have a right to hunt wolves, so I hunt wolves. End of story. Why the long face? You have a pet wolf? Did I kill your pet?"

Beck lunged for the man's throat, gripping his neck. "You killed my—"

A sudden shooting pain in his shin stopped his angry tirade. Beck released the hunter, who had just kicked him with his steel-toed boot. In those few seconds of pain, his wolf battled for reign, yet his *were*self managed to grasp sanity.

Watch what you say.

"Get the hell away from me, you insolent," the hunter hissed. "You shall be glad when I finally kill that monster ghost wolf that's been stalking innocents. And then I can finally save her."

"Save who?"

"Not your concern. You got a bone to pick with me?" the hunter asked, his eyes carving into Beck's soul faster than the knife at his thigh could manage.

Beck shook his head. It wasn't going down like this. Not in a public place where anyone could witness his rage play out. Where he risked releasing the wolf and giving this hunter the challenge he craved.

Forcing himself to take a step backward, Beck shook his head. "No bones," he said. He got in the truck, fired up the engine and backed out of the parking space.

The hunter stood at the side of his car, watching as Beck drove away. Eyes keen and all-seeing. He'd seen something in Beck. But he couldn't have seen the truth.

Maybe.

If the man knew werewolves existed, there was no telling what skills he possessed to detect and hunt them. And yet something about the man disturbed Beck. Who was he trying to save? And how could killing a werewolf serve him that save?

"I have to take care of this," he said to himself. "Before he kills again. And someone I know."

* * *

"That's a lot of kitty litter for a guy who I know doesn't own a cat."

Beck unlocked the front door to his house. Daisy had arrived two minutes earlier and had decided a wait would be worth it. It was. They strode in and kicked off their boots, and Beck set the big yellow litter tub in the coat closet.

"Maybe I have a pet?" he said with a devious glint in his eyes.

"Right. A wolf with a pet cat. I don't believe it. Unless you have a girlfriend I don't know about."

"A familiar?" Beck pulled her in for a kiss that erased any thoughts she might have regarding Beck and a cat-shifting girlfriend. "Sunday and Dean made it work."

"Yeah, well..." She made a show of sniffing near his neck. "If I smell cat on you, I'm going to get jealous."

"Deal."

"I have nightmares about cats. Just so you know."

"Why?"

"Blade has owned a pitiful hairless cat for ages. Got him when I was a teen. You don't know terror until you've woken in the night with a naked creature that looks like a rat staring at you from your chest."

"Is that so? I vow to protect you from bald cats."

"And mushrooms, don't forget that."

"Right. Anything else I should add to my security detail?"

"The color chartreuse puts fear in me, too," she said seriously.

"Noted." Beck gestured to the closet. "The litter is for getting unstuck in the snow. Did I know you were stopping by?"

"No. Just thought..."

The feeling that she wasn't welcome suddenly washed over her. He did have his crazy don't-touch-me-or-I'll-wolf-out moments, but she didn't sense any tension in him. And they had discussed getting together tonight. To bond. He must have forgotten that conversation.

Yikes. She wouldn't bring it up unless he did. She didn't want to jump the gun. "If you have plans...?"

"I don't have plans. And even if I did, I'd cancel them if that means I get to spend time with you. You eat?"

"I had some leftover pizza that Trouble dropped off." She hoisted up the thermos she'd brought along. "I did bring hot chocolate."

Beck swept her into his arms and carried her into the living room. "I knew there was a reason for liking you. You've fed me your love brew, and now I'm completely and utterly head over heels."

He sat on the couch with her on his lap, and Daisy poured some steaming hot chocolate into the thermos cup for him.

"That is so good," he said after a sip. "I'm yours. Completely. Do as you wish with me." He spread out his arms across the back of the couch, opening himself to her. "Wait." He sat up abruptly, took the cup from Daisy and set it on the wood coffee table. "We were going to do something special tonight."

"I thought you might have forgotten."

"I've had so much on my mind lately, Daisy. I'm sorry. I spoke to the hunter earlier when I saw him in the parking lot outside the Piggly Wiggly."

Dread curdled in her gut. "What did you do?"

"We talked. No violence. Promise. Though my wolf wanted to kill the bastard."

"Did he know what you were?"

"I don't think so. He was...weird. He's going after the ghost wolf. Said it was his final kill before he could save some chick. I don't know what the hell that meant."

She placed her hands about the fist he'd formed and

kissed his knuckles. "Tonight all I want you to think about is me."

"Easy enough."

"Will it be? If you shift to werewolf, won't the ghost wolf come out?"

"Uh...hell."

She hadn't considered that could be a problem, but it seemed Beck's werewolf was only able to shift to the ghostly-white form that had been scaring hunters huntless.

Beck blew out a breath and sat back. She slid a hand up under his sweater, seeking the heat from his skin. He placed his hand over hers.

"I want to take the risk," she said. "With your ghost wolf."

"Daisy, I... No. It could be dangerous."

"You won't hurt me. You've already seen me while in your ghost wolf shape, and you walked away. And I'll be wolfed out, so it's all good."

"I don't know. I'm not the same werewolf I usually am. I don't trust myself."

"You said we could bond. I want that more than anything, Beck. To be yours. Bonded with you."

"I want that, too, but maybe we should wait until I can be rid of the ghost wolf."

Daisy nestled her head against his collarbone and closed her eyes. "Love should be daring," she said. "It should feel like we're racing through the forest over the snow and into the stars."

"It already feels like that."

She didn't want to push him. And then she did. Daisy wanted to challenge Beck to win her, to choose only her, to make her his.

He kissed her suddenly. It was an invitation into his heart, one she had answered many a time, yet this time it was tentative, a little unsure. She shifted her hips and straddled his legs without breaking the kiss. Beneath her hands his hard pecs pulsed with his movement. She hugged his hips with her knees. Pressed her breasts against his chest. Melded into him. Became him as their breaths entwined and their heartbeats raced alongside one another.

"If you want me…" She rose and stepped back from Beck, pulling off her sweater to reveal bare skin. She glanced to the patio door. "Then you'll have to come after me."

Dashing to the door, she opened it and skipped out into the chill air. Beck called after her, but she laughed and shimmied down her jeans. She would issue the challenge. She had to. Time was running out for them.

Chapter 27

His beautiful lover with the pink hair and pale skin scampered across the snow. Before reaching the pond, she shifted to wolf shape. She wouldn't stop there. She would shift to werewolf.

And his werewolf would go after her because instinct could not be ignored.

Standing in the open patio doorway, Beck pressed his palms to either side of the door frame. Inhaling the crisp winter air tinged with his lover's feral aroma, he felt the rise of his wild within him. And he let out a howl that was matched by Daisy's wolf.

"Don't hurt her," he said tightly as his body began the shift.

And the ghost wolf tracked across the iced pond, following the scent of the female. It held that scent in its nose, on its skin and fur and in its very being. She belonged to him. She was his mate.

Racing through the trees, the ghost wolf found the female werewolf, who stood bold and proud beneath the moon's glamorous shine. She howled.

The ghost wolf matched her longing cry.

Beck stared up at the ceiling. Morning beamed golden upon the log walls and felt more promising than it had for months. Daisy's scent filled his pores. The scent was tainted with a touch of dirt that he'd noticed on the sheets last night (probably from their wet paws) and pine from the forest (needles they'd tracked in on bare feet).

Closing his eyes, he smiled. Last night beneath the waning moon he had bonded with the woman he loved—and liked even more—and wanted to always have in his life.

Beck had sensed the moment his fears had been overwhelmed by desire. For his werewolf had gone after Daisy. The urge to mate had been fore, and while he only recalled bits now, he knew he had not hurt her. In fact, their werewolves had come together in a vigorous yet loving coupling. The ultimate bond. Howls had seasoned the night air, freezing above their heads and showering them with a sprinkle of faery dust.

Her faery had not come out, much to Daisy's relief, yet Beck had found faery dust on his skin and in his hair after shifting back to *were* shape.

He felt Daisy on his skin still, her warm body moving against his, her sighs entering his pores, her moans of pleasure harmonizing with his. They had given themselves to one another last night, and he wanted no other woman. Daisy Blu was his. He was hers.

If he had to battle each of the Saint-Pierre wolves—including the iron-fisted faery—he would fight and scrape until he was bloody and they understood how much Daisy meant to him.

Turning onto his side, Beck spread his hand across the sheet…but it was cool.

He opened his eyes to find Daisy's side empty. Thinking she might have started breakfast, or even thought to warm up the hot chocolate they hadn't finished last night, he padded naked from the bedroom out to the kitchen. Cold stove. He looked out the window. Her car was still here. Where had she gone?

He glanced out the back window. An eerie fog hung

over the frozen pond. Had she gone for a walk? An early morning run?

If she had waited for him, he would have gladly gone along with her. Daisy did like her alone time. He understood that. It was an introvert thing. But it wasn't practical with hunters roaming the forest. Especially the dead-eyed Denton Marx.

Beck stepped out the back door and immediately picked up Daisy's scent. None of her clothing was lying about. She had probably padded out of the bedroom naked, as he had. Then he noticed something that made his heart drop to his stomach.

Wolf prints tracked across the snow-frosted ground.

Breath fogging in the chill air, he shivered. It wasn't from the cold that brisked over his skin, but rather the feeling of foreboding that tightened his veins and twisted.

Running across the surface of the pond, the loose snow did not promise sure steps from his human-shaped feet. He shifted midstride, and when his foot left the ground, it landed again as a wolf's paw. His senses increased in this shape, though his thoughts quickly ceased to grasp his *were* thoughts, so Beck kept only one thing in mind: Daisy.

The wolf landed on the snow-banked shore. It tracked for a long distance before the awful whining noise of another wolf pricked his ears and he smelled her frightened scent.

The wolf nearly flew over the snowy surface, sensing that this was another whom it must be near. A female he knew well. He had bonded with her; she was a part of him.

Dodging a thicket of wild grass, the wolf slowed as it picked up more scents. Smells of machinery oil and…menace.

Human.

The wolf slowed to a walking pace as it approached the scene. One of the female's back legs was caught in a trap.

The wolf did not smell blood. She whined and struggled against the mortal means of harm.

He growled, showing his teeth as he caught sight of the human, who wore clothing in light colors that blended him into the pale landscape. He smelled of tobacco and oil. The human scent was familiar; he had encountered this one before. Yet now, the human did not approach the female, nor did he hold a weapon trained on her. Instead, he stood by, deadened eyes searching the area, as if in wait.

A trap, the wolf instinctually thought. One he must not go into on four legs.

Chapter 28

The ghost wolf came upon him quickly, shaking his body and stirring and stretching its bones. When fully formed, he howled and leaped for the hunter, who now held a weapon aimed toward him. He felt the touch of an arrow move through his fur, but it did not cut flesh.

Springing from his hind legs, he landed on top of the hunter's body. The weapon slid across the snow. The ghost wolf noted that the female struggling nearby had shifted. Another human caught in a trap? Wolf, maybe? He couldn't be sure. He only knew this human beneath his claws had taken something from him, and he would retaliate by drawing its blood until it ceased to live.

Clamping its maw onto the human's chest only gnawed the thick fabric that was not skin or bone. The werewolf shook the human, ignoring its shouts of fear. The acrid smell of urine spilled across the ground.

"No!"

Startled by the firm female voice, the ghost wolf released the human, but slammed a forepaw against its neck to hold it firmly beneath him. The wolf looked over at the human female, who struggled with the metal contraption and was finally able to pull free and roll away. She could not stand on the wounded leg, and flopped on the snowy ground.

"Beck, no!" she cried.

The wolf understood one of the words. It was related to him. He growled in warning at the female as she crawled toward him, dragging one leg. Only long, bright fur hanging down from her head, the rest of her was bare.

"Beck, this will not change things. Don't kill him!"

The human pinned beneath him kicked up a knee and managed to twist its body and attempt to crawl away. The werewolf stomped on its spine, stopping it as if an insect.

"Call it off me!"

"He's out of his mind in this shape," the female said. "Stop struggling!"

"And let it kill me?"

Beck's howl echoed through the forest and stirred up the crows perched high in the birch canopy. Wings flapped, and a dark wave swooshed low near where he stood.

Daisy dragged herself across the cold ground. Shivering from the pain tormenting her shin—her leg was broken—she bit down hard on her lip to redirect that pain. Her fingers clawed into the snow, and she reached out for the hunter's head. He was weeping now, facedown on the snow. He cried out a name: Sencha. Beck's monstrous ghost wolf crouched on top of him. The werewolf gripped the human about the neck and squeezed.

She couldn't allow him to make the kill. She knew it was not Beck inside the wolf that was calling the shots right now, but that the ghost wolf was fueled by the rage over losing his father. They were connected. Because she and his ghost wolf were now bonded. If it murdered, she would feel the pain of that crime ever after.

"Please." She slapped her hand over the werewolf's paw that squeezed tightly about the hunter's neck. "Listen to me. Look at me, Beck. It's me, Daisy Blu."

The wolf's grip loosened as its red eyes peered at her. Up close he was all white, yet oddly transparent. As luminous as the moon. Faery magic at its worst.

"I love you," she managed through tears.

The scent of blood pierced the air. The hunter's blood.

Daisy gripped the wolf's paw with both hands and tore it away from the hunter's neck. "You love me! For your father's sake, let it go. Just stop!"

The werewolf reared to stand. Daisy saw the claws swoop down before she could shuffle out of the way. Razor-sharp claws cut through the snowy ground, and the meaty paw slapped the hunter's body to the side as if a mere doll. The man's body collided with an oak trunk.

Beck landed on all fours above her. Daisy rolled to her back, instinctively putting up her hands to block an attack—

And then she breathed out, and put her hands down at her sides, making herself lax beneath him. Just last night this gorgeous, bold werewolf had bonded with her were-wolf. She loved him, and she knew he loved her.

She just had to connect with that part of the animal's brain that was still Beck.

"I like you," she whispered. She winced. The broken bones were healing, but slowly.

The ghost wolf sniffed at her face, down her neck and over her breasts. And then it whined that particular noise a wolf made when it was showing submission to another. Ears back, and head bowed, it crawled backward off her.

Straightening, it walked onto its hind legs over to the hunter's weapon. Gripping it, the beast broke the crossbow, and then the arrows, and tossed them aside. The hunter's snowmobile was parked close. The wolf lifted it, and tossed it toward the trees, where it landed in a crooked tangle of branches five feet off the ground.

And then the ghost wolf surrendered to Beck's will. It was the only thing that could truly push back the beast—Beck's determination.

Her lover shifted to *were* form, standing over the human's body. The hunter was not dead, but passed out from fear, and she suspected he'd taken a claw to the throat, but the blood was minimal.

Standing there, naked and stretching out his arms to fend off the final twinges of the shift, Beck yelled out in frustration. Probably anger, as well. And surely grief. He fell to his knees in the snow and yelled again, punching the air.

Tears froze on Daisy's cheeks. She bent to feel at her shin. It was nearly healed, but she couldn't walk on it. She wanted to run to Beck, to embrace him. To make his world a better place.

But the world was what it was. And bad things happened to good people. And good people tried to keep back the bad that wanted revenge. And today Beck had managed that.

"Beck?"

He twisted a look toward her, as if he'd forgotten she was there.

"It's going to be okay," she offered.

Stepping over to her, he bent and bracketed her face in his hands and kissed her deeply. "Sorry," he whispered. "So sorry."

"I was the one who went out on my own." She pressed a finger to his mouth before he could apologize again. His body shook with contained rage. "You wouldn't allow the ghost wolf to murder. You're a good man, Beck. And that is what makes your father most proud."

"Need to make it stop."

"The ghost wolf?"

"The...the pain." He pulled her against his bare skin, and they made body heat. "When will it stop?"

"When the time is right" was all she could say. Because she didn't know. "I'll be at your side all of that time. I promise."

He glanced to the hunter's prone body.

"He'll survive," Daisy offered. "It's just a scratch. Let's go home."

He lifted her into his arms, and walked them through the forest and to his house.

They would be all right.

As soon as the ghost wolf was vanquished.

Chapter 29

Beck raced toward his home, fighting the painful stretches at the back of his legs with every step. It felt as if he were midshift and trying to move on bones that hadn't completely solidified, wrapped by muscles that were too loose. By the time he reached the pond, he was thankful that Daisy hopped from his arms and limped toward the back of his house, his hand clasped in hers.

She dashed inside to the shower.

Now Beck could finally curl in on himself, there in the open doorway of his living room while snowflakes drifted across his shoulders. He wrapped his arms about his bent legs and held back a yowl that he suspected Daisy would hear even through the clatter from the shower. He cursed under his breath as his spine finally found its *were* position. But even as he stood, he wobbled, and caught himself against the door.

Breaths huffed out, panting. He did not feel exhilarated, but rather as if he wanted to drop in a sprawl and close his eyes forever. The ghost wolf had robbed him of vitality. But he would not allow Daisy to see his pain.

Closing the door, he forced himself to wander into the kitchen to make some hot chocolate for her, and by the time the shower had stopped, he was able to stand tall and wander back to the bedroom to kiss Daisy and tell her to go finish the drinks while he showered. He sat on the shower floor as the hot water beat on his aching muscles.

This had to stop. He'd put Daisy in danger today.

She was right. He'd never have to repay the faery a favor as long as the ghost wolf did not accomplish its goal of killing the hunter.

Beck wasn't sure the ghost wolf would allow him that restraint.

He needed to be rid of the monster within him. And the only way to do that was to either kill the hunter or the faery.

He couldn't live with either of those choices.

After drying off and pulling on some jogging pants and socks, he wandered out to the living room.

"The hot chocolate is done," Daisy said from the couch. "I was just resting my leg."

"You stay there. I got this."

Because she had had his back out there, Daisy had stopped his monster. When he'd been the ghost wolf he had known, somehow, that she would not guide him wrong. She had gentled his beast.

But tame it? He doubted that was possible.

"Wolf tamer," he whispered as he poured hot chocolate from the saucepan into two mugs.

"What was that?" Daisy asked as he returned to the couch and settled next to her. She embraced him and pressed her cheek against his bare shoulder.

"I called you wolf tamer." He turned to kiss her. She tasted fresh and sweet, and her wet hair spattered his face when he flicked it over her shoulder.

"The only place I want to tame you is in bed." She winked and kissed his nose.

"Yeah, but I appreciate that you gentled the ghost wolf. Hell, Daisy, if you hadn't been able to do that…" He swallowed. Thinking of the consequences brought bile to the base of his throat.

He sipped the hot chocolate and handed her the mug. He would sacrifice his wolf. He had to. It was the only way to not kill.

* * *

They sat quietly, snuggled on the couch before the fire.
The silence felt good, their bodies against one another, surrounded by the sweet tease of chocolate. Daisy set the mug
aside. Leaning forward, she stroked her shin and ankle. It
was completely healed. She had survived. Yet, even though
she'd been in wolf form and could remember but smells and
feelings about the event, she sensed the hunter had wanted
to keep her alive.

To lure in Beck.

"Is it healed?" Beck asked, kissing her ankle. He stroked
it lightly with his thumb, sending good shivers up her leg.

Daisy nodded. "That feels great."

Could the hunter have known Beck was the ghost wolf?
Beck had shifted back to human form while the hunter had
been unconscious. But Beck had said he'd encountered the
hunter in town, and they had followed the hunter, Beck and
her brothers nights ago.

Was the hunter something more than human to know
about their breed and detect a werewolf while in human
form? If so, he could prove very dangerous.

Had a werewolf harmed one of the hunter's own?

They were missing something about this hunter, and
Daisy felt that whatever it was, it was the key to them solv-
ing this dilemma. As long as Beck knew he didn't have to
kill Marx…

"No," she whispered. Being the ghost wolf would kill
her lover sooner rather than later.

"What's that?" Beck whispered.

"I mean, yes," she said. "Keep doing that."

He placed another kiss to her leg. Sprawling onto his
side, he moved the kisses down onto her foot and biggest
toe, tendering them intently. If he did have a foot fetish,
she wasn't about to argue against it. Lingering in his soft,
stroking touch was beyond luxurious.

"I'm going to do it," he said, grasping her foot in his
big warm hand.

"What?"

"Sacrifice my wolf."

"No," she murmured.

"I have to, Daisy. Unless I want to commit murder."

His confession hurt her. He had surely thought it over. And it was the right thing to do. But it was such a great sacrifice. And could she love a mortal?

She slid down to lie alongside him and kissed his mouth. It was so easy to be with him. She'd once thought that she would recognize a hero when he walked into her life. This one had loped in on four legs.

"I'll support you," she said softly.

"Do you think you could still like a guy who is just a guy? Not a werewolf?"

"I know I can. You are in me now. We've bonded."

"But will the bond remain when I'm no longer wolf?" He bowed his forehead to hers and exhaled. "Is it the right thing to do? I… What will I do as a human? It's so alien to me. Hell, my mother is vampire. I'm soon to have a little brother or sister that will likely be werewolf. And then I'll be the odd one, completely mortal. Is it even possible?"

"With the sidhe, anything is possible." She nuzzled her face against his chest. Comforting. Masculine. Tortured yet a survivor. All hers. And she intended to keep him in the form he should remain. "You're not one-hundred-percent sure. You can't do this, Beck."

"What? But you said…"

"I know what I said. But I can hear the reluctance in your voice. Feel it in your heart." She pressed a palm over his chest. "Kill the faery."

"What? No. Daisy?"

"My father once destroyed the faery responsible for cursing him."

"That was different. She was evil and cursed your parents. I *asked* for the ghost wolf. I can't take another life just because it didn't work out the way I planned it to. Really, Daisy?"

"You're right. I'm sorry. That was desperation talking."

She turned on the couch and snuggled her back to Beck's chest. He wrapped an arm across her stomach, holding her against his warmth.

He stroked her hair away from her face and kissed the curve of her ear. "Wolves and humans get along well enough. So do faeries and humans. Your parents are proof of that."

Daisy closed her eyes. It didn't matter what she chose to become. She'd mourn the loss of one half and rejoice gaining full control of the other. But as for Beck, his choice could destroy his life. Unless...

"I've been thinking about the hunter."

"I wish you wouldn't. The less time you afford Marx consideration the better."

Daisy turned her head to meet his gaze. "I don't think he's completely human. He knows too much."

Propping his chin in hand, he studied her eyes. "Maybe. But what will that serve us?"

"We could get the Council involved. If he's vampire or some other breed and he's hunting werewolves—"

"The Council would punish him and...I'd still be left with this monster growling within me. It doesn't matter, Daisy. The fight is no longer between me and the hunter. I've got to stop whatever is inside me."

"But you have to stop the hunter, too. What about the gray wolves who populate the area? The entire state?"

"The wolves will continue to suffer as soon as the ghost wolf is gone. There's never going to be an easy way to make men stop hunting for sport. Even if we could get the DNR to reinstate the hunting ban, the wolves will always be in danger because kills are made and go unreported."

"Yes. But one less Marx is a bright spot for the packs, if you ask me."

"How do we learn more about him? Wait," Beck said. "I do know a local reporter."

"Who has no clue how to go about researching the man. I'll have Stryke look into it. He knows people who know things. It's worth a try, yes?"

He nodded.

"Can I stay overnight?" Daisy asked sweetly.

"I wasn't planning on letting you leave."

The next afternoon Daisy set down her welding torch just as a knock sounded on her front door. She sniffed, tilted her head. "Stryke?"

"Can I come in?"

"Yes. I'll be right there. Door's open!"

Her brother entered while she tended her equipment and slipped out of the work apron. Meanwhile, Stryke stuck his nose in her fridge, found a half pan of brownies and pulled it out. He was sitting by the counter, fork in hand, by the time she wandered over and grabbed the edge of the glass baking pan before he could spear up a hunk of treat.

"Use a plate, little brother."

"I was going to eat it all," he complained.

"Oh." With a shrug, she pushed the pan back toward him. "Fine. Those are a few days old anyway. They need to go today or get tossed."

"You have some whipped cream?"

She commandeered the Reddi-wip can from the fridge and handed it to him. "So I thought you were going to do some research for me?"

"Already have," Stryke said between bites. "Talked to Dez Merovech earlier. She's a—"

"I know, she's an ancient witch married to the vampire Ivan Drake. Beck's mom is friends with them."

"Dez is a wise witch who knows everything there is to know about spells and curses. Daisy, it freaks me out that you believe Dad's curse is still lingering in you."

"*If* I can believe what the faery said. But Stryke, it makes sense. I can't seem to get a handle on my wolf without my faery interrupting. And vice versa. So I do believe it. Some part of Dad's curse is keeping me from being fully...me."

"And what would you choose?" he asked, setting down his fork and giving her his attention. He had her father's deep brown eyes, and they were soulful, understanding.

"My wolf," she said without hesitation. "But I'd miss the faery."

"Well, if Dez knows her stuff, then maybe we can find someone to break that curse, or somehow lift the lingering remnants of it from you. Then you wouldn't have to choose."

"That would be amazing. And what about Beck's ghost wolf spell?"

Stryke pushed the brownie pan aside and placed his hands on the counter before him, palms down. "Dez told me there's a sort of witchlike person who isn't really a witch, mostly human, that is called a peller."

"A peller?"

"A peller is a breaker of spells and curses. They are rare. Some humans go through life without ever realizing their gift, or so Dez explained to me. They might even end up going down the wrong path, thinking they are psychic or like a ghost chaser or something like that."

"So if we find a peller, this person could break my curse? And lift Beck's spell?"

"Dez said it was possible. And she knew of a peller living close to Tangle Lake, probably Burnham. I guess he looked her up for help finding ingredients for a spell."

"What?" Daisy clasped her brother's hands, but his expression didn't lift to a hopeful grin as hers did. "Stryke, this is amazing. Who is it? When can we go to this person?"

"Daisy." He lifted her hand to his mouth and pressed her knuckles to his lips. "The peller is Denton Marx."

Chapter 30

Denton limped across the snow before the old shed that he had built so many decades earlier. Or had it been over a century earlier? He hadn't broken any bones, but when he'd landed against the tree after being tossed by the werewolf, his body had been bruised and battered. Though he could manage remarkable feats by any human's assessment, self-healing was not one of them.

He paused and reached out for the figment that stood so near, yet so far away. Her long dark hair fell over half her face. She was crying. For the love of all that was sacred, she was crying and he could but stand there and witness that silent pain.

"Soon, Sencha. I am close. I was right about the man and his girlfriend. They are both werewolves. I was able to use her to lure out the monstrous beast that he is. The people in the nearby town call it the ghost wolf. He will provide the powerful last step to the allbeast spell that I can then exchange for your release from the Edge."

He reached for her hair, but his fingers moved through the beautiful brown tresses as if she were a ghost herself. She did not acknowledge the touch. She could not. She was trapped in another dimension. One that she had feared someday falling into during her frequent trips through time.

"Soon we will be reunited," he whispered, tears falling down his cheeks. "And then we will go home. To the time where I was born to live. And the time where you are safe."

* * *

Beck arrived at Daisy's place just as Stryke was finishing off the pan of brownies.

"Lone wolf," Stryke acknowledged Beck after he'd kissed Daisy silly in greeting. "We were talking about you."

"Stryke knows someone who can break spells and curses."

Disappointed the pan was empty, Beck leaned against the fridge and asked, "And who is that?"

"The hunter who is after you," Stryke said. "He's a peller. Breaker of spells and curses."

"How the hell do you know that?"

"I talked to Dez Merovech."

The witch friend of his mother's. Beck knew Dez was all-powerful and revered within the witch community. She'd lived for something like a thousand years. If anyone knew something about Denton Marx, it would be her.

"So our only hope is a guy who wants us dead?"

"Life's a bitch, man." Stryke stood and kissed his sister's cheek. "I gotta go catch up with Trouble. You two want me to send him this way? You're going to need the full force for this one."

"The full force?" Beck asked.

"It's showdown time. You gotta make this peller guy work for you without getting killed in the process. Do you have any idea how to do that alone?"

"I just found out about this. Give me a minute to process, will you?"

"Yeah? While you're processing, I'm sending in the troops. Do not go near the hunter," Stryke said to Daisy, waggling an admonishing finger. "Even if Beck decides to go talk to him, you stay away. You understand?"

"Stryke, I'll be fine."

Stryke turned to eye Beck. "You know she'll try to jump into the fray. She's stubborn like that."

"She's not going to get hurt anymore." Beck pulled Daisy to his side and wrapped an arm across her shoulder. "You're right. This is showdown time. It's got to end today. I can't let the ghost wolf terrorize humans any longer."

"Give me an hour," Stryke said as he wandered to the front door. "I'll gather the troops and we'll meet?"

"I'll be waiting," Beck called.

As the door closed, he turned to pull Daisy into his embrace, but she shoved him away.

"I'm not some helpless pup you have to protect," she said. "I freed myself from that trap last night. And I stopped the ghost wolf from harming the hunter. You need me, Beck."

"I do need you. I need you alive."

"And I need you alive, Beck."

He pulled her to him, and this time she didn't resist, crushing her body against his and tilting her head to his chest.

"I'll have your brothers with me," he said. "I promise you I won't go into this alone. But you have to trust that I can handle this. Please, Daisy?"

She nodded against his chest. "I love you."

"Yeah? Well, I like you."

She chuffed out a weak laugh. "I like you more."

He kissed the crown of her head. He'd never tire of her candy scent. "I'll call you as soon as we've found Marx and talked to him. Promise."

"Fine. I'll...do something to keep myself busy."

"You could work on the sculpture. What about your article? How's that coming along?"

"It's almost finished. I'm going with a fictional slant. Ghost Wolf Really a Man Dressed In a Wolf Costume. I figure I can doctor up a blurry shot of it and maybe add a zipper?"

"Hmm, I like it."

"Yeah, but I can't focus on that right now. I was thinking about baking. It's more relaxing. I need to relax. Not think about you approaching a killer who wants to claim your head as his next trophy."

"Don't say that. It's all going to be great. I promise. Now, where was your brother headed?"

"To Trouble's place. I'll give you his phone number, then you won't have to venture into Trouble's lair."

"That bad, eh?"

"I don't think the guy knows the meaning of clean. It's safer if you don't tread his territory."

"Hey, me and Trouble are tight. Lately, he doesn't punch me quite as hard as he's capable."

She laughed. "Are you sure you want to claim me as yours? Because you know with me, you also get the whole pack. All four arrogant, rough and tough brothers. And the father."

"The Saint-Pierre pack will definitely keep me on my toes. If not humble. I'm in for the ride, Daisy Blu. You okay with that?"

"More than okay."

Half an hour after Beck had left, Daisy was up to her knuckles in flour, eggs and—no cocoa. She had only a tablespoon left and needed much more. So she bundled up in coat, cap, mittens and winter boots, and decided to walk the four blocks to the closest grocery store, which served an ongoing cavalcade of hunters during the winter season.

With a shudder, she strolled by a sign advertising deer cleaning and homemade sausage casings. Sure, she ate meat. It was her nature. But she never began a meal without blessing the source and thanking the universe for the gift.

Once in the baking aisle, she dropped a few extras in her basket. Vanilla, powdered sugar and those snowflake sprinkles looked interesting. Might be cute scattered on top of frosted cupcakes.

At the end of the aisle her senses, overwhelmed by sugary sweetness and spices, suddenly homed onto a familiar human scent. Woodsy and slightly old, like a smoky log cabin. She followed the scent past the cereal aisle and toward the natural foods section. Turning down that aisle, she sighted a tall man with hair tugged behind his head. He wore an odd leather coat and knee-high boots.

Daisy slipped around the end of the aisle, pressing her back against the canned tomatoes display. "It's him."

The hunter who was also the one man who could help her and Beck. And Beck and her brothers had gone off to find him?

She had left her cell phone at home. No way to alert Beck. Maybe she could talk to Marx? Beck had been adamant she not put herself in danger. But what harm could befall her in a supermarket? If anything, the hunter should beware her bite.

Decided, she swung around the corner. Marx stood before the spices, studying the label of a small glass jar. She strolled up to him, turned toward the spices and made a show of looking over the display from cumin to pepper to turmeric.

"I want to make you an offer," she said.

"You are quite the daring wolf," he said under his breath. "I would have thought you'd keep your distance after the other night. Looks like you've healed well enough. I am pleased for that."

Aghast that he'd express such false condolences, Daisy almost swore out loud, but she suppressed her anger. "You were using me to lure in the ghost wolf."

"To much success."

"Your definition of success is lacking. We both got away."

"Yes, but now I know where to find my prey."

He made to turn away, but Daisy gripped his wrist.

Twisting gently within her grasp, the man turned his gaze on her. His eyes were bloodshot. And black, almost demonically black. But he wasn't demon. Dez had said he was merely human.

"Why are you hunting werewolves?"

"Just the one wolf is all I need," he said. "Let go, little girl."

"Why? You afraid of me?"

He relaxed within her grip, his grin curling as he shook his head.

Daisy released him, and he remained before her. She had to look up to meet his eyes, but was not daunted by his height. "If you only need one wolf—and I don't know what for—then take mine."

"Ah? Sacrificing herself for the lover?"

"I'm a half-breed. I'm cursed. I have to give up one or the other. I'll give you my wolf, then I'll become completely faery."

He tilted his head at her. "Intriguing. Faeries can be useful—but...no. I have my sights on bigger quarry. And what I need might only be obtained from a dead werewolf."

She gripped his wrist again, but this time he tugged away from her. "We can make this work," she pleaded. "I know we can. Then no one has to get hurt."

"It's too late for that," he said. He glanced around them, ensuring no one overheard their conversation. "I am concocting an allbeast spell. You won't understand, so I needn't explain my reasons for such a thing. Suffice it to say, I do this to save someone important to me. Now, I apologize in advance for any pain I will bring upon you for taking your lover's life, but it must be done to save my lover."

He swung around and marched off, leaving Daisy shaking in the middle of the aisle.

"The allbeast?" she wondered aloud. "I have to find Beck and stop him. Whatever Marx has planned, this can't be good."

* * *

Bella left Dez and Ivan's house and bundled into her SUV. Ivan had walked her out to the car, even though the sidewalk was shoveled and not icy. She'd spent a great afternoon with the couple, testing Dez's attempts at cheesecake (still not there yet) and listening to Ivan's plans for their new home in Venice. The couple loved Italy, and already owned a few houses around the world. Why not another?

It had all been going well until Bella had asked Dez, in the privacy of the kitchen after Ivan had excused himself to make a few business calls, what she could do to help Beckett.

Dez had explained to Bella what a peller was, a breaker of spells, and had mentioned that a Saint-Pierre had been asking the same thing of her. Was Beck in trouble?

Nothing her son and the Saint-Pierres couldn't handle, Bella had reassured her. And yet, Dez had gotten a worried look. She'd said there was a hunter in town who was also a peller. His name was Denton Marx, and she sensed things about him, but couldn't be sure what those things were.

"He's in the wrong place," Dez had said. "But I don't know what that means."

She had warned Bella to be careful and to not interfere with whatever her son was up to.

"Take care of the baby," Dez had said as Bella had walked down the sidewalk on Ivan's arm.

Now, as she sat behind the wheel, thankful for the seat warmers that heated her butt and back, she ran her gloved fingers along the steering wheel. "I wonder if Beck knows the hunter is someone who can help him break the spell?"

She tugged her cell phone out of her pocket. Shook her head. "I'll stop by. A mother doesn't need an excuse to visit her son."

Time to go straight to the source. Denton had lost all patience. And he couldn't bear to consider the Severo man's lover had offered her wolf in exchange for his life. Severo probably wasn't aware of such an offer.

A real man stood up for himself and for his woman.

Unfortunately for the woman, she would soon be grieving her lover's death.

Couldn't be helped. Denton had worked too long collecting ingredients for this spell to let emotions tumble it now. Just one last element to the spell, and he could summon Sencha back into his arms.

When the allbeast was created it sought the Edge, its natural habitat, and the only way for it to travel into such a place was to replace another, who would then exchange places with the allbeast. Sencha. And once and for all, they could leave this horrible time for good.

He pulled the car down the gravel road to his cabin. One last look at Sencha, then he'd go after Beck. On the passenger seat sat a pistol, loaded with the specialized bullets that contained the nano-silver pellets. He'd gotten them more than a hundred years from now. As well, in the backseat, the crossbow with the same nano-silver-tipped arrows waited. He'd learned that he had to take the werewolf down while in werewolf form. The simple four-legged wolf form wouldn't do. He'd made that mistake once. Though at the time, when he'd shot the wolf in practice, he'd only thought it a natural gray wolf.

He noted the headlights arriving before the Marx homestead. The truck belonged to the Severo werewolf. Denton's heart raced as he shoved the pistol at the back of his pants and grabbed the crossbow. He had not invited anyone here. And yet, he shouldn't expect anything less than a showdown to the final breaths.

Breaths he would steal from the werewolf.

Aiming the crossbow, he vacillated between pulling the trigger and not. He didn't want to kill the man in *were* form. He needed to shift to that monstrous ghost wolf. But an arrow skimming his skin could be just the thing to anger him sufficiently.

Chapter 31

Beck sensed the hunter's decision to pull the crossbow trigger a nanosecond before it happened. He dodged, feeling the arrow skim the hair on his head. Racing for Marx, he slammed his hands against the man's shoulders, pushing him down onto the snow-packed driveway. The crossbow skittered across the slick surface.

A vehicle pulled up the long driveway, and Trouble's howl could be heard from inside the closed truck.

"If the Saint-Pierre boys get hold of you," Beck snarled at the man, "it's all over. What the hell do you want from me?"

"Your werewolf," Denton said. "I need a werewolf's essence to save her."

Beck followed the man's pointing finger. The sky was rapidly darkening, and the space between the cabin and the work shed looked over a vast field, backed by a thin line of pine trees. But he saw something move. Not an animal or bird. It was faint. Was it a woman?

"She's trapped in the Edge," the hunter explained. He kneed Beck in the ribs, but Beck maintained his hold on Marx's shoulder, pinning him to the ground. "I have a spell to release her. But I need a werewolf to complete it."

"So you want to kill me to save her?" Beck asked.

The brothers, all four of them, tumbled out from the truck. Trouble called for Beck to hold him; he was coming.

"Please," Denton pleaded. "She is my— Our souls belong together. She has been trapped for months."

"Yeah? Somehow I don't care to die today." Beck tugged the man upright.

Trouble lunged in and punched the hunter's jaw, splaying him out across the ground.

"Not this way." Beck shoved Trouble away from the unconscious hunter. "We're not going to kill him."

"I heard him say he needed you dead," Stryke said. The brothers filed beside Denton's body.

"He said something about a spell to save her." Beck thrust his hand toward the figment, which still stood off in the clearing. "Do you see her?"

"I do." Kelyn strode over the snow, his footsteps inaudible, right up to the figment of the woman. He reached through the air, aiming for her hair, but his hand went right through her. She didn't turn to acknowledge his presence. "A ghost?"

"I don't know," Beck said. "He said something about her being trapped in the Edge."

Blade hissed and took out a bowie knife, holding it in defense, not over the hunter, but as if he expected something to come out from the surrounding woods.

"I've heard about the Edge," Stryke said. "It's not a place anyone wants to visit. I'd take Daemonia over the Edge any day. What's she doing in there?"

"He said she was his lover. That their souls belonged together." Beck wandered over to where Kelyn studied the figment, but glanced over his shoulder. "Leave him alone, Trouble! Is there some way we can get her out?" he asked the faery as he joined his side. "That seems to be the hunter's goal. Said he needed a werewolf to complete the spell. She's…beautiful."

Kelyn shook his head. "From what you've told me, I suspect she's a wandersoul."

"A what?"

"A time witch. One whose soul wanders continuously

through time. They can't stop. Not unless they find another soul worthy of their love."

"Soul mates?"

"In the truest sense of the term."

"You said she is a time traveler?"

"And the hunter might have come from another time, as well."

"I thought his clothes looked odd, like he was wearing a costume from another time. But what is the Edge?"

"It's another dimension." Kelyn waved his hand through the woman's figment. "Probably landed there instead of her goal time period. One of the dangers of time travel is falling into the Edge. The only thing that'll bring her out is some sort of exchange with an occupant in this dimension, I'm sure of that."

"Like an exchange spell? And that spell requires a dead werewolf."

Kelyn turned and strode back to his brothers.

Beck remained and walked around to stand before the woman. Ghostly and pale, she looked right at him yet didn't see him. Her hair was tangled and her clothing in tatters. The long dress was corseted, and the lace at her wrists hung in tatters. She'd been through hell; he could sense it from her eyes. They looked right through him. She'd given up.

"Another dimension and time travel? This is too weird for me. But if there was a way to save you…"

He placed his palm flat before her. If there were a means to let her know that he stood there, and was interested in helping her…

Beck glanced to the Saint-Pierre men, who stepped in a circle as the hunter roused and sat up. Another set of headlights revealed Daisy's car. But he saw two people in the front.

"This is getting out of hand." He marched back to the

brothers. "Do not harm him," he warned, as he continued on toward Daisy's car.

When his mother got out of the passenger side, he swore under his breath. "What are you doing here?"

"I saw Daisy in town, and she said she was on her way to your house. But then we passed this property and I recognized your truck. Dez told me about the allbeast spell—"

"Mom? You shouldn't concern yourself with this. It's not safe for you here."

"Just because I'm pregnant doesn't make me incapable. Who are all these people?"

"Get back in the car, Mom."

Daisy popped out and strode up to Beck. She looked ready to run into his arms for a hug, so he stepped back and put his hands to his hips. Daisy stopped abruptly before him.

"We're here to support you," she said to him. "The man who killed your father lives here." She looked around his shoulder. "You must want to do the worst."

"I don't," he growled. "But your brothers just might."

"Beck," Bella said. "Dez said the man could help you."

"I know that. But trust me, I'm more valuable to him dead than alive." He turned and stalked away from both of them. It should have been him and Denton Marx tonight. Not the entire Saint-Pierre clan, and his mother.

Someone had to control this situation.

Trouble grabbed Denton, and just when his fist would have collided with his skull, Beck grabbed the wolf and yanked him to a stand.

"At least he has the courage to show me his anger," Denton mocked.

"Leave him," he ordered Trouble and the brothers, who had formed a ring around the hunter. "This is between him and me."

With a nod of his head, Trouble directed the brothers to step back. They did so, but remained alert and on guard.

"Daisy, stay back," Blade said.

"No." She walked up, Bella's hand in hers. "I want Mister Marx to take my wolf instead of Beck's."

"What?" Trouble barked.

"Daisy, you don't get a say in this," Beck warned.

"But I don't need my wolf," she insisted.

Bella nodded in agreement beside her. And Beck silently cursed his mother's newfound independence that should have waited for a safer time to show.

"The wolf is the one part of you that you identify with most," Beck argued with Daisy. "I won't let you sacrifice it."

"What's wrong with your faery half?" Kelyn asked his sister.

"I carry remnants of Father's curse," she explained to the brothers, who had been unaware of her struggles until now. "I can only be either werewolf or faery. I have to choose."

"You've always been more wolf," Trouble said. "And Beck is right. You're not sacrificing anything for this bastard."

"Do you not see her?" Denton pleaded, thrusting out an arm toward the figment. "Her name is Sencha, and she is my love, and she is trapped in the Edge. Her only hope is if I can complete the spell and send the allbeast to switch places with her."

"Not our problem, buddy. Most especially not worth murder," Trouble said.

"She looks so lost," Bella said quietly.

All the men's heads turned toward the vampiress, who cradled her swollen belly. Even the hunter regarded her. Denton gasped.

Noting his reaction, Daisy pulled Bella forward. "This is Belladonna Severo," she said to Denton. "Three months ago on a cold November night, she waited to tell her husband about the child she was carrying, but he never returned home. Instead, his son, that man you want to now kill, returned home with his father in his arms. He'd been shot by a hunter's bullet. A silver bullet."

Denton grasped Beck's gaze before then returning his attention to Bella. "Truly?"

Bella nodded and bowed her head, but then lifted it proudly. "I forgive you."

"Mother, you don't have to say that."

"I mean it," Bella reiterated. "Just because I can forgive does not mean I condone the act."

"But…" Denton's jaw dropped. "I took your husband's life?"

Bella nodded.

"I…" The hunter pressed his fingers over his gaping mouth. He shook his head and looked to Beck for confirmation.

"It was me who charged you that night you killed the wolf," Beck said. "I chased you away from my father's body."

"I hadn't known I had to kill the beast in werewolf form," Denton said quickly. "It was a wasted shot—"

Beck lunged for the hunter, landing them both on the ground as Bella screamed. The brothers formed a circle around the fallen men, shutting them off from the women.

"A wasted shot?" Beck felt his werewolf stretching at his spine. He dug his fingers into Denton's shoulders, but knew it was too late. "I won't do it!"

He shoved the hunter away from him. Beck crept away, his body shifting as he did so. "I have to get out of here. Daisy, don't let them—"

His werewolf came upon him so rapidly, his sweater tore away from his biceps and chest. Managing to step out of his boots, Beck landed on powerful hind paws with each step.

* * *

Daisy pushed Bella toward Blade, the safest place she could be right now. "Protect her."

Blade tugged the vampiress toward Daisy's car.

Daisy saw Denton pull a weapon from the back of his pants. "He's got a gun!"

Kelyn moved swiftly. The heel of his palm landed on Denton's shoulder just as the hunter lifted his arm to aim. The pistol fired skyward, the retort echoing across the snowy clearing.

Beck's werewolf howled. Claws scraped the air. The ghostly beast, eyes glowing red, stalked toward the hunter.

Trouble and Stryke grabbed Denton by the arms and wrestled him into a secure hold while Kelyn took away his weapon and slid it under one of the vehicles.

"Please!" Denton cried. "He can save her!"

"You don't need the ghost wolf," Daisy insisted. "You can take my wolf. You only need the essence, yes?"

The hunter nodded. He glanced to Bella, huddled up against Blade's chest. "Yes."

At that moment the ghost wolf's claws cut across the hunter's chest. Blood oozed through his shirt.

"No!" Daisy raced to put herself between Beck and the hunter.

"Daisy, don't be stupid," Trouble said. "Get out of the way!"

"I'm not moving. He needs to see me. To hear me. Beck!"

The ghost wolf reared and swung around its arm, its claws aimed for Daisy. At Bella's scream, the werewolf stopped abruptly. It howled, lifting its chest and stretching its spine to call out to the moon.

"Hell, he keeps that up I'm going to shift," Trouble muttered. "Then it's all over," he said with a jerk of the hunter's arm backward.

Indeed, the air vibrated with aggression and werewolf

pheromones. Daisy could feel the urge to shift, as well. Not because she wanted to hurt something, but rather because her bondmate called to her instinctual desire to mate. The situation had to be cooled. And fast.

She thrust out a hand, her palm landing the soft warm muscle strapping Beck's chest. "Feel me," she said. "Know me. Your bondmate."

Behind her, Trouble hissed. Well, he had to find out one way or another.

Teeth bared and claws at the ready, Beck's red eyes looked over her head. She knew he focused on Denton. The man who had destroyed his family. Now Marx relentlessly sought to take Beck's life. But it wasn't necessary if she could give him her werewolf. And she would. To save her lover.

Pushing both palms against his chest, Daisy sidled up next to the creature, sensing its need to pull away—and yet it did not. She would hold him until he knew her, and ever after.

Behind her, Trouble swore. Stryke told the oldest to pull it together. Her brother was shifting against his will. It was natural for a werewolf to want to shift when others around him gave off such aggressive vibes as Beck did.

She closed her eyes, curling her fingers into Beck's chest fur and whispered, "I love you. And I like you even more. I am yours. Settle, lover. Feel my hands against your skin. Concentrate on that." If only she could heal him with her vita, but it was too weak even in faery form.

The ghost wolf slashed through the air above her head, and then his paw landed against Daisy's back none too gently. She chuffed out a breath.

"He's going to hurt her," Trouble said.

"No," Stryke warned. "She knows what she's doing."

Daisy spread her arm around the ghost wolf's massive

rib cage and hugged him. The wolf let out a howl that was both mournful and triumphant.

Off by the car, Bella exhaled a sniffling sob.

"I will break your spell, wolf!" Denton shouted. "I will do it. I must. Sencha will... I'm sorry, Sencha."

Daisy glanced over her shoulder to the hunter, whose head hung miserably. Trouble shook off the wolf's ears that had already shifted on his head.

And suddenly the ghost wolf pulled her into a hug that lifted her feet from the ground. And he did not crush her; his embrace was so gentle it must take effort to be so careful in his form.

She grasped him by the neck and nuzzled her face aside his soft maw. "I love you."

She felt his body shift within her embrace. Behind her, Trouble blew out a breath and thanked the heavens he'd not shifted completely.

"Someone grab the guy a coat," Kelyn said as Beck's body shifted back to *were* shape, still clasping Daisy to his chest.

When her lover had completed the shift, he stumbled backward, landing in a snowbank and taking Daisy down with him. Ignoring the others, Daisy kissed him long and deeply. Surrounded by her bondmate's scent, she answered his need for her. To simply be there for him. And within his kiss she found safety and home and love.

"You talked me out of it," he whispered to her. "I wanted to kill him. But your softness, your sweet scent, it calmed me. I don't know what I'd do without you, Daisy Blu."

"Let's not consider what you would have done. You stopped the ghost wolf, and that's all that matters. Marx said he'd break your spell."

"Then let's do it."

Stryke tossed a coat toward Beck. It was too short to cover anything important, so Beck tied the arms about his waist for the time being. His jeans and sweater were shredded.

Stryke stepped beside Daisy and asked quietly, "Is this the tangle you wanted?"

"Oh, yes."

"Good going, sis. You almost got us all killed. You've just taken the lead versus all Trouble's antics."

"Normally that would thrill me. But now? I'm just happy Beck is alive."

"Your bondmate?"

She nodded. "I love him."

Bella rushed to Beck, and Daisy stepped aside to let his mother hug him. "Your father would be proud," she said to her son. "You did the right thing."

"What do we do with him?" Trouble still held Marx with an arm twisted behind his back, on his knees. "Did he really come from another time, Stryke?"

"Ask him."

Denton nodded. "This time is not my own. But I fear I shall never return to the eighteenth century if I cannot free Sencha. My time travel skills were depleted with the trip to the future to obtain the silver ammunition. But, as promised, I shall remove the curse of the ghost wolf from Beckett Severo." He glanced to Bella. "It is the very least I can do for the suffering I have caused your family."

Daisy stepped up to the hunter. "You will return to your time. Because you'll take my wolf to finish your spell."

"No, Daisy," Trouble started, but Blade stepped up behind him, and with but a look, the troublemaker of the family conceded. "You can do what you want, I guess."

"I have to choose one or the other," she said. "I choose to help instead of harm."

"We must work quickly," Denton said. "Twilight is the best time to break a spell. But Beckett must return to his ghost wolf shape. It's the only way it'll work."

Chapter 32

Beck kissed Daisy while everyone around them faded into the distance. It was only he and his gorgeous faery wolf. The woman with whom he wanted to spend the rest of his life. The woman with whom his werewolf had bonded. The woman who made his heart laugh and his life worthwhile.

The woman who had made him stand up to the manifestation of his grief—the ghost wolf—and had helped him fight it. He would forever miss his father. But killing another man in vengeance would never serve his soul, or his father's memory.

And yet now to turn toward the hunter and ask for his help was as far from his understanding as possible. But it felt right.

Because Daisy in his arms was right. She had tamed his wild.

"We must hurry to use the twilight," Denton insisted. "Come, Beckett. Let us do this."

"I like you," he said, and kissed Daisy's forehead. "This is what's right for us." He clasped her hand. "Come with me."

And they strode after Denton toward the open land where the figment of the hunter's lost lover stood. Behind them, the Saint-Pierre brothers stalked as a protective crew that bracketed Bella. Beck felt with everyone he cared about present, it had to be right.

Breaking a spell couldn't do any more harm than he had

already caused. Or so he hoped. It was Daisy giving up her wolf that frightened him.

Denton stopped and turned. Beck walked right up to him. The two assessed one another a moment. The man had killed in an attempt to save his lover. Selfish. And yet, Beck had come close to killing after his selfish request to become something that could scare mortal hunters. Perhaps they were more similar than he dared believe.

"Shift," Denton requested. "And try to control yourself. If you take my head from my shoulders, I can be of no help to you."

"Will it take long?" Beck asked as he toed off his boots and handed Daisy the coat he'd tied about his waist. Everyone present had already seen him naked, including his mother. "I don't have much control over the ghost wolf."

"I'll begin immediately," Denton said. "But she should stand back by the others. Manipulating magic can send off, er...sparks."

Daisy nodded, and stepped back beside her brothers.

"Dude, I've seen your ass more times than a man should," Trouble commented.

Beck flipped him off and turned to Denton. "All right, let's do this."

Daisy felt Bella's hand slip into hers. She slid up close to the vampiress as they watched Beck shift to the ghost wolf. Blade swore quietly as the monstrous creature reached full height and howled at the settling night.

Instantly Denton began a chant before the werewolf. Palms up and mesmerizing the werewolf into his stare, the peller spoke a language Daisy had never before heard. Wasn't Latin. She'd heard that enough times when around witches. Beck's werewolf grew transfixed, as if the man's words alone had bewitched him to a silent supplication.

An intense humming surrounded the two men and the

snow stirred, whipping up around them. Daisy tightened her grip. Bella responded by whispering that all would be well.

"I hope so," she said. "I love him too much."

Bella smiled at her. "I know that feeling."

Suddenly Denton's body flew out of the snowy tornado, landing on the ground near the woman's figment. She didn't regard the goings-on, but merely stood there, as if against a wall, endlessly searching from another dimension.

Stryke took a step toward the fallen peller, but Blade stayed him.

And when the snow fell to the ground and Beck's werewolf stood there, shoulders arched forward and huffing, he was no longer the ghostly white wolf but a brown-furred werewolf similar to her brothers.

Daisy ran for him, and as the werewolf turned and opened its maw to growl warningly, it instead caught Daisy against its chest and hugged her.

An hour later, when the hunter/peller had finally come to after being spit out during the breaking of the spell, he nodded as if he had done well, and wandered toward the woman trapped in the Edge. He put up his palms before her, but his hands moved through her figment.

Beck hadn't let go of Daisy since he'd shifted back to human shape. Stryke had handed him a sweater and some pants. Bella had found the backpack with extra clothing Beck kept in his truck. He'd pulled on his pants, and then had grasped Daisy to his chest, never wanting to let her go.

"It worked," she said against his chest.

"I hope so."

"I know so. We won't believe anything but. Promise?"

He nodded. "I feel…not so exhausted. Like the great drain of the ghost wolf is gone from me. But I wonder now what the faery whom I owed a favor to will think. Will she come after me?"

"We'll deal with that if and when it happens. Now it's my turn."

"You sure you want to do this?" Beck asked. "You can still sacrifice your faery."

"You said you'd like me as a faery."

"I will. I just don't want you to feel as though you owe Marx anything."

"I don't. I'm doing this for her." She nodded toward Sencha. "And besides, I'll always be bonded to you, no matter my form. I love you, Beck."

Daisy saw surprising compassion in Denton Marx's gaze. And she wasn't mistaking it as a desperate greed to get at her werewolf. He was a man who had lost his lover in the worst way possible. Sencha was trapped in some sort of no-man's-land that Daisy couldn't begin to comprehend. But if Stryke had said he'd take Daemonia, the place of all demons, over the Edge, then it was worse than the worst.

She grasped the peller's hands and gave them a reassuring squeeze. "I'm ready for this. Are you?"

He nodded. "I am truly sorry for the trouble I have brought to you and your family."

"I understand, and I can forgive you. Like Bella said, it doesn't mean I condone your actions, but I can see the reason you were driven toward killing."

He winced when she said that word. "Let us begin."

Beck stood beside her. Warmth radiated from his bare chest and sought hers beneath her coat. The guy needed more clothes, but as Denton had explained, this shouldn't take long. She merely had to release her werewolf and invite her faery to stay. Then they could all go home.

And she and her bondmate could begin again.

Scanning her eyes across the waiting faces that stood thirty feet off by the vehicles, Daisy noticed that Trouble did not meet her gaze. He was disappointed she was sacrificing her wolf for the faery. Regret already made her shiver more with nerves than from the chill air. She loved being a wolf. But she hadn't given her faery a chance and, as her mother had said, it was her feminine nurturing side.

Could she abandon the tomboy that she had been all her life and become something else? This was going to be an awkward transition, she felt sure. As Beck had said, she could sacrifice her faery. She didn't need to help Denton by giving him her wolf. It just felt more right than anything. And if she had the power to save the trapped woman, then that was all that mattered.

"Will you step back beside the others?" Denton asked Beck.

Too late to back out now. Daisy nodded reassurance to Beck. Her lover kissed her, then whispered, "You can change your mind."

"No, I'm good. I have to give up one or the other. And you did say you liked my wings?"

"Like them. Love them. Adore them." He kissed her again. "I love you, faery wolf." And he wandered over to stand beside his mother, who wrapped her arms across his middle and tilted her head against his shoulder.

Marx held a glass container about the size of a peanut butter jar, from which he removed a cork stopper. "Say the words I've told you, and I shall capture your werewolf essence."

"So simple as that?"

He nodded, then shrugged. "As far as I know. Your werewolf is neither a curse a spell that I am able to break. I only have Sencha's grimoire that I studied for reference to capturing an essence."

He cast a look over his shoulder at the figment, who had wandered farther away, her head still bowed in sorrow.

"Right then."

Daisy straightened her shoulders and spread out her

arms as she'd been directed. She closed her eyes, and before speaking, said a silent thank-you to her werewolf. It
was all that she knew and was comfortable with. It had
served her well and made her strong. Strong enough to face
this new and unsure future.

"I release my werewolf willingly and with grace. And I
invite my faery to reside upon my soul ever after."

The wind whistled through the trees. Snow swirled upon
the ground, dusting up glittery whorls. The hush of Denton's breath was all Daisy could hear beyond the pulsing
of her heart.

When would it—?

Chest lifting, her arms flung backward. Daisy felt as if
she were being tugged upward by an invisible cord. The life
essence sparkled before her in the air. Her insides flamed,
then cooled instantly. That which sparkled swirled toward
the open jar Denton held and landed within. He capped the
container and nodded.

And Daisy dropped her shoulders and glanced toward
Beck. His hands were spaded before his mouth in a hopeful clutch. She nodded at him and smiled.

"I think it worked," she said, though she didn't feel different. Any more faerylike or less wolflike. "I—"

A raging storm of white moths suddenly swooped over
their heads. It moved toward Daisy, and when she realized
what was happening, she screamed to Denton to protect
the essence.

The white faery had returned.

Chapter 33

At the sight of the crazed storm of moths, Beck shoved his mother into Blade's arms and took off toward Daisy. Before he could reach her, the moths swirled in a tornado upon the ground and formed into the wicked white faery. The sidhe thrust out a hand toward him, which sent a bolt of moths against his chest. Felt like tens of thousands of volts pricking throughout his nervous system. Forced from his feet, Beck landed on the ground, but got up immediately and shook off the annoyance.

"You have reneged on our bargain, werewolf," the faery called.

Behind her, Denton stepped protectively before Daisy.

Beck had cheated the faery out of her boon. But that would have required he ransom his wolf. Become merely human. Or give up his firstborn.

"There must be something you can ask of me," he said, approaching cautiously. He wanted to get close enough to slip around beside the faery and grab Daisy to keep her safe.

"I wanted a werewolf! And I will have one."

The faery spun into a swirl of moths so thick Beck could not see before him. The snowy clearing filled with moths. The swarm's wings cut across his skin, drawing blood at his forehead and his bare chest. He heard his mother's scream. The brothers swore. And when again the moths narrowed into a focused figure of the faery, they streamed toward Denton and the jar of Daisy's wolf essence.

He would not allow Daisy's sacrifice to be used in a

manner she had not intended. She'd wanted to help the
hunter reunite with his lost lover.

Denton tucked the jar inside his leather coat, but try as
he might to hold it closed, the flaps of his coat flayed wide
and the jar lifted out of the pocket.

"No!" Beck called.

Thanks to the distracting shout, the faery turned her
attention to Beck, and Denton was able to grasp the jar.

"Take my wolf," Beck called. He spread his arms wide.
"It is only right you are granted the boon I promised."

"Beck, no!" Daisy shouted. She tried to move toward
him, but a wall of moths blocked her. "Don't do this."

He'd snagged the faery's interest. Though she was not
fully formed, her lower half busy with moths, he stood
waiting as the sidhe moved toward him.

"It is a stronger, more vital wolf than that of the essence
in that jar," he coaxed. And really, he was no man if he
didn't live up to his bargains. For that, he knew his father
would be proud. "Come take it if you dare."

Beck felt the entrance of the faery magic through his
pores as pinpricks boring deeply, seeking the source of his
very being. His essence. His wolf. The one thing that he was.

Muscles tightening in a reactive defense against the rape
of his essence, Beck's fists formed and he thrust back his
head to howl. His wolf cried out to the night, the howl long
and unceasing. Crows stirred from the nearby trees, and a
gray wolf a mile off answered the mourning howl.

And then it was gone.

Beck dropped to his knees. The storm of moths swirled
about him, the wings scraping his skin raw. The fire of his
werewolf had left his body.

Collapsing forward into the snow, he blacked out.

Beck woke. His head was nestled against something
soft, warm and smelling like candy. Pink hair sifted over

his face. A gentle hand stroked his cheek. It felt...safe.
Loving. A teardrop splattered his mouth. He dashed out
his tongue to taste the salted drop.

"Beck?" Daisy whispered. "You're back?"

He groaned and tried to sit up, but his body felt as though
it had been worked over by the Saint-Pierre brothers *and*
their dad. So he merely tilted his head toward the pink
heaven and nodded.

"He's awake," he heard Daisy say.

"Thank God." His mother. She would never abandon
her faith in the god she had worshipped as a human. Beck
smiled. All was well? As good as it could be.

Then he realized he lay in the front of his truck, his head
on Daisy's lap. The heater was blasting.

"He's good," Daisy said to someone else. Probably a
brother.

"Let's head out," Trouble announced. "Stryke, what's
the hunter up to?"

"Working with the spell," Stryke confirmed. "I still
think we should steal Daisy's essence back for her."

"Boys," Daisy called out the truck window. "It's over.
I made a choice. The peller has what he needs to rescue
the woman and go home. And Beck..." she ran her fingers
through his hair, and Beck shivered and snuggled up closer
"...is going to be just fine."

Two days later

Just fine was a matter of opinion. Adjusting to his new
human status was surprisingly bewildering. Beck had
taken for granted simple things such as walking. While as
a werewolf he had moved sinuously, with a grace he hadn't
to consider, this mortal body seemed to fumble upon the
earth. And he felt the clothes upon his body as cumber-
some and itchy.

And he couldn't eat as much, which made him wonder if he'd grow thin and waste away. He'd only eaten a chicken leg, thigh, two wings and a breast tonight. Daisy had been surprised that he'd refused a second helping of red velvet cake.

They had made love for the first time since he'd become human this morning, tucked in his bed, snuggling together against the insistent cold. Man, did he feel the cold now. He could not walk outside without a shirt in this frigid weather.

And the sex. It had seemed the same to him. Spectacular. He and Daisy had kissed, hugged, touched, licked, stroked and…they'd both come a few times, as they usually did when making love.

But would she tell him if he was lacking now? What if he couldn't match the intensity she had known when bonding with his werewolf?

Her father had called right before they'd sat down to eat tonight. Daisy said Malakai wanted to talk to Beck. Of course her brothers had told her father that Beck had sacrificed his wolf. And he was sure one of them had mentioned that they'd bonded, as well.

Beck was pretty sure Malakai's offer regarding marrying Daisy and joining the pack would now be reneged.

He'd face that trial tomorrow at noon, when Kai had requested they meet.

High noon. Seriously?

Daisy hugged him from behind and kissed his ear. He reached back, grasping her hair and letting it slip through his fingers as she pulled away and took the dinner plate to the sink.

"What are you thinking about?" she asked over her shoulder.

That he wasn't going to like being human. At all. And that he hadn't scented her approach from behind, as he usually could. Hadn't gotten a whiff of her sweet candy smell until she'd been right there, kissing him.

"It's the talk with my dad," she decided. Turning, she leaned across the counter and took one of his hands. "It's going to be good."

"Is it? Can you honestly love a human, Daisy? I'm not sure I can deal with myself like this. I'm…nothing now."

"Don't say that. You are the man I like. Werewolf, human or otherwise."

"Says the faery who has suddenly developed a penchant for walking around the house naked."

"I haven't heard an argument from you yet." She stood back and fluffed the ruffle of the apron she'd tied over her bare body while making supper. It just covered her nipples and had distracted Beck so much that he had leaned over to kiss the plump side of her breast more than once during supper. "It's like I'm inside a whole new skin, and it wants to feel the world on it. I want to feel you on my skin." She winked.

How could a man bemoan his condition when his reality offered up a naked faery who loved him, cooked for him and wanted to have sex all the time?

A knock at the door startled Daisy upright. "I wonder who that could be?"

"Whoever it is, they are not going to see you like that." He jutted a thumb over his shoulder. "Go put some clothes on."

She spun around the counter, kissed him and skipped off toward his bedroom.

Beck rose and inhaled deeply. He couldn't get a scent of who stood behind the door. Hell, he could barely smell the burning wood in the hearthfire.

Normally, by scenting out the unseen, he'd be able to sense danger. Or a simple visitor. Gripping the doorknob, he looked aside for a weapon. Wasn't so easy as slashing out a claw in defense now. He hadn't lost his strength, but—hell.

Beck swung the door open to find Denton Marx standing on the threshold, his hands cupped before him. He blew into his hands and rubbed them together. "It is wicked cold in this godforsaken century, do you know that?"

"I thought you'd be gone by now. The eighteenth century?"

"Seventeenth, actually. Might I be invited in, please?"

Beck stepped aside to allow the man in. He brought in a wave of cold that sent a wicked shiver through Beck's body. He quickly closed the door.

Daisy popped back in, clad in one of his flannel shirts and some tight black leggings. Her smile dropped at the sight of Denton. "What do you want now?"

"I have brought something for Beckett," Denton said.

"Where is your lover?" Daisy asked. "Didn't the spell work?"

The hunter bowed his head and clasped his hands before him. "I have not completed the allbeast spell. I have not all the ingredients. Rather." He met Beck's gaze. "I have them, but I don't wish to utilize them. I must find a replacement."

"For what?" Daisy asked. She joined Beck's side, her hand slipping into his.

"For this." Denton tucked a hand inside his jacket and brought out the glass jar that sparkled with Daisy's werewolf essence.

"Is that…?"

"It is, my lady. I combined all the ingredients, and was prepared to uncork and add in the werewolf essence you so graciously offered to me when I felt her looking over my shoulder."

"Sencha?"

Denton nodded.

"I don't understand," Beck said.

"It was the first time we were able to communicate, of a sort, over the dimensions. She swept her hand toward this jar and shook her head. 'Not that one' is what I'm sure she was trying to convey to me. So." Denton offered the jar to Daisy. "I know you have no use for it, as I understand your condition was that you could either keep one or the other."

"Exactly," Daisy said, crossing her arms.

The hunter took Daisy's hand and placed the jar on her palm. He wrapped her fingers about the glass. "I thought you might make it a gift to your lover. If you so choose."

Daisy's bright smile beamed up at Beck.

"Wait." Beck couldn't help but feel elation at the idea of actually getting his werewolf back, but he wasn't stupid. "How can that work? It's not my werewolf in that glass jar."

"It is the *essence* of werewolf. When it once resided in your lovely Daisy Blu's body, her soul made the essence her own. Spinning about in this jar, it is but an essence waiting to be claimed and shaped by yet another soul. You can make it your own, Beckett."

"How do you know this?" Beck asked.

"I have learned much from Sencha and the study of her grimoires. If you doubt me, you have but to try it. If it fails, you have lost nothing. If it is successful..." The man's eyes glinted with promise.

Daisy held the jar up between her and Beck. He touched the glass, and inside, the sparkling essence reacted with a swirl.

"I will leave you two in peace," Denton said.

"Wait." Beck marched to the door, stopping the man with his hand on the knob. "You still need a werewolf essence to complete your spell."

"That I do." Marx did not meet his gaze. And if he had been werewolf at that moment, Beck felt sure he would have detected the sadness that crept about the man's heart. And the resolve that would push him to kill another wolf.

"I have heard about a wolf that has been tearing cattle to shreds farther up north toward the boundary waters."

"Gray wolves don't tear cattle to shreds," Daisy commented.

"Exactly," Denton said. "Not unless it's sickly and an entire pack goes after it. These were healthy beef cattle. Farmers report finding only one set of overlarge wolf tracks. A werewolf like that might not be missed, eh?"

Beck lifted his chin, looking down on the man, who still dared not meet his gaze. He had tormented his family. Killed his father. And now he had offered Beck a second chance.

Stepping aside, he made room for the man to open the door and leave. He watched the hunter march down the drive. Daisy's hand slipped into his. And he heard his mother's voice in his head. *It was the right thing to do.*

Beck called out to the retreating hunter.

Denton turned. Waited.

The pounding of his heartbeat thundered in Beck's ears. His father's last breaths—he would never forget them. Yet at that moment he wished only to move forward.

"I forgive you," he called. "Go in peace."

Marx clasped his hands over his heart, bowed his head, then turned and got in his vehicle. Only when the headlights had receded did Beck turn to catch Daisy in his arms.

"How do you feel?" she asked.

"Lighter. I feel…lighter."

"I'm proud of you."

"He's out of our lives now."

She pressed the glass jar into his hand. "To our future."

Epilogue

Daisy didn't get the internship at the *Tangle Lake Tattler*, despite her exposé on the ghost wolf, which included a photo of the white beast with a zoom on the zipper down its back. Someone had done an extensive investigation into the unclaimed mineral rights in the area and had won the prize. Rocks had won over a man in a wolf suit? Go figure.

She'd stick to sculpting for now. Last week she and Beck had delivered the wolf sculpture to the Ely Wolf Sanctuary. And she'd received a commission for another work depicting a moose and using computer parts for the sculpture. It was a challenge she looked forward to.

Now the twosome stood in the spring-wet grass before Stephan Severo's grave at the back of the family property. Hands clasped, they silently held vigil.

"Forgiveness feels right," Beck said after a while. "I will never forget, but now I can move forward."

"We can move forward," Daisy said. "Will you tell me about the things you used to do with your father someday?"

"Yes. We can do one right now. Go for a run together. You want to?"

Daisy wiggled her shoulders and slipped off her shirt. Her wings unfurled beautifully. "Try and catch me, big boy."

* * * * *

MILLS & BOON®

Why shop at millsandboon.co.uk?

Each year, thousands of romance readers find their
perfect read at millsandboon.co.uk. That's because
we're passionate about bringing you the very best
romantic fiction. Here are some of the advantages
of shopping at www.millsandboon.co.uk:

* **Get new books first**—you'll be able to buy your
  favourite books one month before they hit
  the shops

* **Get exclusive discounts**—you'll also be able to buy
  our specially created monthly collections, with up
  to 50% off the RRP

* **Find your favourite authors**—latest news,
  interviews and new releases for all your favourite
  authors and series on our website, plus ideas for
  what to try next

* **Join in**—once you've bought your favourite books,
  don't forget to register with us to rate, review and
  join in the discussions

Visit **www.millsandboon.co.uk**
for all this and more today!